"Dare I?" Caleb said, lifting his hand to his chest in feigned innocence. "I'm certain I don't know what you mean, Miss Marah."

She advanced on him one step and extended a finger, which she pointed at him menacingly. "You don't have any right to be jealous, Caleb. And that man doesn't deserve an ounce of your contempt."

"Is he a *man*, Marah?" he snapped, the thin wire of control within him finally breaking. "Because all I saw was a dandy who is looking to further his profit through a match with a lady he's not fit to shine the boots of."

Marah's jaw tightened and her eyes narrowed. "Well, he's more of a man than anyone else in the room I saw."

She turned to go, but Caleb caught her arm and twirled her around, unwilling to leave things as they were. She tumbled off balance and fell against his chest. He caught her, holding her steady against him, and everything else around them stopped.

Caleb looked down into her face and he felt her soft body pressed to his and he wanted her with a power that rocked him to his very core. So he dipped his head . . .

And kissed her.

Romances by **Jenna Petersen**

A SCOUNDREL'S SURRENDER
THE UNCLAIMED DUCHESS
WHAT THE DUKE DESIRES
HER NOTORIOUS VISCOUNT
LESSONS FROM A COURTESAN
SEDUCTION IS FOREVER
DESIRE NEVER DIES
FROM LONDON WITH LOVE
SCANDALOUS

A SCOUNDREL'S SURRENDER

JENNA PETERSEN

AVON

An Imprint of HarperCollinsPublishers

AVON BOOKS
An Imprint of HarperCollins*Publishers*
10 East 53rd Street
New York, New York 10022-5299

Copyright © 2011 by Jesse Petersen
ISBN 978-0-06-193500-8
www.avonromance.com

First Avon Books mass market printing: August 2011

Avon Trademark Reg. U.S. Pat. Off. and in Other Countries, Marca Registrada, Hecho en U.S.A.
HarperCollins® is a registered trademark of HarperCollins Publishers.

Printed in the U.S.A.

10 9 8 7 6 5 4 3 2 1

For all the readers who have contacted
me over the past five years. Thank you for
your support, your comments, and your
compliments. They've meant the world to me.
And for Michael, who inspires
me to try, try again.

A
SCOUNDREL'S
SURRENDER

Prologue

1815

When Caleb Talbot looked across the room toward the beautiful blond woman standing with his brother and sister-in-law, he felt many things. They hadn't known each other very long, but already Marah Farnsworth brought out a desire so powerful it nearly took him to his knees. Beyond that, he was racked by guilt over acting on that desire just a few days prior in an encounter that still melted his bones and haunted his restless dreams.

More troubling, seeing her brought out a flutter of something more. Something deeper, more seductive than pleasure and infinitely more terrifying. Emotions he had scoffed at in his friends and acquaintances when they described falling in love with some chit.

The one thing he did *not* feel, as she turned toward him and cast a quick smile in his direction, was happiness. These unwanted and unexpected feelings had come at the most inopportune time. The worst time of his life, truly.

Because Caleb was not who he had always thought he was. It had been only a few days since he found proof that he was a bastard, a child born of some kind of indiscretion on his mother's part, not of his father's loins, but some stranger. Worse, his brother had known and hidden that fact from him for years.

And the truth of all these things rocked him whenever it passed through his mind . . . as it had been passing through his mind on a constant stream for days.

He clenched the glass in his hand until he swore he could feel the delicate stemware creak beneath his palm. And of course, in that troubled moment, Marah came toward him. He watched her move, float really, for women like her seemed to glide weightlessly rather than walk.

"Caleb?" she whispered as she reached his side and looked up at him with impossibly wide and blue eyes that were currently filled with kindness and understanding. Her voice was like music, soothing him.

He shook his head and forced a tight smile down at her. "Marah."

She hesitated for a moment and then her hand reached out to touch his arm. She meant the brush of her fingers as a comfort, but sparks exploded within him, overpowering him with a desire to grab her, tug her against him, kiss her until everything else faded, all the pain dissipated.

But he didn't. He had allowed himself to drown in her once, to confess the dark rage and pain that bubbled within him. He had taken comfort in her body and could offer her no more than that. And she deserved more. More than he could give, at least at the moment.

"I'm worried about you," she whispered.

He blinked down at her. Yes, she was. *Everyone* was. His brother, Justin, who had kept the truth of his parentage from him; his sister-in-law, Victoria, who cast sad looks in his direction when she could bear to tear her loving gaze away from her husband.

The weight of their regard pressed on him, heavy as it amplified his own anger and confusion at being revealed as bastard. He was stifled by it all.

"I'm fine," he bit out past clenched teeth.

She tilted her head, and her expression said she didn't believe him.

"I-I want to help you," she said as a blush filled her cheeks that told Caleb she was thinking of their stolen afternoon together. "How can I help you?"

He stared at her. For a moment he was filled with a ridiculous urge to ask her to run away with him. To escape his past, to escape the secret he couldn't forget. To help him drown out the sorrow with her companionship and her touch and the care he had no doubt she would give.

Even though he had nothing to give in return at present. And he wasn't sure if and when he ever would. The idea of dragging her away, as tempting as it was, was impossible. It would destroy her. Use her even more than he already had.

"I must leave," he said, backing up so that she no longer confused the situation with her touch.

She nodded. "I understand. And I'm sure Victoria and Justin will as well. We all know you need time to digest what you have been told. Perhaps tomorrow . . ."

He nodded. Yes, perhaps tomorrow it would be better. Except, as he gave a brief wave to his brother and slipped wordlessly from the parlor, he recognized that was folly. Tomorrow wouldn't be better. Nor would the next day.

He swung himself up on his horse and rode off into the night. Only as he passed by the street he would normally turn on to go home, he didn't. And he didn't stop at any of his clubs or the homes of his friends. Without thinking he merely steered his mare out of Town.

Toward. . .

Well, he wasn't certain what he rode toward. Only what he left behind. A secret he wished he'd never uncovered, a family that was shrouded in a cloud of lies . . . and a woman whose heart he would break because she would never understand that he was doing her a favor by leaving without a word. By keeping himself from using her as a balm for his grief.

But it was cold comfort as he urged his horse faster toward the unknown.

Chapter 1

Two Years Later

Caleb Talbot snapped his fingers, then motioned to his empty glass, and the burly, scarred man behind the bar nodded swiftly. Lowering his head, Caleb didn't watch as the barkeep worked his magic, he only smiled when the worn hand placed a fresh tankard of ale before him.

He wasn't quite to oblivion yet, but he was edging closer with every passing moment and he couldn't wait until the pleasing numbness arrived and washed away all thought, feeling, and memory.

At the door behind him, a dinging bell signaled a new patron's entry to the tavern, but Caleb didn't bother to look toward the sound as he dragged his drink closer. He had everything he wanted in the palm of his hand, he had no need to involve himself in the matters of others.

"Well, la-di-da," muttered one of the men down

the bar from Caleb. "Look at the fancy one who just came in."

The other man's companion chuckled, though the sound was fed more by menace than by humor. "Bet he could part with plenty o' blunt without any trouble whatsoever."

At the threatening comments, Caleb turned his head and fixed a rather bleary gaze on the doorway. What he saw there cleared his mind of the magnificent fog he had worked so hard to obtain. Without thinking, he shot to his feet, nearly knocking over his ale.

At the doorway, peering around the dingy tavern and appearing as out of place as the Regent in all his finery would have, was Caleb's brother, Justin Talbot, the Earl of Baybary. Caleb's stomach turned at the sight of him, but his heart also swelled with love for his brother and joy to see him, even under these circumstances.

At almost the same moment, his brother's dark gaze fell on him. Justin's reaction was immediate and palpable, a mixture of relief, sadness, anger, and pity. The last made Caleb scowl, his happier feelings gone, and he grabbed for his tankard blindly before he started across the room to his brother. The brother he hadn't seen for over six months.

"What are you doing here?" he growled as he caught Justin's arm with his free hand and pulled him away from the door and into a darkened corner crowded with dirty tables. "This is no place for you."

"Oh, and it is for you?" his brother asked.

Justin pulled his arm free and took a seat. It was clear he had no intention of leaving, so Caleb flopped into the chair across from him and scowled. "I've been to worse."

There was a long, heavy pause before Justin nodded. "Indeed, I imagine you have."

At that moment a buxom barmaid sidled up to their table. She leaned forward, giving both men a long view of her full breasts, lifted by some kind of unseen contraption in her gown. Justin arched a brow at the lewd display, then turned away with bored disinterest. Caleb also looked, but he felt not so much as a stir in his loins.

As if the young woman sensed their indifference, she huffed out a sound of offended annoyance and snapped, "Whadayawant?"

Caleb motioned toward his brother. "A pint for the earl and another for me."

"Oh yes, my lords. Right away." She bobbed out a rather snooty curtsy and flitted away.

Once she was out of earshot, Justin sighed.

"Your tankard is hardly half empty, you needn't have ordered another," he said softly. "But then, it seems you've had enough for both of us already, so perhaps you shouldn't have ordered for me, either."

Caleb glared at his brother as a wave of intense irritation stole what was left of the pleasantness he had obtained from drink.

"So you did all the work it must have taken to locate me, then rode three days from London, in order to *judge* me?" He leaned back in his chair and speared his brother with a look. "Not so very long ago, you would have clapped me on the back and joined me without hesitation."

"Times have changed," Justin said, his angular face softening with emotion as he held his steady gaze on Caleb. "As have you, brother."

"Indeed, I have," Caleb said as he swigged his remaining ale in one long drink. He slammed the tankard down on the wooden table with a bang that brought several faces turning toward them. "Now why are you here? When last we spoke, I told you I didn't want you interrupting your life to find me anymore. That, at least, has not changed."

Justin swallowed hard and his eyes briefly came shut. When he opened them, raw emotion had settled there. Caleb wasn't accustomed to seeing that on his brother's face.

"That is where you are wrong. You see, I-I came here to talk to you about our father."

Caleb tensed. This subject of all subjects was the most delicate and painful to him and Justin full-well knew it. His fist tightened on the tabletop, but he was saved from answering for a moment when the barmaid returned with more alcohol. Before she had even removed the items from her tray, Caleb grabbed one tankard and slugged half of it. She set the other one down in front of Justin and backed away without any more clumsy attempts at flirtation. It seemed even *she* could sense the intensity between the brothers and had no interest in inserting herself in it.

"Our father," Caleb said slowly as the alcoholic haze he had lost when his brother entered the tavern began to return to him. "Don't you mean *your* father? We long ago established he isn't mine."

Justin cast a quick glance around the bar. "Mind your voice, Caleb."

"Why?" Caleb asked with a humorless laugh that instantly faded. "Why does it matter? Why does *any* of it matter anymore? And *why* did you come here? Why couldn't you just listen to me for once in your life and leave me in peace?"

"You, in peace?" Justin said with a snort. "Oh yes, you are the image of serenity here in this disgusting hole that is hardly fit for rats, surrounded by drunks who aren't half the man you used to be, and wallowing in pain and heartache like a child who has lost his favorite toy."

Caleb pushed from his seat in one motion that rocked the table back. Justin was up immediately behind him, and the two men faced off as the other patrons maneuvered to watch, ready to be entertained by a brawl between the drunk and the fancy stranger who didn't belong among them.

"Watch yourself," Caleb growled. "I don't want to hit you."

"Yes," Justin said with a sad shake of his head. "You do. But I didn't come here to start a fight, though I sometimes think it might help if you could just blacken my eye and be done with it. No, I came because . . ."

He trailed off with a pained expression.

"Because?" Caleb prompted, his anger fading as his curiosity about what could bring his brother here with such secrecy and drama intensified.

"He's dying," Justin said, quick and flat, as if he were pulling the wrap from a wound in one sweep rather than tugging at it mercilessly.

Caleb blinked. He must have heard wrong.

"Dying?"

"Our father," Justin whispered.

Those two little words sobered Caleb more fully than even the sight of his brother had done earlier. Without the alcoholic haze, the pain that accompanied Justin's statement threaded through his veins, setting his very soul on fire and doubling his heart's rate almost instantly. He shoved at the painful reaction the only way he knew how.

Denial.

"No. You're lying," he whispered.

Justin swallowed and Caleb was shocked when he saw the sparkling beginnings of tears in his brother's eyes. He stared, his mouth partly open, for he had never seen Justin so undone. Well, once, when his wife, Victoria, was threatened, but this was different. This was heartbreak, but mixed with resolution and an awful acceptance.

"I wish I were lying," Justin choked out. "I wish I would wake up and find this was all a terrible dream. But the doctors say they don't believe he'll last the summer."

"Find better doctors!" Caleb barked. "You have the blunt, spend it!"

Justin's jaw tightened and Caleb saw he had gone too far. His brother's lips were white, drawn tight, and they trembled. Justin looked ready to strike him, just as he had accused Caleb of wishing to do a moment before, but as Caleb had, Justin kept himself in check.

"Don't you think I have?" he asked through clenched teeth. "I've brought in every physician and surgeon in the country with any kind of reputation. Then I transported in a few from the Continent. Hell, I even called in some favors and got the Regent's personal doctor to visit. Nothing has changed. They all say the same thing."

Caleb grabbed for the back of the rough wooden chair he had abandoned a moment before. He clung to the wood, not even registering the splinter that slid beneath his skin when he gripped it.

Justin frowned. "He has . . . he's asked to see you. He *wants* to see you, Caleb. He has no idea why you ran away from the family two years ago. I swore to him that I would find you and bring you home. Please don't make me a liar. Not when it comes to what is likely his final request."

Caleb stared at his brother long and hard as a thousand memories flooded his addled mind. Images of the man he had called his father, both the good and the bad. From the way he had lifted his youngest son high above his head when Caleb was just a boy, to the disappointment that had entered his father's stare when Caleb was about fifteen and had never entirely left, no matter how hard Caleb tried to live up to his father's lofty expectations.

But now the man who had raised him was a candle in the breeze, flickering on the edge of extinguishing. Caleb had avoided him since he learned the truth about his parentage. He hadn't wanted to see him, he hadn't wanted to feel the pain of knowing the marquis wasn't his father.

And in truth, he hadn't wanted to do or say something foolish that would somehow reveal the truth and shatter everything in his father's world.

For all their differences, he hadn't desired that.

Without speaking, Caleb dug into his pockets and found enough blunt to pay for the drinks. He tossed it on the table and motioned his brother to the door.

"My horse is at the inn. Once I've had her saddled, we can depart immediately."

Marah Farnsworth drew in a long breath of fragrant tea before she took a sip, and sighed with contentment. She smiled as she lowered her cup, and the expression was returned instantly by her companion.

Victoria Talbot, Countess of Baybary, had come from London a week ago to visit Marah, and the two old friends had been catching up ever since.

Though it was wonderful to see Victoria, Marah felt rather uneasy around her friend in a way she never had before. For as much as they chatted and gossiped and laughed the way they ever had, there was an unspoken topic hanging between them, coloring every moment they spent together.

"Are you planning on staying here forever?" Victoria asked.

Marah shut her eyes briefly. Ah yes, here was that topic, breached at last. And she did not wish to discuss it any more than she had the first moment Victoria stepped from her well-appointed carriage.

"In this room? I doubt it. There isn't a good place to hang my gowns and I don't think I would be comfortable sleeping on the settee," Marah said, meeting her friend's stare evenly. "Besides, the servants would talk."

Victoria smiled, but the concern that had been flickering in her eyes since her arrival strengthened. "I think you know what I mean."

"Of course I do," Marah said as she set her cup aside and pushed to her feet. She paced to the window and looked outside to the small but tidy garden below.

"No one could ever deny that Baybary is a fine shire," Victoria continued softly. "Lord knows, I loved my years living here, and the people who reside in this little hamlet are some of the finest in the world. Visiting here is always a pleasure."

"Then why harangue me about my choice to stay?" Marah asked without looking back to Victoria.

Her friend sighed softly. "I'm not trying to harangue, my dear. I'm only saying that Baybary is very small, Marah. There isn't much company here for you."

"I don't desire to keep a great deal of company so that matters little to me," Marah insisted, keeping her gaze out the window, though she hardly saw the scene before her.

Victoria hesitated before she said, "You may claim that, but I know you too well. I can see you are lonely."

Marah finally turned and speared Victoria with a look. "Perhaps that is because my grandmother just died."

She hoped the pointed comment would put Victoria off, but her friend's stare didn't waver, nor did she look chagrined.

"She died six months ago, dearest. Your mourning period has ended in the eyes of Society. No one could begrudge you the desire for new scenery."

Marah sucked in a breath. Her grandmother had raised her after her mother died in childbirth and her father abandoned her. She was the only love Marah had known in her life.

As if she read her friend's thoughts, Victoria got to her feet and reached out to touch Marah's arm. "I realize you miss her, but I fear her death isn't what is truly keeping you here, sequestered away from the world. I worry about you."

Marah began to turn away. She didn't want to talk about this, to think about these things, but Victoria's fingers tightened on her wrist to hold her steady.

"Please, Marah, I realize things have been difficult since . . . well, since you were last in London. But it's time you return to the city and live a little. You *will* accompany me and stay in our home. With the illness of Justin's father, the family has much reduced its presence in Society, but that will put less pressure on you. And we are still attending many events where you can be gay and regain some of the light in your eyes that I so miss when I look at you now."

Victoria smiled, and there was a pleading hope in her eyes that touched Marah even if she wished it didn't.

"Come to London," Marah whispered, her voice distant as she pondered that idea.

Her mind naturally went to the last time she had been to the city, two years ago when she accompanied Victoria. They had gone to conduct a shocking ruse and a desperate investigation over the disappearance of a dear friend.

But nothing had gone as planned. Victoria's long-estranged husband, Justin, had interfered and the two had ultimately reunited. As for Marah, there she had met Caleb Talbot, Victoria's brother-in-law. She couldn't help but recall his hands on her . . . and the moment when she realized he had left her life forever with hardly a good-bye.

"I don't know," she said, turning her face as she wiped all the thoughts from her head. They were bothersome and served no purpose. She considered it a weakness when she allowed them to trouble her.

Victoria swallowed. "Please, please come. If not for yourself, then for me."

Marah looked at her friend swiftly. Tears sparkled in Victoria's eyes and there was a deep and powerful fear that darkened her normally light demeanor. These things were not forced or pretended for Marah's benefit; there was no doubt Victoria was truly distressed.

"What is it?" Marah asked, grabbing her friend's hands and holding her tightly for reassurance.

Victoria hesitated before she choked out, "Our

whole family suffers cruelly over the illness of Justin's father. I understated its seriousness when I spoke of it to you before. He—he is dying, Marah."

"Oh no!" Marah said, as she put her arms around Victoria and held tight.

But her thoughts strayed traitorously to Caleb once again. Did he know of this? And after all he had been through, would he regret running away, at least from his family?

Victoria nodded. "It is difficult to see my husband so heartbroken, to visit with the marquis and to be unable to do anything to ease their pain. I could use a true friend to talk to, to turn to."

"Of course, my dear," Marah heard herself saying. "Of course I'll come if you desire and need my company."

She kept a smile on her face, but her rational side silently screamed. The last place in the world she wished to be was London. Her memories of the place ranged from crushing disappointment to stark terror. And she had enough scars to remind her of those things. Without meaning to, she rubbed her wrist, where a raised, white piece of flesh remained from her last visit to Town.

"Thank you," Victoria said, enveloping Marah in a hug that washed away her doubts, at least for a moment. "It means a great deal to me!"

As they parted, Marah forced a smile. She would focus on the good things about this trip and there *were* several.

"I suppose it *will* be pleasurable for me to see some friends," she murmured, trying to convince herself as much as Victoria. "One friend in particular is of great interest to me, for he departed for London himself last month."

Victoria, who had been smiling, now looked much more subdued. The shift troubled Marah. "Are you speaking of Mr. Emerson Winstead?"

Marah nodded. "I am. Once I send word that I'm coming to Town, I'm sure I'll see him."

"I didn't realize you two had become so close." Victoria worried the hem of her sleeve gently. "Your letters mentioned him frequently, of course, but your acquaintance must be increasing if your decision to come to London is in any part due to a desire to see him."

Marah shrugged, though her friend's feelings on the matter meant more to her than she could likely express. "Do you disapprove of my friendship?"

Victoria's brow wrinkled and her hesitation was answer enough. "I only wish I knew a bit more about him. He is a mystery."

"Not really," Marah said, compelled to defend the man. "At least not to me. I met him almost a year ago. He has been nothing but affable, polite, and attentive, and he was so kind when my grandmother passed. He is dependable and *that* is what I desire."

Victoria didn't seem any less concerned, but managed to nod. "Well, if he is important to you, I look forward to learning more about him. And London shall be the perfect opportunity for me to do so. Once we arrive at my home, we'll invite him to call and perhaps we can ensure a handful of invitations for him to a few balls or gatherings, as well. Justin surely has enough influence to arrange that."

"Good," Marah said with a satisfied sigh.

She knew, even if she hadn't expressed it to her reluctant friend, that her relationship with Emerson was developing slowly into something more than mere friendship. At some point she believed he would offer for her hand, and she had every intention of accepting.

Surely *then* she would forget what had happened in London. She would forget Caleb and the way his hands had moved over her skin, and his lips over her body in such wicked ways.

With a shake of her head, she cleared her mind of distracting thoughts. "Then let us go to Town!"

As she enveloped her friend in an embrace, Victoria smiled and Marah valiantly worked to do the same. Facing her past, facing her fears, wasn't something she looked forward to, but once it was done she hoped she could truly forget it all and move on to a future she prayed would hold stability and perhaps even happiness.

Chapter 2

Caleb chewed on the end of his cigar restlessly. He longed for a drink, but since their arrival at Justin's home over an hour ago, his brother had made no offer of one, nor did he indulge himself in any of the tempting spirits locked in the finely crafted cabinet behind his desk.

"Can you really be enjoying that fine cigar if you only choose to maul it?" Justin asked as he looked up from the papers spread out before him with an arched brow.

Caleb removed the offending item from his lips and set it in the ashtray beside him. "I apologize. I suppose it is only anxiety at my return to London that causes my unease."

"Did you not think you would ever come back home?" Justin asked softly, his brow wrinkling as if that idea pained him.

Caleb pondered the question.

"I-I suppose I hadn't ever planned that far ahead.

Once I left the city, I never considered much about my future beyond where I would lay my head each night and obtain my next drink."

Justin drew a long drag from his cigar and puffed out a perfect circle before he responded. "Life is about so much more than those things, you know. You've been given a precious one and you ought to do more with it."

A shrug was Caleb's only answer. His brother did not, *could* not, understand what it was he had endured over the past two years. To discover his entire past had been a lie . . . that had torn him to pieces. No one could really comprehend it unless he had been through it himself.

"Do you have any plans now that you're here, at least?" his brother pressed.

Caleb steepled his fingers before him. "Well, it was a long few days' ride and I admit I thought about my future much more than I have in a very long time."

Justin leaned forward, eyes dark with interest. "Indeed? And where have your thoughts lead you?"

"You are right about me," Caleb mused as he stared at his brother whom he looked so much and yet so little like. "And you may crow about that admission since I know it pleases you."

Justin flashed a quick grin, but didn't interrupt,

so Caleb continued, "I've spent two years doing exactly what you accused me of in the tavern a few days ago. Wallowing."

Justin frowned as if the memory pained him. "It was a harsh assessment said in anger."

"But utterly correct," Caleb said with a shrug. "I wallowed in my parentage. Wallowed in what I lost when I found out the marquis wasn't my father, that I wasn't who I always thought I was. I even wallowed in the fact that you kept all that from me. Even though I know you were blackmailed into marrying Victoria to protect the truth."

Justin nodded. "I do not regret my marriage, but I should have told you myself rather than let you find out the truth by discovering the proof I burned. I should have given you the respect of trusting you with your own past. I *am* sorry."

Caleb acknowledged his brother's apology with a brief nod. "But all my self-pity and indulgence didn't matter. Here we are back in London, and my situation has neither changed nor improved since I left. So I am finished with it."

Justin cocked his head. "Finished with what?"

"I refuse to let my past dictate my life any longer," Caleb explained. "So I'm not my father's son, what does it matter? Why shouldn't I continue on as before and pretend, as you did for so long, that this sad set of circumstances doesn't exist?"

His brother's brow furrowed. "Although I'm happy to hear you say that you no longer wish to run or hide from the truth, I'm not certain that *ignoring* what you know or pretending it doesn't exist is the best alternative."

Caleb frowned. "Well, what would you have me do? Run to our father and confess the truth to him on his deathbed? Confront our mother?"

"Of course not," Justin snapped with a peevish shake of his head. "But there must be something in the middle, Caleb. Perhaps you could find out more about the circumstances of your birth, the family that—"

"And tear apart some other family as ours has been torn apart?" Caleb asked, cutting off his brother with a wave of his hand.

Justin dipped his chin without answering.

"I've returned to London, Justin, as you wished me to do," Caleb continued softly. "This is my decision and I intend to stand by it. I'll return to my rollicking days of yore. Please don't try to stop me or tell me how to live my life."

Justin clenched his fists against his thighs, and Caleb knew his brother well enough to see that he wanted to argue and say more. But to his surprise, Justin only jerked out a nod.

"As you wish, Caleb," he ground out through clenched teeth. "If you feel this is for the best, then I wouldn't dare to interfere in how you run your life. I think I did that far too much in the past."

Caleb shrugged as he picked up the cigar he had abandoned and puffed it. "You only did it to protect me and to protect the marquis."

Justin nodded, but the pain on his face at the mention of his father was palpable, and Caleb's own chest hurt at the thought of the man who had raised him.

"I wish we could have seen him today." Caleb shook his head. "I find myself uneasy about the moment of truth."

Justin nodded. "I hope you don't take today's denial of our company personally. Father still has many good days, but also very bad ones now. If today was a bad day, the shock of seeing you after so long could cause a setback. It's better to wait until tomorrow and allow him his rest. That way he can be happy to see you and not overwrought by the experience."

Caleb couldn't help but shake his head at the idea that his father, so strong in all his memories, had to be tiptoed around in his illness. But he had other worries as well.

"I suppose I shall see Mother, too," he murmured.

Justin's nod of reply was slow. "She doesn't leave his side, even when it is to her detriment. She'll certainly be there and I'm sure very happy to see you if her enthusiasm in today's letter was any indication. As will our sister. Tessa has often asked after you."

"Yes, I received some of her letters."

"But you never replied," Justin said, but without any kind of opinion in his voice, including censure.

Still, Caleb couldn't help but wonder if Tessa had been hurt by his silence. He simply hadn't been able to think of a way to address her without saying too much or being too glib. Silence had been a poor way to solve that problem.

Caleb shook his head. The issue of his family was a complicated one, even in the face of his decision to move on from the truth and pretend it mattered little to him. That would be a thorny task with all of them staring him in the face. Seeing his mother, especially, would be difficult. Her actions had caused all this strife and there was some part of him that longed to confront her about that fact.

"You'll do fine," Justin said softly, as if he read Caleb's mind. "I'll be there at your side and will do everything in my power to assist you."

Caleb met Justin's eyes for a moment and smiled. "You already have. Thank you again for allowing me to stay with you. I had no idea my town home had gone into such disrepair during my absence."

"I have no idea why that would be a shock to you! You haven't taken care of the place for years."

Justin laughed, perhaps the first true sound of it since Caleb had turned and found him searching the tavern three days ago. It was a strangely contagious thing and Caleb grinned in return.

"I suppose. There is much I shall have to set to rights now that I'm here. And it allows me a chance to spend the money you'll surely give me in order to make the place livable again."

Justin rolled his eyes, but before his brother could answer, there was the sound of movement in the hallway. Doors opened and shut, and in the distance Justin's butler, Crenshaw, spoke in low tones.

Justin was on his feet in a moment and Caleb couldn't help but stare. His normally dark and dangerous brother had just lit up like a candle glowed within him.

"Victoria," Justin breathed before he turned and hurried from the room without further explanation.

Caleb followed, but moved with purposeful slowness. He wanted to allow the couple a moment to reunite before he interfered. He stepped into the hallway. At the end of it, in the foyer, his brother held his wife. The two were kissing in greeting and Caleb turned his face as a flash of unexpected jealousy filled him.

It wasn't that he had any feeling toward Victoria. She was a beautiful woman, to be sure, but he'd never experienced anything more than brotherly regard for her. No, it was that Justin seemed so *settled* now. So happy with his wife and the life they had built together after resolving the many problems that had once plagued their union.

It was something Caleb had never experienced before and somehow thought he never would. There was but one woman who had offered Caleb such acceptance, and he had thrown her away in his grief and upset. All the better for her, probably.

He shook off thoughts of Marah. What he wanted now was frivolity and fun. He had no intention of seeking out more from a woman but carnal pleasure. It had been a long time since he indulged in such bliss.

In that moment, the happy couple parted, and behind them Caleb saw what their embrace had hidden. Victoria was home, but she wasn't alone. Standing at a distance was the very woman Caleb had been contemplating. A woman he hadn't seen since he slipped into the night two years before.

Marah Farnsworth.

She hadn't yet noticed him as she stepped forward to greet Justin, so Caleb took the opportunity to drink in the sight of her. She was more beautiful than ever. Her blond locks were bound up beneath a traveling bonnet, but the curling length peeked out beneath the brim, appearing as soft and touchable as they had always been. And her eyes, those dark blue eyes that had offered him solace and understanding, sparkled as she smiled in greeting at her friend's husband.

Time hadn't changed her.

"Marah," he said as he moved forward, almost against his will.

She froze at the sound of his voice and looked around Justin's form toward him. When she saw him, she actually took a long step backward, staggering until Victoria caught her elbow to steady her. She opened and shut her mouth once, then again before she found her voice and whispered his name.

"Caleb."

With those two syllables he was undone all over again.

Marah's heart pounded so loudly in her chest that she could scarce hear anything else above its rattling. The entire world had slowed to half time around her and all her focus had been shifted to that one person, the one man she had allowed near her in any way that mattered . . . only to have him run away from her. Ever since, she had been torn between wishing to see him again and praying she never would.

But here he was, standing not five feet away from her and advancing in her direction with slow, steady steps.

Caleb Talbot.

Their time apart had changed him, there was no denying that. Oh, he was still devilishly handsome, his bright blue eyes still as beautiful, his harsh jaw and full lips as kissable as they had been when they last met.

But gone was his sparkling air of mischief that had always made her smile. Gone was the hint of pleasure that forever quirked the corner of his lips.

Now there was a haggard quality to him. Like a dishtowel wrung too hard and left out to dry. He seemed leaner, but not in a healthy way. Like he didn't eat, like he hardly slept.

And despite herself, despite all her attempts to remain stoic toward him, her heart momentarily ached for him and his pain. She *knew* why he had changed, perhaps she was the only one who had fully glimpsed the heartbreak of what he had discovered about his parentage. Of course, that memory brought others. Like his kiss. His touch. His—

She blinked and viciously ended the stream of her thought. When he left, Caleb had made it very clear that he didn't want her, that whatever they had shared, it meant very little to him. She refused to make a cake of herself over him now.

Clearing her throat, she steeled her heart and steadied her tone before she spoke again.

"Mr. Talbot," she said softly before she speared Victoria with a glare. "I didn't realize you were in Town."

He stared at her for a long, charged moment before he spoke. "I had no idea you were here, either." He hesitated. "You aren't staying with Victoria and Justin, are you?"

"Indeed she is," Victoria said, saving Marah the effort of replying. If Marah hadn't been so furious at her friend, she might have hugged her, for her own tongue felt thick and her mind sluggish. "She is our guest for the remainder of the Season."

Justin let out a slow sigh as he turned toward his wife. "My dearest, circumstances have dictated that my brother will also be our guest for the duration of his stay in the city."

Victoria turned on her husband with a gasp of shock that Marah had no doubt was real. It seemed her friend was as surprised by this news as she was.

Caleb . . . under the same roof as she? Great God, what a disaster!

"No!" Victoria said, then turned to her brother-in-law with an apologetic shake of her head. "Not that you aren't welcome, Caleb, but my understanding was that you would be staying at your own town home."

Caleb seemed to have pulled his emotions into check, for, when he shrugged, it was with the nonchalance of a man who couldn't have cared less who stayed in what house and for what duration.

"I would have, my lady, but when we arrived we found the place in great disrepair. It seems I have been remiss in my duties." He faced Marah slightly when he continued, "But I can see I've intruded here and upset your prior plans. I shall quit the house immediately."

Marah's eyes narrowed. Was he so horrified by the idea of spending any time in the same house as she that he would bolt . . . *again*? Just as he had the last time they were together, only this time he admitted he would go. As if *that* made it better.

The anger she had long fought to suppress momentarily shot to the surface and bubbled over.

"You? *Quit?* How shocking," she said through clenched teeth, unable to keep the bitter sarcasm from her tone.

Caleb spun to face her fully and she saw a brief flash of anger in his eyes, but she was happy to also see a rare glimpse of chagrin as well. Good. She hoped he felt sorry. God knew she had done enough of that since the last time she saw him.

With a flounce of her hair, she turned away before he could retort.

"Do as you wish, Mr. Talbot," she said. "Your actions are meaningless to me. Now, I find I'm very tired from our travels. If you wouldn't mind, Victoria, I'd like to retire to my chambers."

Victoria slowly stared from one fuming houseguest to the other before she nodded. "Of course, Marah. I'll show you to them myself."

Marah nodded to Justin, but completely ignored Caleb as she turned away and followed her friend up the long hallway and to the staircase beyond. But with every step she felt Caleb's eyes burning into her. And it took everything in her not to look back at him.

Marah dipped her hands into the icy cold water in the basin in her room and splashed it over her skin. She was surprised that it didn't sizzle when it met the heat of her anger and humiliation. Grabbing for a nearby towel, she dried the droplets of water that clung to her skin and drew in a deep, cleansing breath before she turned to face Victoria.

Her friend shifted with discomfort, but Marah was incapable of tempering her reaction at present. She'd never before felt so betrayed and ambushed.

"Would you care to explain yourself?" Marah said softly as she placed the bunched towel beside the basin. "Or at least tell me why Caleb Talbot is *here*, in this house?"

Victoria shook her head swiftly, but made no effort to move toward Marah.

"I'm so sorry, Marah. I had no idea that my brother-in-law would be staying here at the same time you were in residence."

Marah arched a brow. From the sick, horrified look on Victoria's face, Marah believed that to be true, but regardless, the response didn't fully satisfy her. After all, it implied other, less savory statements.

"But you *did* know he would be here in London, didn't you?" she asked softly.

Victoria hesitated long enough that Marah knew the answer even before it was spoken, and she pursed her lips in increased displeasure.

Victoria whispered, "I did. At the same time I left Town to visit you in Baybary, Justin departed in the hopes he could locate his brother. His father asked him to bring Caleb home in these final weeks of his life and Justin couldn't refuse that request."

Again, a surge of empathy for Caleb rose up in Marah, but she tamped it down firmly. There was no room for any deeper feeling for the man now. Not when he had made it so abundantly clear that he didn't want or need her regard, her empathy, or her affection.

She blushed before she spoke again. "If you knew he would be here, it follows that you were aware we would see each other, even if Caleb *wasn't* residing within your walls."

Victoria nodded a second time, though the motion was slow to come. "I realized it was very likely that your paths would cross once you were both in Town, yes. After all, Justin is Caleb's brother. Whether he stayed here or not, we would have invited him to join us many times during your stay."

"And yet you didn't share any of this with me when you urged me to join you in London." Marah sucked in a breath, for she feared the sting behind her eyes that said tears were coming. She had cried so much over Caleb Talbot, she resented that she was on the verge of doing so again, even after two years. "*Why* did you do that to me?"

At least Victoria had the sense to look repentant.

She stepped closer, reaching out a comforting and steadying hand toward Marah.

"I'm sorry. Perhaps I *should* have told you, but I feared it might keep you from coming to London. I realize it was selfish of me, but I need you here right now." Victoria drew a breath and continued slowly, "And perhaps more importantly I think you *need* to see Caleb. And he, you."

"Need to see him?" Marah burst out as she paced away from her friend. "Why in God's name would you believe that? He made his feelings more than clear two years ago and again today when he said he would quit the house immediately upon seeing me."

"But you must have seen his emotion when he said it," Victoria said. "I certainly saw yours."

Marah pursed her lips. She had been too shocked to control her expression. She would have to work harder to do so in the future. "No, you are mistaken. There is nothing left between us."

Victoria shook her head. "No, Marah. *Everything* is left between you, and that is why you've hidden away for so long. And we both know that there are many reasons for Caleb's departure from the city, but one of them is *you*."

"What are you talking about?" Marah snapped even as the blood drained from her cheeks.

"You haven't ever spoken of it to me, but I *know* you two shared something powerful and instant two years ago when we came to London. I know when he left, your heart was broken, even if you tried to hide it. You have unresolved matters between you, and I think it would be good for you both if you finally faced them."

Marah spun on her friend, barely stifling a bitter laugh. Oh, how little Victoria knew. She had longed to tell her the whole story of the afternoon she and Caleb had shared two years before, but somehow had been unable. Victoria didn't know the half of what had transpired that day, or in the days and weeks afterward.

That was her private pain. Her personal hell.

"Caleb . . ." Marah shut her eyes as her fingers moved of their own accord to the scar on her wrist. It was a permanent reminder of her last trip to London. "*Mr. Talbot* didn't wish to settle whatever was left unresolved between us when he had the chance to do so. And *I* want to move forward, not look back."

"But you *don't* move forward!" Victoria insisted. "You have been living in the past, locked away in Baybary."

Marah folded her arms. "Then be happy I've broken out of that shell and come here, but do not

press me on the subject of Caleb, Victoria. It's clear
from his behavior today that he can scarcely stand
the sight of me, so there is little use to wishing for
or creating more than that between us. We will be
distant acquaintances from now on. That is all."

Victoria seemed to wish to say more, but instead
she shook her head slowly. "I'll leave you to your
rest, then. Again, I apologize for withholding the
information about Caleb's visit."

Marah looked at her friend. Victoria did look
truly distressed, enough so that it softened Marah's
anger toward her. After all, Victoria was going
through a great deal. It was Marah's job to help
her, and judging her friend for what she had done
did not fulfill that task.

With a sigh, Marah hugged her friend for reassurance. When she drew away, she shrugged. "Just
don't expect to orchestrate some grand reconciliation, Victoria. It won't happen."

Victoria looked at her with incredulity, but said
her good-byes and left Marah alone. After her
friend was gone, Marah went limp against the door.

A grand reconciliation. How often she had hoped
for that, especially in the weeks and months immediately after their last encounter. She had frequently
dreamed that Caleb would ride up to her door and
apologize for abandoning her. That he would offer

her the future of her heart, as she had once dared to dream they could share.

But the years since then had taught her one thing . . . she couldn't depend upon men like Caleb Talbot . . . men like her father. If she wanted happiness, she required stability, so whatever was once between her and Caleb was dead now.

For her sanity, it had to be.

Chapter 3

At a small supper table with only a few occupants, ignoring another person was almost impossible. But Marah was doing an admirable job of it and Caleb would have smiled at her dogged determination to pretend he didn't exist, if only he didn't recognize how fully he must have hurt her to cause this rift between them.

Leaving without a word had seemed like his best . . . perhaps his *only* option the night he'd done it. But now he had to live with the consequences.

Turning his attention instead to his brother and sister-in-law, Caleb sighed anew. The couple were seated close together, utterly engrossed in each other. They weren't eating and they certainly didn't seem to be interested in playing host and hostess. Apparently two weeks apart was enough to send them mad for each other.

He drew in a long breath and returned his focus to Marah. There would be no avoiding conversation if Justin and Victoria wouldn't be of assistance, so it was best to jump right in. Perhaps if he worked hard enough, he could overcome this tension between them tonight and put Marah as much in his past as he had decided he must do with the truth of his parentage.

"I was sorry to hear about the passing of your grandmother," he began.

Marah lifted her gaze from her plate and speared him with dark blue heaven that had always sparked with whatever emotion she felt. Tonight there was pain in those captivating eyes, anger, but also a grief he was beginning to understand even if he didn't want to.

"Were you?" she asked in brusque tones. "I didn't receive a note from you when she died. I hadn't realized she even rated a thought, let alone any sorrow from you."

He frowned. When he had heard of the death, he'd briefly thought of penning a missive. In fact, he'd begun several only to destroy them after deeming them either too emotional or not emotional enough. Ultimately he had talked himself out of the notion entirely.

"I *did* feel sorrow for you, Marah, but struggled to properly express it," he said softly. "And you are correct in my lack of manners. I'm afraid that in the last two years I have lost those little niceties and civilities that dictate social behavior."

Marah took a sip of wine, looking at him with stark disapproval as she did so. "The niceties and civilities are often what make life bearable. And they are present in even the lowest society, so you must have been quite an outcast during your time away."

She meant the statement as a sling against him, and it struck home on a far deeper level than perhaps she had even intended. An outcast was exactly what he had been. What he remained and would probably always remain, if only because he no longer felt comfortable in his own skin.

"I was indeed," he said softly. "But an outcast of my own making, I fear. At any rate, I apologize again, both for the pain of her passing and for my lack of manners in addressing the subject."

She didn't answer, either to accept or to decline his apology.

Caleb sighed. "Perhaps we can strike upon a less painful topic now?"

She arched a brow, though the hardness of her face softened slightly. Caleb couldn't help but smile. It seemed he still possessed the ability to break through Marah's tough shell if he chose to do so.

"What topic do you suggest, Mr. Talbot?" she asked, her tone low. "Should we discuss the weather? The roads? Or perhaps today's fashions? What benign, emotionless matter would strike your fancy?"

She snapped her mouth shut and Caleb could see she regretted her sudden and emotional outburst, but he couldn't help but take solace in the unguarded moment. Marah had been so cold and distant since they first saw each other that he had begun to believe she didn't care for him at all anymore. This momentary burst of feeling, even if it was anger or upset, proved she wasn't as immune to him as she pretended to be.

"You know, this reminds me of the first time we met," he mused, his mind turning back to that afternoon that at once seemed like yesterday and a hundred years before.

She frowned as she lowered her gaze to her plate. "Does it? I don't recall that day, I'm afraid."

"No?" Caleb leaned closer, trying to determine if her bitter words were truth, but unable to read her expression now that she'd turned her face and he could only see her profile. "I do."

Marah's lips twitched as if she was suppressing a smile, and triumph coursed through Caleb. No matter how strenuously she declared their time together two years ago had been meaningless, clearly that was a lie meant to protect herself.

"We were sitting at this very table, if I recall," he continued, becoming more comfortable as he once more found the easy rhythm of teasing flirtation. He'd always been talented in that kind of surface interaction. "We shared a luncheon, I believe, but *you* were very cold."

Marah turned a glare toward him, but there was a tiny sparkle hidden far within her eyes that drove him to continue.

"Only I was very lucky that you turned all your ire toward my brother then, not me."

Justin laughed and both Marah and Caleb snapped their gazes to him in surprise. In truth he had almost entirely forgotten the presence of his brother and sister-in-law. As they had earlier with each other, he had become too engrossed in his companion to pay attention to his surroundings.

Justin smiled first at Marah, but then to Victoria with a knowing wickedness. She returned the expression immediately and undeniable heat sparked between them.

Caleb's brother said, "If Marah was cold to me then, it was nothing less than I deserved for my abominable behavior during her last visit to London. I'm only grateful she did not challenge me to a duel."

Marah smiled and it was a friendly expression.

Despite himself, Caleb stared. He hadn't seen that look on her face for so long he'd almost forgotten how pretty she could be when she was soft like this.

"My dear Lord Baybary," she said with a shake of her head. "You did not deserve half my ire and if you did, you've certainly proven yourself more than worthy in the time since then."

"I've done my best to prove myself," Justin said softly, his hand moving to cover Victoria's on the tabletop.

Caleb couldn't help but notice that Marah looked away from the happy couple's easy display of affection and love.

"You and Caleb were a wicked pair then, my dear. And Shaw only encouraged you," Victoria said with a light laugh of her own. "The stories you told that afternoon were terrible, though they seemed quite engrossing to Marah at the time."

Marah returned her stare on her plate, and all her verve was muted as she shrugged. "That was long ago."

"Not that long," Caleb said.

Looking at her now, it seemed like that playful luncheon was yesterday, not two years past. At first he had only been flirtatious with her in order to assist his brother, who had asked Caleb to create a distraction for "the unpleasant Miss Farnsworth," but by the time the afternoon had ended, Marah had captured his interest in reality. Despite her prickly exterior, Caleb had wanted her with a power that surprised him. He'd never been one to turn his attention toward chilly virgins.

Only Marah had ended up being so much more.

Victoria looked at her friend, but her expression was one of concern. She slowly got to her feet.

"Why don't we go to the library? We can share a bottle of port before we turn in."

Justin laughed as he took his wife's arm. "I like the sound of the second part. We've been apart too long."

Victoria blushed, but then she smiled at Caleb and Marah as the two exited the room.

Caleb got to his feet and turned toward Marah.

"Will you accompany me?" he asked.

She stared at his outstretched fingers, almost as if she feared them. In some small way, so did he. He hadn't touched her since that afternoon two years before when he had . . . well, he had touched her in ways that weren't gentlemanly. Now he anticipated this brief brush of their skin with great enthusiasm.

Slowly she rose from her seat. Their gazes met and she lifted her chin in defiance, refusing to break the stare as she extended a trembling hand and slipped her gloved fingers around his bicep.

There were three layers of clothing separating their skin and the touch was an utterly appropriate one, something one might even share with a sibling. But the moment her warm hand wrapped around his arm, Caleb felt anything but brotherly.

For the first time in too many months to count, the rush of desire flooded his body and his cock swelled ever so slightly. It had been so long since any woman inspired his interest that the feeling was immensely pleasurable and utterly surprising, enough so that Caleb stood stock-still as he sucked in a breath. He was like a green boy and it took everything in him to regain control.

"Are we going to follow Victoria and Justin?" Marah asked softly after a moment had passed. "Or simply stand here all night?"

Caleb suddenly had a long list of wicked activities he would rather pursue that evening, but he pushed them aside. "Of course we'll follow my brother and his wife."

They stepped into the hall and down the short distance to the library where Victoria and Justin awaited them. As they entered the room, Caleb saw his brother's expression. It was troubled, worried, and more than a little confused. But who could blame him? Justin knew very little about what had transpired between Caleb and Marah. She was the one conquest Caleb had never bragged about.

For a short time the two couples talked, but it was obvious Victoria and Justin remained downstairs only out of courtesy to their guests. From time to time Justin slid his fingers along his wife's ungloved hand or Victoria leaned in close to him, and their desire to be alone was palpable.

Eventually the discussion tapered off and the couple became lost in their own world once more, talking low in the corner by the fire.

It seemed their closeness made Marah as uncomfortable as it made Caleb, for she finally slipped to the opposite side of the room and began to examine the high shelves of books as if they were the most interesting things in the world.

"You read Latin?" Caleb teased as he sidled up beside her.

She jerked her face toward his. "I beg your pardon?"

He nodded toward the shelf. "All these are my father's . . ." He trailed off as an unexpected burst of pain at the memory these books inspired hit him. He could almost see his father, spectacles perched on his nose, reading over one of his books. With a shake of his head, he continued, "They are his classic philosophical tomes. Most are in Latin, as you must have noticed."

Marah looked at the shelf again, then smiled tightly. "Ah, I wondered why I didn't understand half of what I was reading. I assumed I was only distracted. I read but a little Latin, Mr. Talbot, and mostly in the context of medicine because of my grandmother's position as a healer, not philosophy."

She turned toward him slightly, as if she expected him to say more. Unfortunately, all thoughts emptied from Caleb's mind in that moment and all he could think about was how utterly delectable her lips appeared.

Did she taste the same after all this time? Would she sigh if he touched her, or recoil?

She cleared her throat, blushing beneath his focused scrutiny. "So—so how do you find London after all your time away?"

Caleb's lips pursed with displeasure. From her expression and the tone of her voice, he could see Marah was only asking him the question to be polite. This was small talk, much the same as she might make with any person she didn't know. In some way, it was an attempt to push him into the category of faint acquaintance. To forget that they had shared not just passion, but an intimate exchange of emotion that he had never experienced with any other person in the world.

He liked her icy demeanor at supper more. There

was something more intimate about her anger than her politeness. Anger implied more feeling.

"Mr. Talbot?" she pressed.

He shook his head. If she wanted a mere acquaintance, perhaps he should follow her lead. Certainly he couldn't and shouldn't be more. Not under the current circumstances of his life. He longed to lose himself in the meaningless existence he had once lived. A woman like Marah would want more than that. She *deserved* far more than he had ever been capable of providing.

"My brother and I arrived only a few hours before you did, but from the little I saw of the city, I found it much the same."

She looked at him more closely than before, her dark blue eyes searching his face and seeing more than he wished to reveal. Finally she whispered, "But *you* are different."

A blush immediately darkened her cheeks and she turned her face. "I apologize, Mr. Talbot, that was an abominably forward and rude thing to say."

He shook his head. "It wasn't," he insisted. "After all, you know a bit more about the situation than most. It was merely an observation and a keen one, I might add. Yes, I am a different man than I was the last time I came to London. You well know why."

She nodded, her face still in profile, but he could see she understood. In some ways she did, and not only because she knew his secret, confessed in a moment of weakness and pain.

That moment haunted him, forcing him to relive it briefly, but in powerful detail. Victoria and Marah had come to Town two years before in a desperate attempt to find a missing friend. But their investigation had gone wrong in the end and the pair had been attacked by a man obsessed with the woman they searched for. The bastard had abducted Justin's wife, but left Marah behind.

She had been bound. Bloodied.

Caleb could still feel the way she had shook in his arms while he tended to the wounds around her wrists left by her cruel attackers. She had confessed her terror, on the edge of hysteria, and clung to him like he was her savior. It was the first time he'd ever felt like another person truly *needed* him and that he could provide more than frivolous joviality and empty companionship.

At first he had talked to soothe her, but somehow her presence had soothed *him* and he had found himself confessing the secret he had only just discovered that same day. He had whispered that his father wasn't the marquis. He hadn't meant to say it, but once it was out there was relief in trusting her.

Because she hadn't judged him. She had given him nothing but acceptance and comfort. And that had led to a surrender of a different kind.

But these bare, stark facts weren't why she identified with him now. No, she understood because he could see she, too, had changed since her last visit to the city.

In part that was his fault. Perhaps more than in part.

"Victoria says you'll see your father tomorrow," she whispered, drawing him back to the present as she let herself face him.

Although she had been distant earlier and dismissive a moment ago, Caleb now saw the one emotion he had been missing in her. Empathy. Not pity, for he wouldn't have welcomed that, but a deep compassion.

He nodded, ignoring the powerful ache that troubled his heart at the thought. "We wished to see the marquis today, but he was unwell. My mother told Justin in her message that it would be better to come tomorrow."

Marah was silent for a long moment, but then suddenly and unexpectedly her hand came out and covered his. Her touch made him want her, just as it had earlier in the evening, but this time there was something more. That same feeling he had felt two years before: that with her, he could surrender. And that he was capable of offering her more than mere passion.

"I'm sorry, Caleb. Truly."

Hesitant, he covered her hand with his own and smiled down at her. "Thank you."

The moment stretched out, as quiet as the silent room, but as meaningful as any deep and probing discussion. Finally Marah shook her head, like she was waking from a spell. She looked down at their clasped hands and slowly slid hers away. She took a long step back.

Caleb held back a curse. He could see she wanted to bolt, perhaps even excuse herself for the night, but he wasn't ready to release her, not when he'd had a glimpse of the closeness they once formed, but had been lost when he left. He searched wildly for a topic of conversation that would force her to stay out of innate politeness.

He choked out, "And what of you? How long has it been since you were in London?"

Her expression fell and the blood left her face. "Since—since—"

She stopped, and with one hand she caught the other and gently rubbed her wrist. Caleb stared.

The sleeve of her gown lifted slightly when she brushed it and now he saw the faint pale ridge of a scar there. With a gasp he caught her hand and lifted it, pushing the fabric aside so he could see the mark better in the light.

The scar was faded but he could see how painful it had once been. He'd had no idea that the wounds he tended that long-ago afternoon were so deep.

He stroked his fingertip along the delicate skin and only looked up when Marah gasped softly. She was staring at him, eyes wide and face even paler than before. Her breath came in sharp heaves and her hand shook as she withdrew it.

"I'm sorry," he said as she pushed her gown sleeve back over the mark. "I'm sorry for that."

She jerked her face up. "*That* was not your fault."

"Other things were," he said without meaning to.

Marah spun around, putting her back to him. Caleb watched, helpless, as she drew in several long, shaky breaths, watched her fight for control. After a few awful moments, she turned back to him with a smile that was very obviously forced.

"Victoria says I've lived in the past for too long," she began, casting a quick glance to their utterly distracted companions, neither of whom had even noticed the intense interaction of their guests. "Perhaps she's right. But there *is* a future for me, and I think there is one for you, as well. But only if we forget about what happened before, and find some way to move forward."

Caleb shut his eyes briefly. Marah was only repeating the very speech he had made to his brother that afternoon, but somehow that gave him no comfort. Now that she was here and he would be forced to see her on a regular basis, the idea of forgetting what they had shared seemed almost impossible. How was he to forget what she had tasted like? How soft and sweet her sighs of pleasure were? Not to mention how quick her mind was . . . how much he *liked* her.

When he looked at her, those things came back to him so powerfully that he could have shut his eyes and relived the entire afternoon they had shared in vivid detail.

"Caleb," she whispered, drawing his attention back to her. "Let us agree not to revisit the past again."

He stared down at her. Her jaw was firm and her eyes were clear. She believed this course of action to be best and was determined to stick with it, regardless of his response.

"It is an admirable desire, Marah, but—"

"No!" she interrupted, her voice breaking. "*Please* do this one thing for me. Shake my hand, Caleb and let us pretend that we have only just met. Let us be acquaintances alone from this moment forward."

She held out a hand for him to seal the bargain she required. Her fingers shook, the only outward signal that what she was asking was difficult or painful for her. But even her hesitance did Caleb no good. One look in her dark eyes and he could see that once they clasped hands on the bargain, she wouldn't look back. She was stronger than he was. Strong enough to do as she promised and pretend they had no shared history, no personal connection.

He stared at the delicate fingers, still outstretched toward him. And with difficulty and more pain than he expected, he took them.

"Very well," he said with a stiff bow as he shook her hand.

She nodded as she withdrew from him, and then she took a few jerking steps toward Justin and Victoria.

"I'm very sorry to be so rude," she said, her tone falsely bright. "But I should excuse myself. Today was trying, and a soft pillow sounds heavenly at present."

Victoria shook herself away from her obvious

distraction with her husband and moved toward her friend with both hands outstretched.

"Of course, my dear. You *do* look tired. A good night's sleep will make all the difference."

"Yes," Marah said with a smile as she nodded toward Justin. "Good evening, my lord, my lady."

Slowly she turned on her heel and faced Caleb, but this time all the emotion had been washed from her face. She stared at him, and he *felt* her fulfilling their agreement.

"Good evening, Mr. Talbot."

He swallowed hard as he inclined his head. "Miss Marah," he choked.

And then she was gone, disappearing from his sight out the door. And he knew nothing would be the same for him ever again.

"I suppose you shall follow her," Justin said as he came forward.

Caleb jolted. "She would never allow it."

Victoria's eyebrows rose slowly as she stared at him. "I believe Justin meant you shall follow her lead and take to bed early, as you had a trying day of travel yourself."

For the first time in years, Caleb felt the heat of embarrassment at his cheek. To say such a thing out loud and in front of one of Marah's best friends was inexcusable.

"Of course," he murmured. "I'm sorry."

Victoria nodded, but there was a gentle pity in her eyes that Caleb wished he couldn't see.

"You haven't seen her for a long time," she said softly.

"Not since—" he cut himself off. "Two years."

"Much has changed since then, for you both," Justin said as he slipped an arm around his wife.

"Yes," Caleb said with a sigh.

"You know she . . ." Victoria cast a quick glance at her husband before she continued. "Marah met someone about a year ago. He is a man of no rank, but great fortune, named Emerson Winstead. He seems to have taken a strong interest in her."

Caleb stared at his sister-in-law but he no longer saw her. All he saw was this faceless man touching Marah the way he had once touched her. He saw her pleasure and it caused him nothing but pain.

"What kind of man is he?" he asked with a shake of his head.

Justin shrugged. "Although I have investigated, there is little to know about him, I'm afraid. But Marah is determined to like him."

Caleb nodded, but now the nausea and the ache that had begun in his belly doubled. "Well, I wish her the very best. And now I think you are correct,

I should go to bed myself. Tomorrow is certain to be a trying day for us both. Good night."

Without waiting for a response, Caleb hurried from the room, hoping his brother and sister-in-law didn't see his emotions reflected on his face and wishing he was stoic enough not to feel them at all.

Chapter 4

Caleb walked the length of the small parlor, then pivoted to repeat the action. He had been doing this for the past quarter of an hour and had counted fifty-three times that he had restlessly paced the room. Justin sat on the settee across the chamber from him and his brother watched his every step, almost as if he was counting them as well.

Finally, with a shake of his head like he was waking from a dream, Justin stood up.

"How are you holding up?" his brother asked.

Caleb stopped mid-stride, the nervous accounting of his steps dissolving from his mind. In just a few short moments he would be escorted upstairs to see the man who had raised him.

He would be forced to face the very thing he had run from, hidden from for two long years. But there would be no more of that. Not when he had to look the marquis and his own lying mother directly in their faces.

And behind those thoughts of grief and anxiety were others about a person not even in this home. Ever since Victoria and Justin had revealed that Marah had a beau, that idea had been crowding into Caleb's thoughts and even his dreams. It mixed with his other anxieties until they were all a confused, jumbled, bitter brew in his belly.

"Caleb?" Justin whispered, his tone heavy with concern and empathy.

He shook his head as he realized his brother had asked a question he hadn't answered, but then he had no answer to give. He had no idea *how* he was holding up, or even if he *would* once the moment of truth came.

The door behind them opened and both men turned to face the intruder. A petite young woman stepped into the room. For a brief moment Caleb didn't recognize her, though from her fine clothing, it was clear she wasn't a servant. She stared at him, her brown eyes filling with tears. It was only when she spoke that her identity became clear.

"Caleb? My God, it is really you," she sobbed as she crossed the room and wrapped her arms around his neck.

Caleb hesitated and then let his own arms close around the slender form of Tessa Talbot, his younger sister by five years.

"Tess, you look wonderful!" he said as he drew back to look at her closely.

His sister was edging toward old maidenhood after five unsuccessful seasons, but she was a beautiful woman. The two years he had been away hadn't changed that. If anything she only had a maturity about her now, a sophistication that was often lacking in girls of seventeen and eighteen who splashed onto the scene with giggles too loud and gowns too garish. But she was much thinner than he remembered and her face had a sadder, more serious look to it.

"You don't look well," his sister said as she stepped away. "Roaming aimlessly, abandoning your family doesn't suit you, brother."

"Tessa," Justin said sharply.

Their sister turned toward him and Caleb saw the unspoken communication that passed between the siblings. Seeing their connection hit him like a punch in the gut. He no longer shared that with them. Perhaps a small bit with Justin, who had never stopped reaching out to him, but not anything like the close bond they had shared before. The years away while he pondered the truth about his parentage had cut him from his family almost more than his secret had.

An aching loneliness burned around his heart,

merging with a guilt that nearly took him to his knees at that realization. How much worse would it be when he saw his parents?

"Come, they are waiting for you upstairs," Tessa finally said with another frown toward him.

Justin motioned Caleb to follow her as she exited the parlor, and Caleb acquiesced. As he stepped onto the landing and then up the winding staircase to the second floor of the home, he couldn't help but feel he was a prisoner being taken to execution, with his sister as escort and his brother behind him as jailer meant to keep him from bolting.

The feeling only increased as Tessa stopped at the door to his mother and father's chamber. She turned toward him with a shaky, tearful smile.

"Papa will be so happy to see you. He's been asking for you every half hour since he awoke this morning. And Mama is waiting for you at his side." Tessa tilted her head to look at him. Caleb shifted with discomfort beneath her stare, wondering what thoughts passed through her mind. Then his sister lifted her hand and gently touched his face, her anger with him faded, at least for the moment. "Don't look so worried, Caleb. It won't be so bad as all that."

Caleb shut his eyes. Oh, if only she knew. But he smiled down at her with difficulty and then turned toward the door. After a few long, calming breaths, he turned the knob and stepped into the chamber.

It was darker than he had expected, and Caleb stood in the doorway for a long moment before his eyes adjusted and he was able to see clearly. The fire burned low, and across from it his father's bed was outlined by a solitary lamp burning on the side table.

"Is that him?" came a weak voice from within the chamber. "Has he come at last?"

For a horrible moment, Caleb considered turning on his heel and fleeing the room rather than facing the man in that bed. He was certain he could have a horse and be gone before anyone caught up with him, only this time he would be careful never to be found again.

But then his rational mind retook control. Running hadn't been a successful way of dealing with this situation for all these years. As he'd told Justin, it was time to stop and reclaim his life. And part of that reclaiming was to face the man who had raised him and find a way to pretend he didn't know the truth.

"Yes, my lord," he said as he entered the room. "It is Caleb."

A rustle sounded from beside the bed, and then a woman stepped into the light. Caleb stared as his mother, Phillipa Talbot, rushed forward. In the brief moments before she launched herself at him in a crushing embrace, he noticed that she, like his sister, had lost a great deal of weight. And she had a haunted expression that made her once happy face very long and pained indeed.

She held him, shaking like an autumn leaf about to break away from the tree, but said nothing for a long moment. And despite his anger with her at the lie she had created, despite his utter lack of understanding of why his mother would do what she had done, Caleb allowed himself to hold her.

When his arms came around her, a hundred memories assaulted him at once. Ones of his mother's comfort, of her laughter, of all the special things she had done for their family over the years. Despite not being the heir, despite being born into this family as a middle child who was neither to be groomed for inheritance nor babied, he had never once felt neglected or uncared for, thanks to his mother.

Finally she released him and stepped away, swiping uselessly at the tears that clouded her eyes and overflowed onto her pale cheeks.

"Oh, Caleb," she murmured. "My boy, my precious boy."

He dipped his head at the endearment she had

used for him as a child. He'd almost forgotten it.

"Mother," he managed to say gruffly, but could say no more. He had too many questions to dare it, for he didn't think she would appreciate such an inquisition with his father lying not three feet away.

Caleb turned toward the bed and faced the man who lay there. It took everything in him not to stumble away at what he saw.

The skeletal person who lay within the folds of blanket couldn't be the same bold, powerful man who had raised him. It wasn't possible.

Illness had made the marquis' skin sallow and stretched it along his face until it was almost translucent. His dark brown eyes, the ones Caleb's brother and sister shared, proving they were of their father's true blood even if Caleb wasn't, were cloudy and dilated with pain.

The thin, pale hand lifted from the blanket and reached for him. Caleb took it and was shocked by how light and cold his father's touch was. There was no strength left in it and very little life.

"Caleb," he finally said, and the voice, at least, was the same as Caleb had remembered. That deep, resonating voice that could bring down the house in anger or soothe the slightest pain with compassion and grace.

"Hello, my lord," he whispered, taking the seat beside the bed that his mother had begun to motion toward wildly.

"Are you here? Or is this is another dream?" the marquis asked, but it seemed every word took great effort, and he let out a pained sigh at the end of his question.

"It is no dream, sir," Caleb choked as emotions he'd vowed not to feel overcame him.

Had his father truly dreamed of his return, only to awaken disappointed by his absence? The idea of it smashed Caleb as hard as any fist in a bar fight ever had. In fact, it stung more than any physical injury in his experience.

Caleb swallowed past the lump in his throat and turned toward his mother slightly. "Is he in great pain?"

She hesitated, her eyes tearing up before she nodded wordlessly.

Caleb flinched. "And can they give him nothing to relieve it?"

His mother smiled at him sadly. "He refused his laudanum this morning. He said he did not wish to sleep through your visit."

Caleb stared at his mother for a moment before he looked back at his father.

"You wouldn't have your ease?" he whispered as he reached forward and gently brushed a long lock of gray hair away from his father's face.

"The drug makes me . . ." His father struggled for a moment. "Tired. Far away. And you have been far away from me for so long already. I was . . . afraid this might be . . . the only time I would see you. I didn't want to . . . forget."

Caleb sucked in a harsh and painful breath, not only at the laborious way his father was forced to speak, but at the guilt his words brought. Here he had been wallowing in his own anguish and his father bore his own far larger share with such silent strength.

"Well, you needn't worry about that," Caleb finally choked. "This will not be the only time you see me. I intend to come here every day. After a week you shall have had your fill of me and will be telling the servants to inform me you are not at home when they bring you my card."

His father wheezed for a moment and Caleb tensed. Dear God, had he come at the very last moment? Was this his father's death rattle? And why had he waited so long to return home?

But after a brief moment of horror, Caleb realized his father wasn't dying, but laughing. The rattling, awful sound was the closest he could come to a chuckle. Behind him, his mother gasped.

"That is the first time he has smiled in months," she whispered.

Caleb gaped at his father. This grimace was a *smile*? It was nothing at all like the broad, mischievous grin he recalled from his youth. And this wheezing sound that was now his father's laugh was but an empty, hollow shell of the booming chuckle that had filled their halls over the years.

The wheeze faded and his father's lids drooped slightly as he settled deeper into the pillows. "I promise to kick you out if I grow tired of your presence," he said with difficulty.

Caleb nodded, taking the moment of his father's distraction to swipe at a tear that had somehow escaped and now clung to his cheek. "Very good. Now let me sit with you, sir. I would greatly love to hear about your adventures while I was away."

His father opened one eye and speared him with a look. "I'm not certain I will be very entertaining."

Caleb smiled. "Then let me tell you some of mine."

The older man nodded slowly as he closed his eyes. Behind him, Caleb heard the door click quietly, and when he looked over his shoulder, he realized his mother had left the two of them alone. So he looked down into his father's haggard face and began to speak.

* * *

Caleb had no idea how much time had passed when he finally stepped into the hallway and stretched his back. As if they had been listening for the sound of the door, his family stepped from the parlor across the hall. Still blinking from the brighter light, Caleb stared at them, gathered as a group before him.

The anger he had sensed in his sister earlier remained on her face, though there was love in her eyes and empathy as well, as she looked at him. Justin simply appeared worried, his face lined by anxiety.

As for his mother . . . she seemed drawn. Exhausted. And resigned, as if she realized her time with her husband was coming to an end and she had somehow managed to find peace with that fact. Caleb knew he shouldn't begrudge her that little comfort, but he found himself angry that she could once again distance herself from the man who had raised him.

"How was he?" his mother asked, breaking the silence.

When she spoke, it was as if everyone in the hallway exhaled at once, relieved that the awkward moment had passed at last.

Caleb shrugged. "He is tired. He dozed in and out during our time together, but I welcomed it, for the sleep seemed to ease his pain. He engaged me seldom, though when I stopped talking, he always encouraged me to continue. He seems to have fallen into a deeper sleep now."

His sister nodded. "Yes, what you describe is how he is now."

His mother stepped forward and took his hand. Caleb stared down into her face, loving and abhorring her with seemingly equal measure.

"How are you, my son?" she whispered. "You were in there for three hours, you must be overwhelmed."

He slipped his hand free gently, unable to bear the touch meant to comfort him. He ignored the way her lips trembled when he did so.

"I'm fine. He is the one who suffers," he said. "But I *am* tired. Justin, I know I promised I would find another place to stay immediately, but I find I'm not up to the challenge after this day. Perhaps I could trespass upon your hospitality one more night?"

Before Justin could reply, their mother said, "You are staying with your brother?"

Caleb let out a sigh before he nodded. "My own town home is in great disarray. Until it has been aired, cleaned, and restaffed, I won't be able to stay there."

"Then come here," his mother said, her face lighting up with real pleasure for the first time since his arrival. "Stay with us in your old chamber. I could have it ready for you before your things were sent from Justin and Victoria's home. Tessa and I would love to have you."

Caleb's gaze flashed to his sister, who seemed less certain that she would enjoy such a thing, and then to his brother before he shook his head.

"No, I think it would be better for everyone if I stayed where I am. As long as my presence is no trouble to Victoria and Justin."

The two brothers locked gazes, and Caleb could see Justin's disappointment. Caleb turned away from it, ready to hear his brother shun him and force him to go to a place he did not desire, but instead Justin said, "Of course it's no trouble. And it is getting late now, so perhaps it is best to leave you settled where you are."

Their mother's expression fell, but she nodded. "I suppose you are right. Everyone is in such high emotion, there is no reason to rush around changing what is working out. But if you change your mind—"

Before she could finish, Caleb bowed. "Of course. I will consider your offer."

His mother's lips thinned, but she said nothing further even when his sister wrapped her arm around her gently. For a long moment the family stood in silence, but then Caleb shifted.

"Justin, might we return to your home now? I assume Victoria must be awaiting a report on how the day went."

Justin nodded and Caleb almost felt badly for using his sister-in-law to force his brother's departure, but Victoria had been feeling ill that morning and hadn't accompanied the gentlemen to their meeting. He knew Justin was concerned for her health and wanted to check on her.

"Yes, we *should* return," Justin conceded.

Their mother and sister escorted the two men downstairs. Caleb watched as Justin embraced each woman. Caleb wished he could be so unguarded, but instead he nodded his farewell to each and stepped outside.

He was surprised to find the sun setting. Time had slipped away from him today, as much as it ever had when he drank it away. Only he preferred the drinking, for it numbed the pain he felt so keenly at present. There was yet another reason to forget all these troubles and return to the carefree life he'd once led.

Stepping into the carriage, he let out a long sigh. His brother settled in across from him and the carriage rolled into motion.

"Caleb—" Justin began when they had moved along a few streets.

He lifted his gaze to Justin. "You are disappointed in me, there is no need to begin an entire treatise about it. I don't think I can bear it at present."

Justin pursed his lips. "I'm not disappointed. Great God, Caleb, it was the first time you have seen our family since you found out the truth about yourself. To be honest, I expected much worse."

Caleb laughed, but there was no humor in the sound. "Did you think I would enter the house and scream out the truth from the foyer, demand satisfaction, perhaps challenge someone, *anyone* to a duel?"

Justin shrugged. "There was much I feared. But instead you remained quite calm about the entire situation."

Caleb shut his eyes as he thought of the jumbled images of his time with his family. "Our sister holds a great deal of resentment toward me."

Justin nodded. "She, like everyone else, knows nothing of the circumstance which caused you to leave so abruptly. Tessa thinks you abandoned our family and yes, she is angry about it, despite my attempts to defend you since your departure."

"Well, I appreciate your efforts, even if they were fruitless." Caleb rubbed his eyes.

"If you want to end her anger, I suppose you could tell her the truth," Justin said after a pause, his voice barely carrying.

Caleb jerked straight up and stared at his brother in shock. "Tell her? You and I have already discussed this. I have no intention of pursuing the truth of my birth, either by revealing that I know of it to anyone in our family or by making any attempt to uncover more about the particulars of it. You of all people should know why that isn't prudent or even possible. You kept this secret for years."

"For all the good it did us," Justin said with a shake of his head. "I deserve your rage for keeping what I knew from you. You, of all people, deserved to know it."

Caleb looked at his elder brother for a long time. They had been best friends as much as siblings over the years. During his time away, he had missed his brother, even when he was furious at him.

"I *was* angry at you in the beginning," he admitted softly. "Perhaps that anger even lingered beyond my initial shock. I couldn't comprehend, no matter how I tried, why you would keep me in the dark about who I am. Why you wouldn't simply con-

front the truth head-on and be done with it. But
after today . . ." He trailed off as he remembered
his father's sickly cough and his drawn face. "After
today I'm more determined than ever to pack the
past away and forget about it."

"I still worry about this 'solution' you propose,"
Justin said softly. "It may not be as easy to put away
your emotions as you believe. I would hate to see
you put on a path to destruction."

Caleb choked out a laugh though he felt no good
humor. "Even before I knew I wasn't my father's
son, I was well on my way to destruction, Justin."

"That isn't true," Justin said softly.

"No?" Caleb tilted his head. "How many times
did you pay out my debts? Or help me escape an
angry husband who discovered his wife was philan-
dering with me?"

Justin shrugged. "It isn't the same thing."

"Perhaps not, but the fact is I was never a saint,
Justin." He smiled, a thoroughly false expression.
"And I look forward to returning to those wicked
ways again. At least when I destroyed myself
with pleasures, I didn't hurt any innocents in the
process."

He flashed briefly to an image of Marah, but immediately pushed that thought aside. At all costs,
he had to forget what they had shared as much as

he should forget what he knew about himself. That was what she required and it was for the best, even if it currently seemed like an impossible task.

"Perhaps you're right," Justin conceded with a shrug. "Perhaps you'll be able to simply pack away the emotions that have chased and tormented you for two years. Perhaps within weeks you will be as carefree as you once were and I won't worry about you any longer."

"You don't sound very certain," Caleb said with an arched brow.

Justin shook his head. "I hope I'm wrong to hesitate, but I still believe you deserve the answers you refuse to seek. And that until you have them, you won't be able to forget what you know about yourself and what has happened in the past."

Caleb was silent for a long moment as his brother's words sank in. He feared Justin was correct, though he wouldn't ever state that out loud.

"It doesn't matter," Caleb finally replied as the carriage moved into the drive of Justin's home and slid to a stop. He fumbled for the handle of the door even before the footman could reach it. "After a few drinks all of this will be numbed. And numbness will have to suffice."

Chapter 5

Marah tightened her wrap around herself as she moved through the cold halls toward the library. In the three hours since she retired to her chamber, sleep had not come to her, no matter how many old tricks she employed to invite it. Counting sheep, drinking warm milk, drinking *brandy* . . . none of it had done any good. She had still lain in her bed, staring at the filmy canopy above, her jumbled thoughts swirling in her head.

The topic of her thoughts was the most troubling part of her sleeplessness. She wasn't worrying for Victoria, who had been ill that morning, though she seemed recovered enough by the afternoon. She wasn't thinking about Emerson and the fact that he had sent word he would soon call on her. She wasn't even thinking of London or planning all the activities she would do and people she would see while here.

No, the thoughts clouding her mind were all

about one person and one person only. Caleb.

He and Justin had returned home from their family's estate in London around supper time. Marah knew that because she had been sitting in a front parlor pretending to sew, when in reality she had been staring out the window waiting for them.

She'd had no time to talk to Caleb, though, for he had gone directly to his chamber and hadn't come back down, even for food. She had no gauge of how he was doing or feeling about seeing the man he had called father up until two years ago.

But if Justin's behavior was any indication, the visit had been a painful one. The earl only picked at his meal, lost in an uncharacteristic melancholy that made Marah even more fearful about what had occurred that day. But she was too afraid to ask Justin about his brother's well-being. It was as if stating her concerns out loud would make her unwanted feelings toward Caleb all the stronger.

And she *did* still feel those old unwanted feelings. There was empathy in her heart for him and sorrow for the pain she knew he suffered. And then there were *other* emotions that she violently shoved aside as she pushed the door to the library open and came into the dark, cold room.

In the grate, a low fire had burned away almost to nothing, but it still gave Marah enough light to see some of the shelves as she crossed to them. She needed the most dry, boring tome she could find. Certainly that would put her to sleep and banish thoughts of Caleb at last.

She squinted through the darkness as she scanned the titles. This one was too interesting, that one too exciting. Goodness, this one was definitely too naughty!

She turned to face another high shelf and continue her quest when a slight movement from the chair beside the fire caught her eye. She wrinkled her brow and moved closer to inspect what she had seen. Was that a cat? The movement repeated and she jumped in surprise as her eyes adjusted further and she realized it wasn't a pet, but a person who shifted in the darkness. The very person whose unwanted image had kept her up half the night.

Caleb sat beside the fire, slouched down low in the chair so that he almost faded entirely into the darkness.

She lifted a hand to her chest as if the touch could soothe her suddenly pounding heart.

"I didn't see you there," she said when the glittering flash of his bright stare made her realize he was fully aware of her presence. "You frightened me."

He said nothing in return but inclined his head slightly as if acknowledging her statement. Marah pursed her lips in frustration at his lack of reaction. She didn't like that he was in the darkness, his expression hidden by shadow.

"Let me give you more light," she said with false sweetness as she turned toward the hearth.

She grabbed a small log from the bin and tossed it onto the grate. Immediately the smoldering coals caught the dry wood and a flash of light filled the room. She turned toward Caleb, who was squinting at the renewed brightness, but the instant she did, her irritation toward him faded.

His expression spoke volumes about his heart, probably more than he wished to share, especially with her. But there it was, all over his handsome face whether he intended to reveal so much or not.

Marah's grandmother had been a healer in their village, a midwife, and at her side Marah had seen heartbreak before. But this emotion in Caleb's eyes went beyond that, deeper into something with far more despair. There was no hope on his face, only pain and utter surrender to the idea that nothing would . . . or perhaps *could* ever get better.

"What do you want?" he slurred as he lifted his eyes to her.

Marah pursed her lips. Even if she hadn't noticed the empty bottle of whiskey on the floor beside his chair, his surly tone made it clear that Caleb had been drinking. And his glassy eyes ended any doubt she might have had about his inebriated state. The rational part of her reminded her that a drunken man was a dangerous man, especially in his highly emotional state. She should leave him in peace and forget what she saw.

But she couldn't do that. She didn't want it to, but his quiet sorrow touched her and she couldn't help but edge closer to him.

"M-may I sit with you?" she whispered.

He arched a brow, but then jerked his head toward the chair opposite his. She took her place quietly and tilted her chin to look at him more closely.

"I thought you wouldn't *want* to sit with me, Miss Marah Farnsworth," he said with a shrug. "We are but mere acquaintances, are we not?"

Marah drew back. So her words the previous night had somehow struck home with him, though she didn't know why. He hadn't wanted her before, she had no idea why he would suddenly decide he wanted her now. Pride was the only thing she could think of. Somehow her rejection the day before had stung his pride.

"I wouldn't be able to abandon an acquaintance who was in the state you are in." She looked at him. "Even if it was only for one night, I would offer to be a friend. I think you need one."

"A friend," he mused as he slid his chair just a little closer to hers. It was a slight movement, one that might even be explained away, but Marah still stiffened at it. And stiffened further when he added, "I have pictured you in every way imaginable over the years, but the last way I would ever see you was as my *friend*, sweet."

Marah's breath caught in her throat at the openly flirtatious tone of Caleb's voice and the forward words he had chosen when addressing her. It was entirely inappropriate, especially given that she had specifically said she didn't want him so close. But it still thrilled her.

Immediately she hated herself for being moved by such a simple, silly charm that Caleb Talbot had been turning on women since he was out of short pants. His words were meaningless and she knew it. She didn't want to be one of those foolish girls who threw propriety and good sense to the wind at the empty compliment of a handsome gentleman. Over the years she had come to know that she required more stability than that.

She cleared her throat and decided to ignore his statement. "You and Justin were out for a long time today. I assume that means you finally saw your father."

The dark flirtatiousness to Caleb's expression

faded away instantly and the sorrow she had been so drawn to at first returned.

"I saw the marquis, yes," he said with a slow nod.

Marah shut her eyes briefly. Her own father had walked away from her the moment her birth caused the death of his wife. His only contact with her after that was a large sum of money deposited in an account to maintain her comfort and provide for her future.

After his death, his family had continued that tradition of basic monetary support, but a lack of love or attention. She had longed to know more about them, to ask why they couldn't love her, even a tiny bit. Even now, she wondered about the other family she didn't know. If they knew she was in London. If they gave a damn.

Yes, she knew a great deal about loss and regret. But that wasn't something she'd ever shared with anyone else, even Caleb in those open, heated moments of two years before. Perhaps *especially* Caleb.

There were some pains she kept private.

She leaned forward slowly, draping her elbows over her knees. Now their heads were less than half a foot apart and she could smell the warm, clean fragrance of his skin. She shivered and refocused on her attempt to help him, rather than the unwanted and surprising desire to do far more wicked things.

"The marquis *is* your father, Caleb," she whispered.

His gaze snapped to her face and anger briefly flashed there. "You know damned well he isn't. We both may wish to forget what happened between us that afternoon, but you can't deny what I confessed to you."

Marah nodded, recalling how pained Caleb had looked when he told her he had discovered the marquis wasn't really his father. She had thought she would never again see him so broken.

She was wrong.

"Of course I remember," she whispered. Her hand stirred but she forced herself to keep it in place rather than touch his fingers or his cheek in comfort. That was too familiar. Too dangerous. "What I meant is that a father is the man who raised you and loved you. The blood you share or don't share is often an entirely separate issue."

Certainly it had been in her own case.

"Perhaps," Caleb said softly, but his expression softened somewhat. The edge of his pain was muted by her words, but it was only brief, not a lasting ease.

They sat quietly for a few moments, the only sound in the room the crackling of the wood as it burned down lower in the coals. Marah was surprised that the silence between them was not un-comfortable or uneasy. In fact, that realization put her on edge. She shouldn't feel comfort of any kind with this man. He was not one to be trusted with such things.

She pulled back a little. "I realize this is diffi-cult," she began, ready to offer some platitude and then depart.

"It is," Caleb said before he covered his face with his hands. His head dipped down, his shoulders slumping in such defeat that Marah felt the effect of it. "Marah, he is dying. He is dying and the past hangs between us. No matter how much I want to forget, seeing him today made that so terribly, painfully clear."

She was no longer able to keep herself from reaching for him. When she took his hand, his fin-gers closed around hers, clinging to her like she was a lifeline that had been tossed to him on a stormy sea. He looked at her, but his eyes were wild and she strove to find some words that would soothe him.

"But Caleb, you are here now. You still have time with him and that is a gift. Take comfort in the fact that you didn't come home too late."

"Sometimes I fear I am too late, though," he whispered. His voice cracked in the dim quiet. "We've been distant a long time. Even before I knew the truth and ran from it, our interactions were strained and forced. What if I can't recapture a relationship with him before he is gone?"

Marah stared at him. She had never expected Caleb to expose so much of his soul to her. The one and only time he had done so before was an anomaly. Or so she had thought. But here he was, spilling his heart, if only because the bottle had loosened his tongue.

"All you can do is try," she finally said as she cupped his face gently.

He didn't answer. Instead his fingers came up and he touched her hair. At first the touch was questing, almost questioning, but when Marah couldn't find her voice to resist, his fingers moved into the locks and tugged, moving her toward him.

She could hardly breathe as his mouth moved closer and closer. He was going to kiss her and she wanted him to. She wanted him to do that and so much more. She blinked as the full ramifications of that desire hit her.

With difficulty, she turned her face and his lips brushed over her cheek instead of her mouth. She shuddered even at that touch and got to her feet.

"W-we agreed to forget the past," she whispered, staying back from him as she adjusted her shawl so that he wouldn't see her body's traitorous response to him. Her nipples were hard against her night-shift; she was sure they would be outlined clearly if she dropped the protection of the heavier wrap.

His gaze came up to her, dark and angry, as well as needy and filled with want. "Yes, we did."

"Acquaintances don't kiss," she said, lifting her hand to her cheek where his lips had touched her. Could someone be branded by a kiss? She feared she might be.

He arched a brow. "Don't they? I have several lady acquaintances I once kissed regularly."

She winced at his cold statement. But she was glad for it, too. It reminded her that to him, she was really no different than any other woman whom he might drown his sorrow in. The fact that he had tried to kiss her tonight hadn't been about love or tenderness.

Caleb had always been about need, especially when it came to her. He saw her as a way to fill a void, to forget a pain, but when the need passed, he was far too willing to let her go.

"Then perhaps you should find one of those women to help you," she murmured, her tone lacking any heat of anger. She surprisingly felt none, though the idea of Caleb making love to someone else turned her stomach.

"Is that what you want?" he asked as he pushed

to his feet, though he didn't advance on her. He simply stood, staring at her, his bright blue eyes holding her hostage.

She shrugged. "It would be wrong of me to confuse matters between us. I can't be your comfort, Caleb. Not like this, not again. Now if you will excuse me, I shall return to my chamber where I belong. Good night."

She didn't wait for his response. All she could do was hurry from the room. It was only when she was halfway up the stairs that she realized she had never found a book to bore her into slumber. But it didn't matter. She had a feeling that even the most tedious tome couldn't help her now. And if she by some miracle found the rest she desired, her dreams would be of one thing and one thing only:

Caleb's touch and all the pleasure he would have given her if she hadn't pulled away from him.

Chapter 6

Caleb groaned as he entered the breakfast room. Late morning sunshine poured through the windows and he squinted his bloodshot eyes to block the light, even as his head pounded and his stomach churned. As he staggered toward the side bar, he searched for a pot of tea or, God willing, coffee, but found the area to be empty.

A door opened behind him and Justin's butler, Crenshaw, stepped into the room on nearly silent feet. "I apologize, sir, the breakfast dishes were cleared away an hour ago, but the kitchen would be happy to prepare you some eggs or anything else you desire."

Caleb sucked in a breath as nausea overwhelmed him. "God, no eggs," he moaned as he took a seat at the table and rubbed his temples in an unsuccessful attempt to quell their throbbing. "And please do stop shouting, Crenshaw."

The butler's eyebrow slowly arched, but he gave

no other outward reaction to Caleb's demand. Instead he lowered his tone and said, "Of course, sir. Then what *could* I fetch for you, sir?"

Caleb covered his eyes. "Coffee."

"A slice of toasted bread might also help to calm your stomach, Mr. Talbot," the butler suggested.

Caleb nodded without looking at the other man. "Bread. Good. Thank you."

As the servant stepped away, Caleb let his head drop onto his arms on the tabletop. It had been a long time since he'd had a drunk powerful enough to bring on such queasiness. He'd almost forgotten how awful the feeling was.

He could scarce remember the previous night, except for one awful part: Marah coming to him. He had almost kissed her, *that* he recalled with perfect clarity. He'd been close enough to feel her breath on his cheek and see her eyes dilate with a desire as powerful as his own. But that desire hadn't been fulfilled because Marah had rejected him.

The thought of her made his head pound harder and the room spin even faster. With a moan, Caleb burrowed his head further into his arms. Another drink was probably the only thing that would cure this feeling, but the idea turned his stomach even more.

"There you are," a voice said from behind him.

It was female and it sounded like the screech of a bird of prey to his sensitive ears.

Lifting his head, Caleb turned to find Victoria leaning in the doorway. Her arms were folded and she looked him up and down with a delicate sniff that spoke volumes of what she thought of his current state.

"And don't you look a sight," she continued as she stepped into the room. "I hope whatever you did last night was worth the pain you must be experiencing now."

Caleb rubbed his eyes. "I don't remember."

"That's the trouble, isn't it?" his sister-in-law asked softly. "Burying yourself in spirits means you don't remember, but you never fully forget, either."

He nodded. "So true, my lady."

She folded her arms. "But now that you are finally awake, I think it would do you some good to join us for luncheon."

"Luncheon?" Caleb repeated. "Is it that late?"

"Just past noon," Victoria said with a nod.

He glanced toward the servant entrance to the room. "Er, Crenshaw arranged for me to have some coffee and some toasted bread."

"Good, perhaps once you have had that, you'll be ready for hardier fare." Victoria smiled. "I'll be certain whatever you have asked for can be brought to you in the Lilac Room, where we are having luncheon."

Caleb shrugged. "I'm sorry, Victoria, but I'm not really in the mood—"

"We have a guest, Caleb," she interrupted, her raised voice raking across Caleb's nerves. When he rubbed his throbbing eyes, she smiled slightly, which made him believe she might have done that on purpose. "*That* is why I am so persistent."

"A guest?" Caleb stifled a groan at the idea of having to face anyone in his current state. He could hardly remain upright. "Then I'm certainly in no condition to join you. Look at me, Victoria."

She arched a brow as she did so. "You *are* a wreck. Didn't Justin's valet help you?"

"It has been so long since I had a valet, I fear I appall him beyond measure." He sighed. "And I may be beyond even his talents this morning."

She stifled a laugh. "Wreck or no, I think you'll want to meet our guest. Once you do, I doubt your mind will be so focused on your sad appearance."

Caleb's brow wrinkled. Although his head continued to ache, Victoria had piqued his interest. "Is that so?"

She nodded as she motioned toward the hallway. "It is. This person will be of great interest to you. Come."

With a frown, Caleb pushed from the table and followed Victoria into the hallway. She was quiet as she escorted him down the hall to the Lilac Room, thus named because its terrace looked out over a blooming burst of beautiful lilacs Caleb and Justin's grandmother had planted there years before. Even from the hallway, Caleb could smell their fragrance through the open terrace door and it unexpectedly soothed him.

As they entered the space, Caleb came to a stop in the doorway. Seated on one of the settees was Marah, but she wasn't alone. Close beside her . . . far *too* close . . . was a man. Perfectly dressed and impeccably coiffed, he was as slick a gentleman as Caleb had ever seen.

Instantly Caleb hated him, even before he knew his name.

"Mr. Caleb Talbot, may I present to you Mr. Emerson Winstead," Victoria said, her eyes locked on Caleb as she said each word. "Mr. Winstead, my brother-in-law."

Winstead rose to his feet and extended a hand. "Ah, Mr. Talbot, a pleasure to meet you."

Marah also rose and Caleb remained speechless as he stared at her. *This* was her beau? This—this dandy? As if she could read his thoughts, she returned his stare with an even and cool expression of her own.

"Caleb," Victoria snapped after a moment of awkward silence had passed.

Caleb returned his attention to the man before him. With a smirk, he took the offering of his hand and they shook. "Mr. Winkles. Good to meet you."

"Winstead," Marah said softly. "And you needn't trouble yourself by joining us, Mr. Talbot. It's clear you aren't fully recovered from last night."

He arched a brow as he settled into a seat. "My dear, I'm not certain I'll *ever* recover from last night."

He winked at her and reveled in the blush that filled her cheeks. He liked that he forced her to recall their near-kiss with her "beau" sitting right next to her.

"No, no," he continued with a wave of his hand. "I couldn't be a poor sport and not join you. I look forward to talking with your friend."

Winstead returned to his place beside Marah and smiled, but Caleb could see there was as little warmth on the other man's face as there was in his own heart. He wondered at the cause. Did Winstead simply sense that Caleb wanted the same thing he so obviously did . . . or had Marah become so close to the other man that she had spoken of Caleb before?

He wasn't sure which answer he wished to be true.

"So, Watson," he said. "I don't think I've ever met you before. You don't mix in our circles much, do you?"

"Winstead," Victoria said with a smothered smile.

"It's quite all right," Winstead said smoothly, though he never took his eyes off Caleb even when he spoke to Victoria. "No, Mr. Talbot, I'm afraid I haven't moved in your circles at all until very recently."

Marah glared at Caleb. "Mr. Winstead is a self-made man. I so admire someone who takes the initiative to better themselves. What an intelligence and grace that must take."

Winstead smiled at her, clearly taken with her compliment, though from her glare, Caleb could see it was directed more as a barb toward him than praise for her companion.

"Lady Baybary," Winstead said. "Will your husband not be joining us, as well?"

Victoria shook her head. "Unfortunately, no. He was called away on urgent matters this morning."

At that, Caleb turned his focus to his sister-in-law. "The marquis?" he asked, his heart leaping to his chest.

She shook her head. "No, not your father, Caleb.

We would have woken you if that were the case. It was a matter with one of his investments." Her smile was brief but warm before she continued, "I assure you he was very unhappy not to be able to join us."

Winstead's brow wrinkled with displeasure, which he quickly smoothed from his face with an overly affable smile. "Of course I understand. Sometimes these things come up."

"Ah," Victoria said as the door opened and a servant signaled to her. "It appears our luncheon is ready. Shall we move to the tables outside?"

She motioned to the open terrace doors, and Winstead nodded as he got to his feet. Without hesitation he offered Marah an arm, and after a brief glance toward Caleb, she took it. He stared as the couple exited ahead of them.

"Breathe, Caleb," Victoria said at his side. "You'll turn blue if you don't."

He glared at her as he took her arm and followed the other two to the table. They were all seated, and within moments food began to arrive. Caleb hardly ate, partly because his stomach still churned, but also because he found himself distracted by his observations of Marah and her suitor.

He didn't like Winstead. He could admit that a lion's share of his feelings were because of the man's obvious intentions toward Marah, but that jealousy wasn't Caleb's only hesitation. Winstead was a dandy. The cut of his jacket was too fine, the colors he wore matched too perfectly. Caleb had always liked nice things, but he'd never been obsessed with fashion. He thought it odd if a man took too much time interested in his own image in the mirror.

There were far too many other things that caught his fancy. Like the young woman sitting beside Winstead. Marah kept her gaze purposefully away from Caleb, but he still sensed that she was aware of him. When he wasn't looking, he felt her stare on him, and when he was, she tensed.

"So, Wintergreen—" he began.

"Winstead!" both Victoria and Marah said at once, though Victoria's tone was filled with more humor than Marah's.

"—what is it you *do* that has made you a self-made man who Marah so admires?" he asked without correcting his mistake.

Winstead took a sip of wine before he answered, "My father was involved in shipping, Mr. Talbot. I took what little money I inherited from him when he died and invested it in more ships. Within a few years, I'm happy to say I had more than tripled my initial investment. Now I import and export several commodities for both private parties and the

Crown. Slowly but surely, I'm gaining a reputation for myself."

"And quite a fortune, I would imagine," Caleb drawled.

Winstead looked at him, and again Caleb was struck by how very *unfriendly* the other man's eyes were when he looked at Caleb, despite his smile or his perfectly chosen and utterly polite words.

"Although I wouldn't be so uncouth as to talk about money at a table with ladies present, I admit my lifestyle is comfortable. All I'm missing now is a wife and family to share it with."

As he said the final words, Winstead turned his head slightly and glanced at Marah. She pretended not to notice his regard, but her cheeks filled with color as she stared at her plate.

Caleb stared as his stomach churned even more furiously than it had earlier in the day. Victoria had said that Winstead was a suitor and that Marah was determined to like him, but he hadn't thought things had progressed so far with them that Winstead might be considering marriage. And from Marah's lack of reaction beyond a blush, this wasn't news to her. She was aware, or at least had guessed of the other man's desire to form a more permanent union with her.

And since he couldn't imagine Marah leading

anyone on, that meant she was open to the future Winstead described. To becoming this other man's wife, to bearing his children.

Servants entered the room and cleared away the final dishes from their luncheon, but Caleb barely noticed their intrusion. He just couldn't tear his gaze away from Marah; he just couldn't stop picturing her in a wedding chapel pledging herself to another man, or in a bed waiting for another man's touch, or holding another man's child, or in the twilight of her years as another man's companion at the end of his days.

He saw all those things in the flash of a moment, and his hands shook with anger and jealousy that was powerful enough to take him by surprise.

"Thank you again for the lovely meal, my lady," Winstead said to Victoria with a quick nod.

She smiled in response. "Of course, Mr. Winstead. And now are you two ready for our walk?"

Caleb straightened up. "Walk?"

It was Marah who turned toward him. Her eyes were narrowed as she said, "Victoria is playing chaperone for Mr. Winstead and me while we take a turn through Hyde Park."

Caleb clenched his fists beneath the tabletop, even as he jolted out a quick nod.

Winstead got to his feet. "I'm very pleased to

have met you, Mr. Talbot, and I hope we'll be able to repeat this again soon. After all, anyone who is an important acquaintance of Marah's must be equally so to me."

Caleb pushed from the table and rose to his full height. "Well, I'd say Miss Marah and I are not mere acquaintances."

Now Marah rose to her feet, her chair screeching across the floor loudly. "Caleb!" she snapped.

Neither man looked at her.

"No?" Winstead drawled, his expression never changing. "Well, even a *distant* friend of Marah's is of interest to me."

"I'm sure," Caleb said with a laugh that held no humor.

Marah moved toward the two men with a scowl. "Victoria, perhaps you could show Mr. Winstead to the foyer. I'll meet you both there in a moment. First I'd like to discuss something with Mr. Talbot."

Victoria came forward, her own glare focused on Caleb even as she said, "Of course. Mr. Winstead, will you follow me?"

Winstead smiled at Caleb and then offered a quick bow. "Good day, Mr. Talbot."

"Whisperton," Caleb said as the other man offered Victoria an arm and the two left the room together.

As soon as they had gone, Marah stalked to the terrace doors and yanked them shut with enough force that their glass shivered. As she spun back on Caleb, he stared. She was livid, there was no doubting that. Her skin was flushed pink and her dark blue eyes snapped with emotion.

"How dare you?" she said, her voice no more than a harsh whisper.

"Dare I?" Caleb said, lifting his hand to his chest in feigned innocence. "I'm certain I don't know what you mean, Miss Marah. Or how I could have offended you so deeply."

Her hands came to her hips. "Don't treat me like I'm a fool. From the moment you came into the room you were rude to my friend, dismissive, mocking, and eventually you two made idiots of yourselves by posturing like bulls."

"Was *that* him posturing?" Caleb said with a snort.

She advanced on him one step and extended a finger, which she pointed at him menacingly. "You don't have any right to be jealous, Caleb. And that man doesn't deserve an ounce of your contempt."

"Is he a *man*, Marah?" he snapped, the thin wire of control within him finally breaking. "Because all I saw was a dandy who is looking to further his profit through a match with a lady he's not fit to shine the boots of."

Marah's jaw tightened and her eyes narrowed. "Well, he's more of a man than anyone else in the room I saw. Good day, Caleb."

She turned to go, but Caleb lunged toward her. He caught her arm and twirled her around, unwilling to leave things as they were, unable to leave her slur against him unanswered.

But when she turned, she tumbled off balance and fell against his chest. He caught her, holding her steady against him, and everything else around them stopped.

The previous night he had been addled by liquor and also by certainty that Marah would allow him to kiss her, despite any denials she had made of him earlier. Today he was under neither of those influences. He looked down into her face and he felt her soft body pressed to his and he wanted her with a power that rocked him to his very core.

If he offered her a chance to resist, she would, but without the choice . . . well, he had a sneaking suspicion that the bright emotion in her eyes was more than just anger. She wanted him. He felt it in the trembling of her body and the beating of her heart.

So he dipped his head and kissed her. At first her

lips remained tight and thin beneath his, but when he darted his tongue out to gently trace the crease of her mouth, she parted her lips with a soft sigh. He delved into the space she had offered and the stiffness in her, the resistance faded. Her fingers fanned out from the tight fists against his chest, curling as she tilted her head and granted him even more access to her mouth.

He gathered her closer, holding her to his chest in an embrace rather than a prison and let out a low, hungry moan. She tasted the same. She felt the same. And he wanted her the same way he had wanted her two years before. A primal urge to take and claim, one more powerful than he had felt with any woman before, rose up in him and washed over him until he couldn't see or feel anything but her.

But before he could do anything about that desire, before he could seduce her any further with his kiss, her palms flattened against his chest and she shoved him away.

He released her immediately and she reeled until her back was firmly to him. She stood that way for a moment and then turned back to him to spear him with a glare.

"I thought I made it clear to you last night that I don't want this. Not from you," she said, her tone steely even though her lower lip still trembled ever so slightly. "If I didn't, let me state it again: I *don't want you*, Caleb."

"No?" he drawled, stepping back until he leaned against the terrace wall. He folded his arms. "I think you do, angel. Despite yourself. You can't deny that when I kissed you, you melted."

Her lips thinned into an angry line, but a dark red color also filled her cheeks and streaked down her throat to disappear beneath her gown's neckline. Finally she shook her head.

"Fine. It would be stupid of me to pretend that a libertine like you can't recognize when a woman wants him. Perhaps I do desire you."

He straightened up with a grin of triumph, but she waved him off and continued, "But I would like to think that I am more than just the carnal needs of my body. You and I have proven already that we are not a compatible match."

Caleb's brow wrinkled. He wasn't certain that was true. They had never really *tried* to be a match, which he could admit was his own fault. "So you will pretend you have no interest in me?" he asked.

She nodded. "I have plans, you see, Caleb, and you are not part of them."

He moved toward her. "But this Winstead fellow is?"

She smirked. "I *knew* you remembered his name.

And yes, he is a part of the future I envision for me. He is good-natured, capable of taking care of me, and above all else, he is *stable*. So whether or not I have an occasional attraction to you really matters very little."

Caleb stared at her, the nausea he had felt earlier in the day returning once more. But he had no intention of letting her know how much she had stung him with this declaration to unite herself with another man. Partly to protect his ego, but also because she was right. He had no right to jealousy. Certainly *stability* wasn't something he was capable of offering if that was what she required. He never had been.

"It sounds like a wonderfully loveless and passionless union you plan for yourself, then," he said, his tone more forced and tight than he would have liked. "And I suppose if that is what you require then you are correct: I'm not the man for it."

Her cheek twitched, but Marah made no other outward sign as to her feelings on the subject. "I'm glad we're in agreement. Now I'm off to my stroll. I hope we won't have to have this conversation again."

He nodded once as she turned away. "Trust me, Miss Farnsworth. We won't."

Chapter 7

The day was as beautiful as one could hope for a romantic outing between a lady and her beau. The sun sparkled down on Marah, warming her skin as she walked with Winstead along the lake's edge. Victoria strolled a few feet behind them, offering them privacy, but for all the fact that she was almost alone with a man she claimed to wish to marry, Marah's mind wasn't on her companion.

Instead she kept playing and replaying her infuriating encounter with Caleb over in her mind. Blast the man for kissing her! She could still taste him on her lips, still feel his hands closing around her back and holding her so close that it felt like there was nothing between them at all.

For two years Marah had been contemplating Caleb Talbot's kiss. She had fantasized about it, cursed it, and dreamed of it. In order to regain some sanity, she had ultimately told herself that the kisses they shared two years before couldn't have been as pleasurable as her memory recalled them to be. She had decided that girlish delight had forced her to believe they were more passionate and powerful and intense than was truly possible.

But now she couldn't deny one fact: Caleb's kisses *were* different from what she remembered. But they were better, not worse.

"You are distracted, Miss Marah," Winstead said softly, drawing her from her reverie.

Marah drew a deep breath to calm her suddenly raging heart and smiled at him. "You are correct, I fear. I *am* distracted and I feel I must apologize, both for my lack of attention and for the abominable rudeness earlier of my . . . my . . . Mr. Talbot."

"There is no need for you to trouble yourself with such thoughts," Emerson said with a comforting pat of the hand that gripped his inner elbow. "In truth, I wasn't so very surprised by Mr. Talbot's outrageous behavior. Everyone knows he's been gone from all good society for a very long time. And the rumors of how he conducted himself even before his sudden departure from London weren't ones to give me hope that he would prove to be a gentleman."

Her lips pursed as she sent a side glance toward Emerson. She hated that his censure of Caleb, well-deserved after his shocking demeanor today, actually annoyed her. She despised even more that she felt a strange urge to *defend* Caleb in the face of this man's view of him.

"Are you quite all right, my dear?" Emerson asked as he turned toward her. "You are suddenly pale."

She shook away her unwanted reactions and nodded. "Of course. I was simply thinking that I wouldn't want you to hold an ill view of Mr. Talbot . . . for . . . for the sake of the earl and his wife, who are dear friends of mine."

"Who could judge someone so important as the earl and his lovely bride by the conduct of his libertine younger brother?" Emerson said with a shake of his head.

"I'm not sure I would say *libertine*," Marah responded with a wrinkled brow.

Why did she continue to defend Caleb? It was unconscionable! Especially since she had used the very same word to describe him not two hours before.

Emerson's expression softened. "Of course you wouldn't be so judgmental. I sometimes fear you see only the best in those around you. It is one of your most remarkable qualities, and I admire it and you immensely."

Suddenly his stare became very focused on her face, and heat flooded Marah's cheeks. In the past year Emerson had been a friend to her, he had been a comfortable companion, and though she believed he would offer for her hand, he had never been overtly romantic with her. Now his unwavering gaze held hers, and within it she saw the first glimmerings of what might be called desire.

And yet she wasn't thrilled by this. No, instead she found herself shifting restlessly, made uncomfortable by the expression instead of excited or pleasantly anxious for what might come next.

But to her surprise, *nothing* came next. Instead of moving in for a kiss or taking her hand or saying something tender, Emerson suddenly focused his attention on a spot just over her shoulder.

"Why look there," he said. "I believe I see Lord Underhill and his cousin entering the park together."

Marah looked out of politeness rather than interest and saw the portly form of Lord Underhill and his relation standing a few hundred yards away.

"Indeed they are," she said with a forced smile.

Emerson nodded. "I am very close to making a bargain with them on some investments. Would you mind very much if I engaged them for a moment? I find it always helps a deal along if the parties have a friendly acquaintance."

Marah blinked, but then nodded. "O-of course. I shall wait here for your return."

He patted her shoulder and then took off across

the lawn toward the other men. After he was gone, Marah let out a low sigh and turned to look out over the water.

"Admit it, Marah, you feel a bit of relief that Mr. Winstead has gone."

Marah spun to find that Victoria had joined her. The other woman's pretty face had a rather smug smile on it, and Marah glared at her friend.

"No! Of course not!" she protested, though in truth Victoria was right. It *was* relief that had flowed through her when Emerson decided to tend to his business rather than tend to stealing a kiss.

Victoria stood beside her for a long moment without comment before she added, "And you realize that a man truly smitten wouldn't have even noticed the people around him. He would have been too caught up being with his ladylove to see anything but her."

Marah folded her arms with a huff of angry breath. "And why should I listen to you? *You* are nothing but a troublemaker!"

"Me?" Victoria lifted her hands to her chest with a laugh.

"Oh yes," Marah said, looking around them quickly to ensure that they weren't going to be overheard by anyone else. "You may pretend that you are all innocence, but *you* are the one who invited

Caleb to join us in our luncheon today. Admit it."

Victoria's eyebrow arched delicately. "Very well, as long as *you* admit you couldn't keep your eyes off of him."

"I did no such thing," Marah said with a gasp. When Victoria leaned away with an incredulous expression, Marah shook her head. "And even if I couldn't, it was only because he acted like a brute to our guest, nothing more."

"Nothing more," Victoria repeated. "Of course nothing more."

Marah spun away with another rough sigh. "Oh, I don't want to talk about *him* anymore."

"Very well. Would you like to talk about him instead?" Victoria asked, yanking her head toward Emerson.

Marah followed the direction her friend indicated. Emerson was standing with the two gentlemen he had left Marah for and they were laughing loudly. She had always found Lord Underhill to be rather garish and rude, so Marah winced at the sight of her hopefully future husband so enamored with the man. She had a sudden vision of having to host the fool in her home and bear his presence at her table, all in an effort to support Emerson's business.

But she refused to show Victoria that reaction

and hear her crow, so she faced her friend with a shrug.

"And why *wouldn't* I wish to talk about Emerson?"

"Because one only has to spend two minutes in a room with the two of you to see you have little interest in him," Victoria snapped.

Marah let out a sound of outrage. "Of course I have an interest in him. He is a . . . *friend*."

"And that's all?" Victoria pressed. "You have designs only to keep him as a friend?"

Marah shook her head. "Perhaps not. At least not for very much longer."

Victoria rolled her eyes. "Oh Marah! You cannot truly wish to marry this man."

Marah struggled for a moment. She was closer to Victoria than she was to any other person in the world. Her friend had always been able to catch her in lies and Marah hated telling them, for it made her guilty and awkward.

Finally she shrugged in reply to her friend's statement.

Victoria laughed. "That isn't an answer." She hesitated, and suddenly her laughter faded and her face grew serious. "Or perhaps it is."

Marah frowned, embarrassed by Victoria's close scrutiny and the pity that lined her face in that moment. She had to explain herself, to make Victoria see why this union was a good plan. Perhaps to remind herself as well, since she was so confused by Caleb's uninvited kiss earlier.

"Victoria," she whispered, drawing closer both for privacy and in a hope for true understanding. "I have lived a lifetime surrounded by undependable men who have disappointed me at every turn. You might be correct, Emerson doesn't make me shiver, but he also hasn't let me down."

"Like Caleb did," Victoria said softly, not a question, but a statement. "Has it ever occurred to you that the reason Mr. Winstead is incapable of letting you down is that you don't care for him one iota. That to disappoint, one has to have feeling involved, like you do for Caleb."

For a moment Marah didn't reply because her mind was clouded with images of Caleb kissing her, both today and two years ago. Of him talking to her, confiding in her, holding her, making her laugh.

She shook away the thoughts. There was no use reliving those things. They were over. They had to be. "No, Caleb had his chance."

Victoria frowned before she wrapped an arm around Marah's waist and squeezed her gently. "I'm sorry to interfere, Marah, I truly am."

Marah laughed, her good humor returning for the first time since she had arrived and found Caleb in London. "No you aren't! You thrive on interference!"

Victoria grinned. "Only a little. But in all seriousness, I don't wish to run your life. I only worry about you. You see, if I hadn't given Justin another chance, my life would have been empty indeed."

Marah turned on her friend and gently cupped her face. "It would have, I agree, for your happiness glows within you in a way that makes you even more beautiful. But I'm not you. I think I must be more pragmatic about my mate. All of us cannot expect your good fortune to find true love and a union of souls with our partner."

Victoria opened her mouth as if to protest, but Marah lifted a hand to silence her.

"Here comes Emerson," she said, trying to ignore the little sinking feeling in her heart as he strode toward them. "I'd like to continue with our walk."

Victoria's brow wrinkled and her face was still lined with worry, but she nodded. "Of course."

Marah squeezed her friend's hand and then moved to greet Emerson with a smile. As he retook her arm and they began to walk again, she frowned. There was no denying that her best friend was troubled about the direction of Marah's life. But the one thing she hated, the one thing she didn't want to admit, was that she was troubled, too.

The carriage rocked and Caleb lifted a hand to steady himself as it moved around a tight corner on the busy London streets. After another emotional evening at his father's bedside, the last thing Caleb wanted was to be flung all over the vehicle until his body was as bruised as his spirit.

Justin gave him a quick glance, and his brother's face softened. Caleb frowned. He must look a wreck if his brother looked like he wanted to comfort him as he would a child.

But instead of doing something so humiliating, Justin grinned. "So, Victoria tells me you met Marah's Mr. Winstead today."

Caleb groaned. *Marah's* Mr. Winstead. The very idea turned his stomach. It was not a topic he wished to discuss, especially since the stinging memory of that morning's events still made him want to break things. Preferably Emerson Winstead's smug face.

"I did indeed," he said as he scrubbed a hand over his eyes.

"And you were abominably rude, apparently," Justin continued with another sly smile.

Caleb jerked his gaze to his brother. "Why

shouldn't I be? You can't possibly *like* that pompous, posturing jackass, can you?"

Justin's brow arched. "Well, I've done extensive research on the man's background and temperament and I haven't found any reason to interfere, if that's what you mean. And it doesn't really matter what I think of him. Marah likes him."

Caleb scrunched further into the seat and folded his arms. "So she says."

"And *you* haven't any right to be angry about that fact," his brother insisted.

Caleb shut his eyes with a long sigh. "So she says," he repeated.

Justin slapped Caleb's knee and forced Caleb to look at him with a glare. "What?"

"Come now, you had your chance with her, didn't you? You didn't want it. And now you claim you don't want *her* at all. Didn't you tell me, not two days ago, that you wished to return to your flagrantly dissolute lifestyle? Wine, women, the occasional song . . . that's the life for you, isn't it?"

Caleb glared even harder, for he knew his brother was trying to goad him into admitting he wanted more. That he wanted Marah. And he did, but he wasn't about to state it out loud. What he wanted she wouldn't give and he shouldn't take. Not again.

Slowly he straightened up. "Thank you, Justin, you've reminded me of my plan. You're right, I *do* want to return to the carefree life I once enjoyed. Tonight is as good a time as any to start that. Come, I heard Alyssa is holding a fete at her home. We should go."

Justin laughed. "Oh no, my friend. I have no interest in that."

Caleb frowned.

"That's right," he said, his tone mocking. "You're in love."

Justin frowned, but only nodded. "I am. These little diversions no longer hold interest to me. I have something at home that far outshines everything Alyssa or those of her acquaintance can offer me."

Caleb glared at his brother, suddenly overwhelmed by jealousy. "Well, go home to your wife then," he snapped. "But drop me at Alyssa's first."

Justin was quiet, but then he reached behind him and tapped on the carriage wall to signal the driver to stop. As the carriage slowed, Justin nodded.

"Very well. I'll send the carriage back for you once it has dropped me at home."

"Thank you," Caleb ground out.

After Justin had spoken quietly to the driver, the vehicle moved again. The two brothers sat in silence, though Justin didn't have to speak for Caleb to know he was being judged. He bristled beneath it, and when the carriage stopped a second time, this time in front of a large, beautiful town home in one of the most fashionable parts of London, he was relieved.

"Good night," Justin said softly as Caleb pushed past him into the night.

Caleb grunted his reply and walked away from the vehicle, sucking in gulps of the cool night air in the hope it would clear his mind. Tonight he wanted to drown himself in pleasure, frivolity, spirits. He would forget Marah and he would forget his father and he would just *feel* pleasure as he hadn't allowed himself to do for years.

He stepped into the front foyer and smiled. Yes, this was better. This was where he belonged.

He moved into the throng of people who spilled from the ballroom into the hallways. Unlike a normal ball, the women here wore scandalously low-cut gowns and they flirted openly with the men. And when the situation got steamy . . . well, Alyssa had always been more than open with her chambers.

In fact, as Caleb moved through the crowd to the ballroom, he saw a few guests had already begun the best part of the evening in Alyssa's front rooms. Through the doors he heard moans and sighs.

Those around him greeted him, some in surprise, but all with good spirits, and soon he had a drink in his hand and a grin on his face as he listened to the men around him tell tales of their conquests over the past two years of his absence.

"Caleb Talbot, how rude of you to intrude upon my party without even coming to speak to me first."

Caleb turned at the sultry voice that spoke to him and smiled as he watched Alyssa Manning cross the final few feet that separated them. She had her hands extended to him in greeting and there was nothing but warmth and promise on her face.

She had once been London's most celebrated courtesan, indulging in wild affairs with important men who had settled her well over the years. And why not? She was a beautiful woman, with blond hair and blue eyes that sparkled with humor, intelligence, and sensuality.

Once, a few years before, Caleb had gone to her bed, not as a protector, but just a lover. Their affair had been brief but pleasurable and they had remained as good friends afterward as they had been before.

He took her hands with a smile. "My dearest Alyssa, how beautiful you look."

She tilted her head as she looked him over and, though her smile stayed, her eyes seemed troubled for a flash of a moment. "You have changed, Caleb, but you are as handsome as ever. Come."

She took his hand and drew him away from the crowd toward one of the small rooms connected to the ballroom. Caleb smiled, for these chambers had always been for one purpose and one purpose only. It seemed he would have his relief after all, and surely he would forget Marah once that happened.

Alyssa closed the door behind them and turned toward him. "I heard about your father, Caleb," she said softly. "I am sorry."

He shook his head. "Thank you."

When he said nothing more, Alyssa nodded. "But you don't want to talk to me about that."

"No," he said softly as he took her hand and drew her closer. "Will your current protector be angry that you took me in here alone?"

She smiled. "I have no protector now, Caleb. I no longer need one. If I take a lover now, it is for pleasure." She punctuated the statement by placing her hands on his chest and leaning closer. "*My* pleasure."

Caleb tilted her head up and dropped his mouth down on hers. She parted her lips and the kiss deepened. He sank into it, waiting for the hard, harsh, tingling demands of pleasure to wash over him and take away all other feelings. But even as he kissed her, even as Alyssa rubbed her body against him with suggestive arches and sighs, he felt nothing. No stirring in his loins. No aching of his cock. No boiling of his blood.

He drew away and stared down at Alyssa. She lacked nothing, and yet he felt nothing.

"Caleb?" she murmured as he stepped away.

"I'm sorry," he said as he turned his back to her.

She stepped closer, but made no attempt to touch him. "How long has it been since you were with a woman?"

He shut his eyes, picturing Marah as she shivered in pleasure beneath him on the settee in his brother's house. Her eyes holding his as she gasped when he breached her. Unlike when he kissed Alyssa, the memory stirred his loins.

"A long time," he choked.

"Who is she?" Alyssa said softly.

He spun on her with a frown. "Who? There isn't anyone."

Alyssa smiled. "I've been in the business of pleasure and love a long time, my dear. I can recognize when a man is using me to forget another woman. And when he fails."

Caleb pursed his lips. He didn't want to believe that Alyssa was correct, but the fact was his body refused to do what his mind screamed at it to achieve. For two years he had not been with a woman. He hadn't *wanted* any woman and he had told himself it was because of the high emotions of his situation.

But that wasn't true. And now he had to face it. It seemed, at least for now, that the only woman who made him ache, who made him ready, was Marah.

"But perhaps I'm wrong," Alyssa said with a smile meant to soothe him. "You've been gone a long time from the wild life, and maybe you are simply having trouble coming back. Perhaps after a few weeks, you'll be back in this room with me, making me forget every other man who ever touched me."

He smiled. "That would be a feat indeed."

"Now, come back to the party and indulge in my spirits and talk to your friends and enjoy yourself." She patted his cheek before she held the door open for him. "It seems you need that escape."

"Indeed, I do, Alyssa," he said as he walked into the crowd once more. "Indeed, I do."

Chapter 8

Although the orchestra was more than proficient, their beautiful music clanged in Marah's ears as she stood at the edge of a dance floor, watching other couples spin around in each other's arms. Well, it wasn't really *couples* she was watching, but one irritating man.

Caleb had not been without a partner all night. The ladies he had danced with had each been more beautiful than the other and there was a group of women who simply stared at him, either awaiting their turn in his arms . . . or plotting their futures with him.

"You are staring again."

Marah folded her arms, pushed out a huff of breath, and turned on Victoria with a glare. "I don't know what you mean. I was simply observing the dance, I wasn't staring at him."

"Him?" Victoria said as she arched a brow.

Marah's cheeks grew hot. "Them. Anyone. No one. I wasn't staring, that's all I meant."

"Of course." Victoria chuckled.

"Ladies."

Marah turned to find Justin approaching them, a broad smile on his handsome face. In one hand, he held a drink, which he offered to her. "I brought you punch, Marah."

She smiled as she took the drink. "Thank you."

Justin turned to Victoria. "And to you, I brought my hand. My lady, will you dance with me?"

Victoria laughed as she took the hand he offered. "I would very much like to dance with you."

He leaned forward and whispered something in her ear. Victoria's laughter faded and a blush filled her cheeks, but she nodded in response and then tossed a quick smile to Marah before the couple moved onto the dance floor.

Marah couldn't help but stare as Justin swept his wife into arms and they began to move in perfect accord and tandem. Each step was in time and there could be no doubt, by the way they stared into each other's eyes, that they were desperately, and rather unfashionably, in love with each other.

Marah forced her smile to remain on her face, but in truth she had to admit that jealousy was one of her reactions as she watched the happy couple. The kind of love they shared wasn't something she could ever expect. Certainly not from Emerson, who had never shown much interest toward anything except, perhaps, making money. And not from Caleb, who had shown her much passion but little else.

Suddenly she felt a touch on her elbow and snapped from her reverie to find Caleb at her side. She jerked herself away from him before she could control the action and stared. They hadn't been alone since the afternoon he kissed her after their luncheon with Emerson. That was three days past and he had been gone from the house with his father during the day and God knew where at night.

"Good evening," Caleb said softly, though he didn't smile.

She nodded, trying to relax. "You startled me, Mr. Talbot. Hello."

He moved into place beside her, watching the dancers bob by to the beat of the music.

"You aren't dancing," he finally said.

Marah stiffened, but forced herself to be cordial. "I suppose I'm not."

"Isn't your beau here?"

Now she cast a quick glare at him. "You know very well that Emerson isn't in our circles and likely wouldn't be invited here."

"Emerson," Caleb repeated. "How familiar of you."

She growled out her frustration and turned to go, but Caleb caught her elbow. "Come now, Marah. I was only teasing. Don't go."

She glared at him, but when she saw that a few people around them were staring, she didn't storm off. There was no reason to cause talk.

"I don't appreciate your teasing. Nor your statements about my friend, *Mr. Winstead.*"

"I didn't make any statements," Caleb argued. "In truth, I thought Victoria and Justin said they intended to arrange for some invitations for the gentleman. That was all I meant when I asked if he was here."

Marah looked at him, trying to decipher if he was lying or telling the truth. She couldn't tell, so she murmured, "Oh."

"Not every comment should be construed as an attack, Marah," Caleb said softly, his gaze fixated firmly on her face.

Marah's cheeks grew hot and she looked away. Suddenly this conversation felt very intense and entirely inappropriate for the setting. She shook away her discomfort and searched for a less meaningful topic.

"*You* have had no lack of partners tonight, Mr. Talbot. I believe you may be this Season's most eligible bachelor if you continue on in this fashion."

He shrugged and she could see he truly cared little for the pursuit of the women he had chatted and danced with. That fact gave her a thrill that she promptly squashed.

"Well," he said, "you know the ladies of the *ton*, they are always on the hunt. I am foreign game, so I interest them presently, but soon they will go back to their regular quarry."

"I don't know," she said with a glare at one of the girls who was still mooning at Caleb from across the room. "You might be surprised."

Caleb's smile fell and there was a troubled line to his mouth, but then he shook his head and glanced down at her as the orchestra ended one song and after a beat, changed to another. The couples on the floor joined hands as they filtered on and off.

"Will you dance with me, Marah?" Caleb asked.

Marah stared at the dance floor. She wasn't entirely proficient in dancing and she had seen enough of Caleb tonight to know he was very good. She didn't want to make a cake of herself. And she also wasn't certain she could stand having his arms around her even while they turned around and around the floor. Being so close to him . . . it was difficult.

"I'm not sure."

Caleb slipped a finger beneath her chin and tilted her face up toward his. "Please?"

She swallowed as his bright blue eyes focused entirely on her. In that moment, she recognized just how much she wanted to be held by him, especially in this entirely appropriate place where she could pretend it didn't matter. That it was all for the dance and not because she wanted to be in his arms despite all her claims to the contrary.

Finally she nodded. "Yes."

He didn't respond but simply grinned, took her hand, and led her to the dance floor.

Caleb had spent an evening being flirted with and flirting in return with dozens of beautiful women. Any of them were appealing, but he hadn't felt truly comfortable until he slipped his hand around Marah's waist and gently urged her into movement as the music began to play.

From the first step, it was obvious Marah wasn't an experienced dancer. She was uncertain and timid as he led her into the first turn of the dance. But she had a natural rhythm and delicacy to her movements so that soon she was making the turns and moving her feet in time.

He smiled at her as she became more comfortable. "You know," he said, "this is the first time we have done this since we met."

"I suppose that is true. Honestly, it isn't something I've done very often at all," Marah said as she glanced down at her feet quickly and her brow wrinkled with intense concentration. "Though I'm certain you have already noticed that from my fumbling."

"Nonsense, you are doing fine," Caleb said, moving his head to force her to look at him, for he knew that would make her forget her feet and move more naturally. "Though I wonder why you haven't danced more in your life."

She shrugged, her grip on his arm tightening as they spun into the next movement.

"Well, as you know, I didn't grow up with Society such as this," she explained. "When my father abandoned me to the countryside with my grandmother after my mother died, she was more interested in teaching me about useful herbs than having me tutored in dancing or dead languages."

Caleb tilted his head as he looked at her closer. "I hadn't really thought of that."

She glanced up, her mind taken from her steps for a brief moment. There wasn't any judgment to her face or in her voice when she said, "Why would you? In truth, Caleb, we don't know each other.

Circumstances forced us to believe we did, but we . . . we don't."

His brow wrinkled. She was right, of course. Marah had been dropped into his life by a most odd collection of circumstances and he had bonded to her in a moment of grief and pain for them both. He felt a powerful draw to her, but so much of her remained a mystery to him. A mystery he longed to solve with growing intensity.

Her gaze flitted away, as if the intensity of his stare suddenly made her uncomfortable. She swallowed and said, "We've seen each other so little in the past few days, I haven't had a chance to ask you how your time with the marquis has been going."

Now it was Caleb who was made uncomfortable by the subject and he actually missed a step in the dance before he managed to gather himself.

Aside from Justin, he hadn't engaged in discussion about his father with anyone. Even when Alyssa had brought it up a few days ago, he had dismissed the topic before he was forced to go into it with any real depth. But with Marah, he felt less trapped by the situation. He could be open with her and knew she would offer him nothing but quiet support in return.

"I won't lie and tell you it isn't difficult," he said slowly. "But despite his illness, the time we share together is good. He hasn't always approved of me and my actions, but now we seem to be past that."

Marah's smile was gentle. "I'm glad to hear it."

He nodded. "I believe my mother intends to have the whole family for supper tomorrow night."

"Yes, I heard Victoria talking about it earlier in the evening after she returned home from her visit with your father and mother."

He glanced at her and suddenly wondered what his sister and his mother would think of her. What his father would say about her beauty and charm.

"You are quite welcome to join us, you know," he burst out without thinking.

Marah came to a stop and Caleb realized the music had ended, though in truth he hadn't even heard it for the past few moments. He'd been too focused on her, and that didn't stop even as the other couples jostled around them in their attempts to leave the open floor.

"Yes, Justin kindly extended that invitation to me as well, but I don't know," Marah said with a blush. "I wouldn't want to intrude."

Caleb took her hand. She stared as he lifted it and he felt her tremble ever so slightly when he tucked it into the crook of his arm and drew her away from the dance floor before the orchestra began its next piece.

"Please do come," he insisted. "I believe my mother and my sister might like the company. Having a guest for supper will bring them a touch of normalcy in this difficult situation."

Marah's lips parted and he could see he had touched on her natural desire to help others. But she still struggled. Because of him.

Finally she nodded. "Of course I'll attend if you think it would please your family."

"Good," Caleb said with a flash of a grin. They stood staring at each other for a long moment until Marah shifted and flitted her gaze away from his. With a shrug, Caleb said, "I, er, I promised the next to Victoria, so I suppose I should go collect her."

Marah smiled as she peered out over the crowd. In the distance, Caleb found Victoria standing beside Justin. His arm was around her and her face was upturned to his as he whispered something to her. Without hearing a word of it, Caleb knew exactly what was said, or at least the sentiment of the unheard words. A whisper of love and devotion and desire that was so comfortable that it didn't seem odd or difficult to say or hear it.

And he flushed as he purposefully kept his eyes away from Marah as he said, "That is, if I can tear her away from Justin."

"Well, good luck with that," she murmured, also

keeping her stare from his as she fumbled with the hem of her sleeve. "Good evening."

He cast a quick glance over his shoulder at her before he nodded. "Yes, good evening."

But as he walked away, leaving her behind, he wondered how good an evening he could really expect to have. The woman he wanted was out of reach and it seemed no one else could stir even a fraction of his interest.

Chapter 9

Marah fidgeted in the comfortable carriage seat as the vehicle made another smooth turn and brought them ever closer to their final destination for the night. Across from her, Victoria and Justin both stared at her, their expressions twin ones of concern.

"You look as though you are being taken to the gallows," Justin said with a chuckle that broke some of the tension in the carriage. "I promise you my mother hasn't executed anyone in months."

Marah smiled and relaxed a fraction at her friend's teasing, but in her chest a tightness remained.

"I'm sorry to be anxious," she said. "I only worry about intruding, especially at such a difficult time. I wouldn't want you mother to wish I hadn't come."

"Nonsense," Victoria said as she leaned across the carriage and placed a gloved hand on Marah's. "The marchioness and I exchanged missives this

morning and she was very much looking forward
to having a guest."

Justin nodded. "She told me as much herself this
afternoon during my visit. They haven't had much
company since my father took ill, I think this has
given her something to look forward to. A moment
of normalcy."

Marah nodded. "Yes, that is what Caleb said, as
well." She frowned as her gaze slipped to the empty
seat beside her. "But he isn't even here."

Victoria tilted her head, and from her pitying
expression it was clear Marah had revealed a bit
more of her heart than she intended.

"He plans to meet us at his parents' home," Victoria explained. "I believe he wished to take a bit
of extra time with the marquis before our arrival."

Marah made a noncommittal sound, but inside
her heart fluttered. She hated to admit it, but she had
been disappointed at the idea that Caleb wouldn't
be in attendance tonight. Since their kiss a few days
before, she had seen so little of him. That she might
observe him in this setting had been an interesting
idea to her.

The carriage pulled to a stop and there was
hustle and bustle as servants assisted and orders
were called. Marah found herself looking toward
the open door of the large and stately city estate.

She couldn't see inside from this distance and she wondered if anyone was watching them as they moved up the drive toward the home.

Justin and Victoria entered first and Marah stepped in behind them. In the foyer were two ladies and immediately they began to hug and welcome Victoria and Justin, but standing off to the side, watching *her*, was Caleb. Marah smiled as he approached her and took her hand gently.

"Good evening," he said softly.

She blushed as she nodded. "Good evening."

Before they could say anything else, the group turned to them and Marah withdrew her hand from Caleb's to greet her hosts.

The two ladies were beautiful indeed. Lady Stratfield, Caleb's mother, had dark hair with a bit of gray touching it and lovely green eyes that did not match either Justin's dark brown ones or Caleb's bright blue. But there was a deep grief around her, a cloud that darkened her face.

His sister, Tessa, had the look of their mother about her, married to a sharp intelligence that made her eyes sparkle as they moved over Marah with a quick pass.

"And this must be Miss Marah Farnsworth," Lady Stratfield said as she extended a hand in welcome. "Victoria has told us so much about you, my dear. We are very happy to finally have you in our home."

Marah managed to find her manners and her voice as she nodded. "I thank you for having me, my lady," she said softly.

"This is my daughter, Lady Tessa." The marchioness motioned to the other woman, who stepped forward with a wide and welcoming smile.

"Good evening, Miss Farnsworth. What a beautiful gown!"

Marah smiled as she glanced down at the dress she wore. She had agonized over the choice for hours and changed at least three times before settling on the deep blue that seemed somber enough for a house in grief but pretty enough that she didn't feel like someone's poor relation.

For a moment the group chatted in the foyer, but soon enough Lady Stratfield ushered them to a parlor for a quick drink before their supper. As they settled into their seats, Lady Stratfield smiled at Marah once more.

"You are a dear friend of Victoria's, are you not?" she asked with a brief smile at her daughter-in-law that was immediately returned.

Marah could see that their relationship was on the best terms. She was happy for her friend in that regard, for she knew Victoria had once wondered if that would be true.

"She is my closest and most cherished friend," Marah said with a smile. "We met during her time in Baybary."

Lady Stratfield's face lit up. "Oh, Baybary. A delightful shire. When we were first married and Lord Stratfield was earl how I loved that place. We split our time between London and there until just after Caleb's birth when Asa took over as marquis."

From the corner of her eye, Marah saw Caleb shift, his fingers tightening on his glass as he shot his mother a dark look that he hid as quickly as he had expressed it.

"I agree, I love living there," Marah said slowly as she forced her stare from Caleb.

"And who is your family there?" Tessa asked as she sipped her brandy.

Marah swallowed. This was the question that always made her uncomfortable when it was asked of her by those of rank. Still, she lifted her chin and said, "I stayed with my grandmother, a woman of no standing. You wouldn't likely know her, she was but a healer and a midwife."

She waited for Lady Stratfield or her daughter to react to that statement. She had no doubt they would be polite because of her relationship to Victoria, but many people of elevated status who didn't know of her family ties to the Viscount Farnsworth looked down upon her when they thought her common.

But neither lady made any indication that this news surprised or disappointed them in any way. Their smiles remained the same as ever, without even a quiver or twitch to reveal a deeper feeling on the matter.

"Marah's grandmother was the best of women," Victoria said softly.

Marah smiled at her friend as Justin briefly caught her hand. It was when Victoria had lost a child that they had met. Though her grandmother hadn't been able to help Victoria, the three women had been bound by the experience. And though she doubted Lady Stratfield or her daughter knew that part of Victoria's past—she had once kept it secret even from Justin—they nodded in unison.

"My lady," a servant said as he stepped into the room. "Supper is served."

The family rose as Lady Stratfield nodded to the footman. She moved toward Caleb, but to Marah's surprise he frowned and turned to his brother. "Justin, why don't you escort Mother? I'll take Victoria."

The marchioness only hesitated for a moment, but the sadness in her eyes was clear in that fraction of time. Still, she turned to Justin with a smile that hid her hurt and let her elder son take her from the room. Caleb and Victoria followed, which left Marah with Tessa.

The other woman, who had until that moment been so vivacious and light, now glared at her brother as he walked from the room.

"I don't understand how he can treat her so, especially when her heart is breaking over Father," Tessa whispered.

Marah shifted with discomfort. The other woman was speaking to herself more than to Marah, but it was more than this glimpse into a stranger's heart that made her uneasy. Marah knew something that Tessa Talbot did not. Something that the girl would likely never know even though it involved *her* family.

She smiled. "Shall we follow, Lady Tessa?"

Tessa shook off her emotions and smiled at Marah, though she could see it was but a shadow of her previous joyful grin. "Of course, my apologies."

Marah walked from the room with her, talking quietly as they made the short journey to the dining room. But as they did, she couldn't help but look ahead of her at Caleb.

Tessa was right that by his behavior he was hurting his family in the very depth of their pain. And even though Marah had some understanding of why, she was still left feeling as though Caleb's attempts to pretend the past didn't exist were only causing more trouble, more pain, and more heartbreak for everyone.

Including himself.

Caleb fiddled with his wineglass as the servants drew away the last of the dessert plates. Although the food had been as fine as any meal he had eaten in this house, all of it had tasted like sawdust to him, and now it sat heavy in his belly. His emotions wouldn't allow him to enjoy this night. When he looked around the table, he was keenly aware that he was a disappointment to everyone he saw.

There was his mother whom he had hurt tonight and since his return with his dismissal. It didn't matter that he avoided her because he feared he might pose questions to her that could never be taken back and should be left unasked, she still shrank with anguish every time he rejected her.

There was Tessa, who glared daggers at him as often as she embraced him. She had no idea of what he knew or how it made him feel. All she could see or understand was that he was hurting people she loved, and her natural reaction was to fly at him and defend them with everything she had.

Victoria and Justin were more subtle, but he could tell they didn't like that he was out every night, that he came to their home drunk, that he slept past noon and avoided their table whenever he could.

And then there was Marah. She had softened toward him, but there was no denying how much he had hurt her. He had taken her innocence, he had been dishonorable by abandoning her, and now the fact that he desired her even more than ever only underscored his dissolution. She kept telling him she wanted nothing from him but an acquaintance and he kept picturing her spread across his bed, naked and willing.

"Thank you again for allowing my intrusion," Marah said with a broad smile for his mother. Her voice drew Caleb from his musings.

His mother returned Marah's expression instantly and without hesitation. "We loved having you, my dear. But I'm sorry you won't meet my husband. You probably know that he is quite ill, though he did try his best to join us. But it was too much for him."

Caleb's expression fell at the same moment as his mother's. He had been in the room, telling the marquis more about Marah, when the old man had made the effort to rise and ready himself for a pretty guest. He hadn't even made it past sitting straight up in bed.

He looked at Marah briefly. "He did very much wish to meet you," he mused.

His gaze slipped to his mother and the two looked at each other for a long moment. She seemed to read his thoughts, for there was no surprise on her face when he said, "What if we bring Marah to him?"

The surprise he hadn't seen in his mother was instantly recognizable in everyone else in the room. Justin, Victoria, and Tessa all drew back, almost at the same moment.

Tessa found her voice to respond first, "Are you entirely irresponsible, Caleb Talbot? Father is far too weak for visitors."

Justin nodded slowly. "I tend to agree. And I can't picture him being comfortable with an intrusion into his private chambers."

Marah shook her head. "As much as I would love to meet the man who raised Justin and Caleb, I would never want to be responsible for causing him upset or even making his illness worse."

Caleb's mother turned toward her slowly. "You are a dear girl, but there is nothing in the world that could truly make him worse . . . or better now. And although I appreciate all the concern of everyone, I know your father. When he was denied the ability to meet with a guest, it underscored to him the finality of his condition."

"He was always so proper when it came to guests," Caleb said with a chuckle. "He always wanted to be the one to greet them and make them feel welcome in our home."

His mother crossed the room, holding out a hand to Marah as she did so. "Come, Miss Farnsworth. We shall go up and I will go in to the marquis. If he is sleeping or tells me he isn't up for guests, we'll forget the entire plan. But if he expresses an interest in having this moment that will remind him of healthier days, you may come in."

Marah swallowed and Caleb understood her discomfort. It wasn't often that an unmarried lady . . . or a married one, for that matter, was asked to enter the bedchamber of a powerful man of Society. To converse with him while he was in his nightshirt. But he could also see how intrigued she was by the notion of meeting the marquis, this man she had heard so much about over the years.

He tilted his head. "If you are too uncomfortable, no one will judge you if you say no."

"Of course," his mother instantly said, lifting her outstretched hand to her chest. "We would never have you do something that brought you distress."

Marah arched an incredulous brow toward Caleb, which he ignored as he continued, "It is unorthodox, I know, but I do think it will give him a brief moment of happiness, a glimpse at the life he once led."

"You are daft," Tessa insisted as she tossed her napkin down and pushed her chair back from the table with a screech. "I'll have no part in this. It was a pleasure to meet you, Miss Farnsworth, but I shall say good night."

With that she stomped from the room, her footfalls echoing up the stairs until a chamber door slammed far in the distance. Marah cringed at the sound as she turned toward Justin and Victoria.

"Do you feel as strongly against this idea as your sister seems to?" she asked.

Justin shifted. "It isn't standard or perhaps even proper, of course, and I still worry that so much excitement will cause my father grief . . . but I wasn't here earlier when Mother and Caleb discussed a guest's visit. If they say his reaction and desire to meet with you was so strong . . . it must be true. I defer to their judgment."

Victoria nodded. "And your own comfort, my dear."

Marah turned from them and faced Caleb and

his mother again. She smiled first at the marchioness, but then her gaze fell on Caleb. "If you think I could help him, it doesn't hurt to ask if he'd like to meet me."

"I think we'll wait for you here," Justin said as he slid his chair closer and slipped an arm around his wife's shoulders. "I wouldn't want him to feel overwhelmed by guests."

His mother smiled as the rest of them got to their feet. The marchioness grasped Marah's hand and guided her to the hallway. Caleb followed, unable to hear them as they talked in low tones ahead of him. But he could watch them. He could see that her offer still worried Marah, but she did this regardless because it seemed to please his mother.

Because it pleased him.

But his thoughts left him as they all stopped outside his father's door. His mother released Marah and entered the room, closing the door behind her. Caleb slipped into the place beside Marah. He looked at her from the corner of his eye. There was so much he wanted to tell her, wanted to advise her on how to interact with his father if she did have the chance to pass through the door, but she looked nervous enough at this strange situation. There was no need to make her more anxious as she waited.

So instead he reached out and briefly squeezed her hand. "Don't worry," he whispered.

She glanced at him swiftly, but when he made to remove his hand she clung to it a moment longer before she dropped it away and sucked in a breath as his mother rejoined them in the hallway.

"Well?" Caleb said, uncertain why he so wanted his father to meet Marah.

The marchioness nodded. "He is as stupefied as Miss Farnsworth here by the oddness of this situation, but he seems intrigued by the notion that he could greet his guests without leaving the comfort of his bed. He's ready for you now, my dear. Won't you follow me?"

She opened the door again as she said the last and motioned to Marah as she entered. Caleb followed her, almost colliding with her as she came to a sudden stop just within the chamber door. He had grown so accustomed to the darkness of his father's chamber that he hardly noticed it anymore, but now he saw the room through Marah's eyes and recalled his own feelings when he had first entered the chamber not so long ago.

He leaned in over her shoulder and whispered, "Brighter light bothers him. Your eyes will adjust momentarily."

She nodded, but she was staring toward his

mother as she went to the bed and said something to the figure who was propped up there, waiting. Then she turned back and motioned toward Marah.

"Miss Marah Farnsworth, may I present my husband, the Marquis of Stratfield."

Marah hesitated, and for a brief moment Caleb wondered if she had become overwhelmed and would run. He certainly couldn't blame her if she did the very thing he had done not so long ago. Between the oddness of this situation and the pressure put on her to make a sick man happy, it was much to ask of her.

But the moment passed, and then she stepped into the room and made her way to the bedside.

"My lord, how happy I am to have this chance to meet you," she said.

Caleb marveled as she maneuvered so his father could see her well and then bobbed out a quick curtsy in deference to him. She didn't behave as if it was odd to be here, she didn't recoil at his state, she simply acted as if this was all perfectly normal.

His father smiled up at her. "Hello, my dear, I've heard so many wonderful things about you from my son that I'm happy to have this chance to meet you. Even under these odd circumstances."

His mother motioned delicately and Marah seated herself in the chair beside the marquis' bed and laughed. "I am certain Justin exaggerates about my character. You will likely find me very dull in comparison."

"That is not the case so far," the marquis said, his breathing labored and his words slow, but as Caleb moved closer, he could also see a light in his father's eyes that hadn't been there in all the times he had come here. "And it wasn't Justin who praised you so high. It was Caleb."

Marah hesitated, and in the dim light Caleb saw her swallow hard. She cast a quick glance up at him and then back to the marquis. "Caleb spoke of me? Well . . . I appreciate his compliments to you. He has often spoken of you as well, sir."

Slowly Caleb backed away to stand at the door beside his mother as the two continued their conversation. Even from a distance, he could see his father was brighter as he spoke to Marah. And she occasionally laughed, never taking her eyes off her "host."

"This has made him happy," his mother said softly.

Caleb nodded. "He was always a social man. In the moments when his mind is unclouded and his pain is less, he must feel trapped by this bed and his illness."

"He *did* love to mingle and talk and occasionally

flirt in a harmless manner with a pretty girl," his mother said with a light laugh. When Caleb spun to face her, she shrugged, but he could see her smile. "Well, Miss Farnsworth *is* a very pretty girl."

"Indeed she is," Caleb said, barely suppressing a sigh.

His mother opened the door quietly. "And a very kind one. Someone should go down to Victoria and Justin, but Miss Farnsworth will need an escort."

Caleb looked at Marah and his father and then he nodded. "I would be happy to wait for the lady."

His mother's eyes went wide, but then they softened a touch. She looked toward the slender woman who was sitting with his father, smiling and talking to him in tones they couldn't hear.

"It is not proper to leave her with *you* as chaperone."

He arched a brow. "I don't think much in this situation is 'proper,' madam. However, of the two of us, Miss Farnsworth does know me a little, and when she is finished with the marquis she might be more comfortable with a—a *friend* waiting for her."

His mother hesitated a fraction while her gaze slipped to Marah once again. Finally she shrugged one shoulder. "Very well. I'll return downstairs while you wait for your . . ." She looked at him evenly. "*Friend*."

Then his mother was gone, the chamber door shut behind her, and Caleb was alone with the two people who muddled and confused him most. His father, who had raised him and yet not sired him. Who brought out all the love and all the anger that Caleb had ever felt as he watched him die.

And Marah. He wanted her, but couldn't have her. She made him want to stay with her, and yet he was forced to run.

Before his tangled thoughts could grow even more indulgent and maudlin, Marah rose to her feet.

"I should leave you to your rest, my lord," he heard her say. "I'm so pleased I was able to meet you."

"As am I," the marquis said as he extended his weak hand to her. She hesitated for a brief moment, but then she took it. "Good-bye."

Caleb heard her suck in a breath at the finality of his father's farewell. After a brief pause, she whispered, "I think I shall say good night, my lord. I much prefer good night to good-bye."

His father smiled, but said nothing as she released his hand and made her way back across the room toward Caleb. As she reached him, Caleb was shocked to see that tears filled her eyes. He quickly led her to the hall and closed the door behind them to offer them privacy.

Leaning closer, he murmured, "I'm sorry. We shouldn't have asked so much of you."

She lifted her face toward his. "I'm not crying because I was forced to meet or spend time with your father, Caleb. I'm crying because when I said good night, he smiled at me with such an indulgent expression. He knew that he would never see me again. And I knew it, too."

Caleb stared. In the few moments Marah had spent with his father, she had felt the same things he felt every time he opened that door to his father's chamber. In her eyes he saw a mirror image of the grief, the loss, the sadness that made his own chest ache.

"You may be correct," he said softly as he cupped her chin with one hand. "You may never have the opportunity to spend another moment with him, but I can tell you, Marah . . . tonight you made him happy. Meeting you brightened him and lifted him. That is the best gift you could ever give him."

He hesitated as he caught her one solitary tear on his thumb and swiped it aside. "And me," he finally added in a low whisper.

He leaned down, close enough that her breath

stirred against his cheek. Close enough that he could smell her warm skin and feel her heartbeat double. He wanted to draw her to his chest and crush her in his embrace. To lock his lips with hers until he felt like they were one person.

But instead he moved his lips to her cheek and gently kissed the smooth flesh there. Marah shivered ever so slightly, before she turned her face. But unlike the first time he'd attempted to kiss her the day after their mutual returns to London, tonight she turned her mouth toward him, not away. His lips brushed hers, her arms came around his neck, and then her mouth parted ever so slightly beneath his.

Caleb brought his arms around her, cradling her body against his not roughly, as he had initially imagined, but gently. And his kiss was just as tender. He parted his own lips, but didn't delve into her, he didn't try to drown himself in her taste or her feel. Tonight he just kissed her and drew from it as much comfort as he hoped he gave in return.

For the first time, Marah didn't pull back or turn away. Her fingers lifted to the base of his skull and she threaded her fingers through the thick hair there, massaging his scalp with her nails until he shivered with pleasure. She met each kiss with an eager one of her own, holding tight to him as her body began to shake.

Caleb didn't know how long they had stood there, and he had no idea how much longer or further they might have gone, because from behind them on the stairs he heard someone cough and then Victoria's voice called out, "Marah, Caleb?"

They broke apart swiftly and Marah turned away, first smoothing her shaking hands over her skirts and then touching her pink cheeks as Caleb said, "Yes, we were just about to come down."

"Oh good," Victoria said, still on the staircase. "I'll go back and tell the others."

Her footsteps faded as she walked away and Marah turned back, her eyes wide and bright. "Do you think she saw us?"

Caleb looked toward the stairway. "She was far enough down that she couldn't have."

Marah nodded, but from the nervous flit of her eyes toward the end of the hallway, Caleb could see the answer didn't satisfy her. Truth be told, it didn't fully satisfy him. There was no reason for Victoria to call for them from the stairs, to avoid coming up to intrude, unless she *had* seen them locked in an embrace and was doing her level best to avoid embarrassing them by pretending not to have seen.

He doubted she would keep her silence on the matter forever, though. Victoria spoke her mind, which Caleb respected, but also didn't look forward to if her mind had opinions on his confusing relationship with Marah.

"Come, we should join them before they suspect," Marah said, shaking her head as she hurried away from him toward the stairs. He followed her, catching up in a few long strides and they walked side by side, silent and awkward, together to the parlor.

As they entered the room, Caleb's mother instantly stood and crossed to Marah. She enveloped her in a hard hug before she released her.

"Thank you for that, my dear. And know you are always welcome in our home and by our family." His mother touched her cheek. "You are a friend to us forever."

Marah smiled, but Caleb saw her gaze flit to him briefly before she turned her face. "Thank you, my lady. If I helped in any way, I'm very happy to have done so."

"It has been a long and trying night," Victoria said, her gaze on Marah in a way that made Caleb even more certain that his sister-in-law had only feigned not seeing his kiss with her friend. "I think we shall return home."

Justin nodded. "Yes." He turned toward Caleb. "Will you join us in our carriage? I'm sure mother's stable can tend to your horse until our return tomorrow afternoon."

Out of the corner of his eye, Caleb saw his mother nod. For a brief moment he considered going home with his brother . . . with Marah. But if he did, he feared it would only increase his upset. After all, upon their arrival to Justin and Victoria's home, Marah would go to her bed and he to his own. Alone. The idea of that was especially troubling after tonight.

"No," he finally said. "I think I will go out. I'll return home later."

Justin hesitated, his mouth thinning to a worried line, but then he nodded. "As you wish, brother, of course."

Justin motioned the ladies toward the foyer, but as everyone said their good-byes, Caleb saw Marah look at him. The warmth, the openness, even the desire he had seen on her face in the hall before she kissed him, were gone. Now she looked angry. She looked hurt.

And though he knew it was for the best, the loss of her brief acceptance stung him to his very core.

Chapter 10

"**A**re you certain you are ready for this?" Victoria asked softly as she leaned toward Marah and poured her a cup of tea.

Surprised, Marah snapped her gaze to the group around them, but all the ladies Victoria had invited to tea continued to chat and giggle. None seemed to have heard Victoria's concerned inquiry.

"Of course," Marah insisted. "I'm perfectly fine."

But as Victoria turned her attention to another guest with an incredulous shake of her head, Marah stifled a sigh. Her statement was exactly the lie Victoria seemed to believe it was. There was nothing *fine* about how Marah felt.

Thoughts of the previous evening's events had kept her up all night. Whether it was the warmth with which she had been welcomed to Caleb's family or the strain between him and his mother or the odd and yet moving time she'd spent with his sickly father, all of it had kept her tossing and turning in her bed.

Being with their family had been such an enlightening experience, making Marah realize just how much she'd missed, sequestered away with her grandmother in the small shire of Baybary. She hadn't ever attended that kind of family supper, punctuated with friendly stories and meaningful glances and smiles.

It made her wonder . . . did her father's family share those same kinds of nights together? Did they talk about him as a boy? Did they ever wonder about her as she sometimes wondered about them in moments of weakness?

She blinked and forced the thoughts away. There was no use wishing for what one couldn't have.

Only that was what she seemed bound to do, for the other thoughts that troubled her, the ones that had made her yearn for sleep and yet fear the dreams that would surely come, were of Caleb.

Somehow, everything between them had shifted last night. She had been able to observe him in a way she'd never experienced before. She'd seen the strain with his mother, the boiling conflict about to erupt with his sister, and his heartbreaking love of the man who had raised him. He had, in some way, let her into his world, and she had allowed him to do it.

She had even been so foolish as to kiss him, even though it went against everything she claimed to wish to avoid.

And then, in true Caleb fashion, he had left her, likely to go cavorting with courtesans and drink himself into oblivion. Whatever they'd shared had, as always, meant far less to him than it did to her.

So now, rather than being "fine" as she claimed when Victoria asked, Marah was angry, she was hurt, and she felt so foolish that she wanted to go hide for a while. But she couldn't. This tea had been planned since her arrival and she wouldn't embarrass Victoria by running away to pout like a petulant child.

The door out in the hallway opened and she heard Crenshaw's low monotone in the hall as he greeted what was likely a late-coming guest. She settled into her chair and leaned a little closer to the ladies beside her, ready to attend more carefully to their conversation and forget her troubling thoughts.

She wasn't given a chance. Before she had even said hello, the butler stepped into the doorway and intoned, "Mr. Caleb Talbot, my lady."

Marah's gaze jerked to the entryway as Caleb strode into the room. He was wearing the same clothing as he had been in the previous night and he had a scruffy, yet utterly handsome appearance that both aroused and annoyed her. She pursed her lips and forced herself to look away as he bowed with flourish to the room.

"Ladies."

The women around her actually began to titter as a few greeted him in return. Marah actually heard one, Lady Jericho, whisper to her companion, "A handsome one, that. Wild as anything, but the right woman will settle him down."

Heat flooded Marah's cheeks as she stared at her clenched hands in her lap. The "right" woman obviously hadn't been she. It never would be.

"What are *your* thoughts on Mr. Talbot?" Lady Jericho said as she turned toward Marah with a suddenly focused stare.

Marah shifted, for the woman had been stealing glances at her since her arrival. Aside from which, her tone wasn't low at all, and Caleb's gaze flashed to the two of them as he moved to greet a few of the guests.

Marah frowned. "I'm afraid I don't know him well enough to render an opinion, my lady."

"You are his fellow houseguest, you must have some thoughts about him, *Lady* Marah," the other woman continued.

Marah stiffened. Had this woman just addressed her as the daughter of a peer? No, it had to be her imagination. Victoria hadn't introduced her as such, but as Miss Farnsworth.

"Come, Francine," one of the other women said with a cluck of her tongue. "You called Miss Farnsworth Lady Marah."

Lady Jericho smiled, apparently pleased that someone had noticed her social gaffe. "That is because *I* know who she is. Lady Baybary may have introduced her to us as a woman of no connection, but that isn't true."

Because Lady Jericho made no effort to temper her tone, the entire room was now staring at Marah, including Caleb. She shifted beneath the scrutiny as she made a lame attempt to deflect the attention.

"I-I don't know what you could mean—" she began, but Lady Jericho's cackle kept her from finishing.

"Of course you do!" The older woman's brow arched. "My dear, I am a very good friend of your grandmother."

Marah caught her breath as the blood that had flushed her cheeks suddenly flowed away. Her head spun as she stared at the woman who was stripping her bare in ways she had no idea were possible.

Caleb stepped forward. "I believe you are mistaken, Lady Jericho," he said, his gaze never leaving Marah's face. In his eyes she saw concern and empathy, and she would have appreciated them if only he hadn't continued and made the situation worse. "Miss Farnsworth's grandmother recently passed away."

The women of the group let out a collective gasp and then all their gazes pivoted from Caleb to Lady Jericho and Marah.

Lady Jericho shook her head emphatically. "You should not say such slander, Mr. Talbot. Why, I saw the lady's grandmother just yesterday afternoon. The Dowager Countess Breckinridge was in perfect health."

"Breckinridge?" Another of the women raised a hand to her lips. "Then that makes *Lady* Marah the daughter of . . ."

"The late son of the earl and countess," Lady Jericho finished. "He was only earl for a short time before his own death and the younger brother took the title, but according to *my* sources he was legally wed to Lady Marah's mother. Which makes her the daughter of one of the richest families in country!"

The last Lady Jericho said with a crowing and

triumphant grin, and Marah's heart seemed to stop. She could hardly hear anything above the roaring in her ears as she stared around the room at the faces of the women in attendance. Expressions of shock, increased interest, horror, and scandal greeted her. And why not? It wasn't every day that one found out someone one thought was utterly common was actually as elevated as they were.

And once they overcame their surprise and realized that her father's family had all but cut her off entirely, she could only imagine the whispers that were sure to happen after today's exposure would turn into roars in every ballroom and backroom of the *ton*.

She pushed to her feet, her vision spinning as she looked around her in a panic. She just wanted to get out of this room. To get away and breathe fresh air until she could figure out how to respond to this secret she hadn't ever intended to come out.

"Excuse me," she murmured past a thick, useless tongue before she tossed Victoria an apologetic look and then staggered from the room and down the hall to the closest chamber with a terrace.

But as she stepped into the fresh air, tinged with the scent of flowers on the breeze, Marah felt no respite from her horror. Things better left alone had just been dragged into the light. And she feared she could never go back to the way things had once been.

Caleb watched as Marah fled the room, helpless in the face of her obvious upset at the revelation of this shocking news. Around him the women began to whisper and titter, their interest piqued by the idea of a member of an influential family whom they hadn't even known existed. And Marah's reaction only made them worse, for it was one more thing to talk about behind their fans.

Caleb turned toward Victoria. She was still staring at the space where Marah had last stood, her expression one of horrified guilt. He approached her and took her arm gently in an attempt to soothe her.

"Will you go after her?" Victoria asked softly. "I'll stay here and try to minimize the damage."

Caleb stared. He was the last person anyone generally sent on a mission of comfort, but he nodded because minimizing damage was something he was even worse at.

As he moved to release his sister-in-law, she sighed. "I never meant for all of this to happen when I asked her to come to London. Between you and now this . . . I fear she may never forgive me."

Caleb's stomach turned at his part in Marah's pain, but he patted Victoria's hand before he slipped from the room and down the hallway in the direction Marah had gone. The door to one of the parlors was open and he moved to it. He stepped inside, but found the room empty, though the terrace door was open. Drawing a deep breath, he went outside.

Marah was standing at the wall of the veranda, staring out over the greenery of the yard and toward a few city buildings that peeked above and around the treetops in the distance.

He stopped to stare before he said her name. From her posture, her upset was clear. Her shoulders were hunched like the weight of something great was bearing down on them. Her head was bent, as well. For the first time he saw her as . . . broken, and it made his heart hurt, for one of the qualities he had always been drawn to in her was her strength. She had shown it during Victoria's ruse two years ago, she had shown it during and after the attack on her, and she had shown it since her return to the city.

He shut the terrace door behind him. When the door clicked, Marah jumped, though she didn't turn to face him.

"I'm so, so sorry, Victoria," she murmured.

"Victoria is the one who is sorry, I assure you," Caleb said softly.

Marah spun at the sound of his voice and stared at him. "Y-you? *You* came for me?"

He nodded. "Of course. But don't fret, Victoria stayed behind to try to minimize the damage done by Lady Jericho's crowing."

Marah let out a groan and covered her eyes with a palm. "There is no minimizing this! Surely you must see how quickly the story will spread. It will be made even worse since I ran from the room like a ninny."

They were quiet for a moment and then Caleb dared to move a long step closer. Marah didn't recoil, but she slowly lowered her palm from her eyes and looked up at him in silence. She was waiting for . . . something. Maybe for him to judge her, but all he wanted to do was know more.

"Marah, I thought your grandmother died," he said, gentling his tone as much as he could.

There was a flash of pain to her expression at the thought, but she nodded. "Oh, she did. But that was my mother's mother, the woman who raised me in Baybary. The woman to whom Lady Jericho referred is my father's mother."

"And is she really Countess Breckinridge?" he asked.

Marah nodded silently, her face stricken.

"Which would make your father . . ."

Marah turned and her voice became faraway and so sad that Caleb felt the pain of it.

"Arthur Farnsworth, also known as the Viscount Farnsworth when he met my mother. Right after my birth and my mother's death, his own father died and he became Earl of Breckinridge, although he didn't hold the title long. He died within five years himself. It is his younger brother who holds the title now."

Caleb swallowed. From her broken expression he could see just how tender a subject this was. And yet he was compelled to know more.

"I never knew," he said softly.

She shrugged, her eyes still concentrating on someplace far off in the distance. "Few do. It isn't something I talk about often. My grandmother . . . the one who raised me . . . she insisted I be called Miss Farnsworth, not Lady Marah, though I suppose that is my proper address, as uncomfortable as I am with it."

Caleb nodded. It was odd that he and Marah had shared the most intimate of moments, that she knew his darkest secret, and yet this tidbit of information about her past came as a complete shock to him. A shock and a shame, for it was utterly clear that despite all Marah's offerings of solace and comfort, he had selfishly never asked her about herself, nor offered anything in return.

Until now.

"Will you tell me about it?" he said as he motioned to the stairway that led to the garden below. "While we walk?"

Marah stared at him, her eyes wide with surprise. "I'm not sure . . ."

He smiled. "You know, you hold *my* secret in your very protective hands. Perhaps you will trust me with some intimate knowledge of you in return."

Her eyes widened and he read her thoughts like they were written across a page before him. She was thinking of the afternoon two years ago when they had made love. His intimate knowledge of her went beyond any other man's and that was a triumph, at least for the time being.

"And if that reason doesn't suit you, how about this one? The air will do you good," he insisted as he held out his elbow in offering.

She shrugged as she slipped her hand into the crook of his elbow. "Very well. I don't relish the idea of going back inside to face that parlor of vultures so soon. Perhaps a walk *will* help me gather myself."

He maneuvered them down the stairway into a small garden just behind the house. Marah seemed to relax with every step as she drew in a long breath of the fragrant air and then she began to talk.

"My father met my mother during a hunting expedition," she explained, her voice low. "He had fallen from his horse and injured himself. The shire doctor was far off, so the men with him sent for my grandmother, who was a well-known healer and midwife in Baybary. Even the very richest women in the shire called on her to birth their babies, some even came to the shire from other places for her assistance."

Marah smiled and Caleb heard the pride in her voice, the utter love for this woman who had taught her strength and independence.

"When she came to tend to the hunting party, she brought her daughter with her for assistance."

"Ah," Caleb said with a laugh. "And your father fell in love."

Marah shrugged. "I don't know. My grandmother never approved of their marriage, so she rarely said anything pleasant about their courtship. I assume he must have felt something for my mother. After all, she was far beneath him in stature, he should have known a marriage between them would be a difficult path. He could have simply taken her as a mistress or even made her empty promises to obtain what he desired. Instead he married her within a few months of their first meeting, despite all my grandmother's objections."

Caleb frowned at the sadness in her stare, but didn't interrupt again.

"His family disapproved the match even more than my grandmother did. Although they had no legal means to cut my father off from the title, they did limit his funds and stopped inviting him to functions in order to express their utter distaste for his bride. Angry, he apparently sequestered himself away with my mother in London. Within months, she was with child. My grandmother wished for her to come home, to let her deliver the baby . . . *me*."

Caleb shook his head. "But he wouldn't allow it."

"He thought the London doctors would be better equipped. But when I arrived, there were complications. I was saved, but my mother bled to death."

Caleb felt a stab of pain at the guilt in her eyes and the flat sorrow in her voice when she said the last sentence.

He touched her hand. "That wasn't your fault."

She stared at his fingers touching her skin and

then pulled away gently. "My father believed otherwise. As soon as I was strong enough to travel, he showed up on my grandmother's doorstep and handed me off to her. He returned to his family in London and reentered Society almost immediately. From what I understand, his family never spoke of his marriage or of me again. The only acknowledgment any of them made toward me was a payment twice yearly."

Caleb stared at her. "So you've never met them?"

There was a long, painful hesitation before she finally shook her head. "They never *wanted* to meet with me."

Her heartbroken tone told him how much that fact hurt her. "I'm sorry," he whispered.

She shrugged. "I've never received a note or an acknowledgment in the entire span of my life. Even when my father died, my grandmother read about it in the local paper weeks later. No one contacted us with the news."

"But you are family," he insisted with a wrinkled brow.

He could hardly imagine having no contact whatsoever with his family. Even when he had run for two years, his brother had found him multiple times and his sister had written to him at least a few times a year. He had cut himself off, but not been shunned in any real or complete fashion. He had always known his family was there, waiting for him.

"And *you* also have another family," Marah retorted. "Who you have no intention of meeting, yes?"

Caleb released her arm and paced away, stung by her mention of that secondary family he had vowed to forget existed. "But this is different, Marah."

"No, it is the same," she protested as she moved to the closest bench and sank into it with a sigh of exhaustion. "There are too many complications for both of us in finding the families we don't know. For me, I will only encounter censure and denial." She shivered. "I admit I don't think I'm strong enough to bear that. For you, it will open up wounds you fear to explore. So we are at an impasse. Only now that Lady Jericho has so triumphantly declared my true identity, I fear there will be consequences for me."

Caleb frowned. "Yes, that may be true."

She sighed a second time. "I should probably just go home to Baybary. Return to my grandmother's cottage and the life of simplicity I had there."

Caleb moved closer and took the seat beside her.

She straightened up, but didn't draw away as he reached up to brush a lock of hair away from her face. "So you would run, just as I did?"

She shrugged one shoulder. "Running seemed to work for you."

He stared at her. There was no way she could possibly believe that to be true. "Running only hurt everyone in my life . . . including me. I don't recommend it."

She was quiet for a moment. "Then what do you recommend, Caleb? How do I forget? How do I pretend this away? You are the expert, advise me."

Her words should have stung, but there was no heat to them, no cruelty. Caleb stared at her and there was only one thing he wanted to do. Only one action that would, as she asked, make her forget. Make him forget.

He cupped her cheeks gently and tilted his head as he moved in toward her. He wanted to kiss her. He wanted her to kiss him. He would settle for that although his body burned for more, the way it seemingly only did for her.

But just as his lips were about to meet hers, Victoria cleared her throat from behind them. "Marah?"

Marah jerked to her feet and stumbled away from him with a blush. "Victoria," she said, her voice cracking as she faced her friend. "I'm so sorry.

I never meant to ruin your party or embarrass you."

Victoria stepped forward and embraced her. "Stop. You've done nothing wrong, my dearest. I only wanted to check on your welfare and see if you would come back. I believe your sudden departure has only made the women more curious. I think if you come back with me and face them, we can end the subject just by refusing to address it."

"That won't end the subject," Marah said with a sigh as she shot a look toward Caleb.

"No, but it will end it for today," Victoria said softly. "Will you come with me?"

Marah nodded. "Yes." She turned to go but then moved back toward him. "Thank you, Caleb."

They were three simple words, with little meaning just on the surface. But the way they were said, the look that accompanied them . . . it touched Caleb to his very core. It made him feel, for the first time in too long to recall, like he had done something worthwhile.

He nodded, untrusting of his voice at present, and watched as she walked away. But even when she was gone, her presence troubled him. This encounter troubled him.

He had spent years pondering Marah's sweetness, his attraction to her, and punished himself for the fact that he couldn't give her what she needed.

But now that she had shared her past, he found himself drawn to her more than ever. And more than just physically.

They had something in common. A pain that few in their circles could understand for they had never endured it. And he felt closer to her than ever, even though he didn't want to.

Chapter 11

Three days had passed since Marah's true identity had been revealed by Lady Jericho, and as Crenshaw entered the parlor with another high stack of invitations that mentioned her especially, she moaned.

"This is becoming ridiculous!" she cried as the servant left the room. She crossed to the table where he had set the cards and letters and flipped through them.

"Well, not *all* of them are related to Lady Jericho's revelation," Victoria said, but her voice was weak indeed, and Marah sent a scowl over her shoulder at her.

"Everyone in good society is fully aware that your family is gathered close due to the marquis' illness. You told me they have limited their invitations to you this summer, haven't they?"

Victoria sighed behind her. "Yes."

Marah gathered up at least twenty-five invitations and spun around to hold them up. "And does *this* look limited to you? It is more than double what you were receiving before my secret was revealed."

Victoria pursed her lips, but Marah set the things aside and continued before she could argue. "Do you remember when I took Betsy and went out to the seamstress yesterday to find a bit of ribbon to have added to my yellow morning gown?"

Victoria nodded. "Yes, you and your maid were out for about an hour, why?"

Marah raised both eyebrows. "When I returned you were resting and I didn't want to bother you, so I never told you that I was approached on the *street*."

Victoria struggled to her feet with a look of concern. "By whom?"

"Some gaggle of awful ladies who were cooing and purring over me like I was some magnificent new animal they'd just discovered and wanted to turn into a coat!"

Victoria sat back down, resting her hand on her belly with a sigh. "Goodness, I thought you were trying to tell me you'd been molested by some strange man."

Marah stared at her friend. Victoria was pale enough that she must have been truly worried for

Marah's welfare. She moved to the couch and took her friend's cool and slightly clammy hand.

"Are you well, my dear?"

Victoria smiled and sat up straighter, though Marah could see it was only an attempt to placate her.

"Of course. It's just a slight headache. I'm very well, I only worry about you."

Marah dipped her chin, hating herself for her utter absorption with her own problems. Victoria was dealing with so much. Not only did her friend go to sit with her father-in-law nearly every day, but she had been struggling with her own bouts of illness. Marah had even seen the doctor going in and out of Victoria's chamber from time to time. Still, she didn't always trust city physicians.

"Would you like me to examine you?" she asked softly. "You know I trained a bit under my grandmother. I might be able to give you some herbs to help if you—"

"No," Victoria interrupted. "I appreciate it greatly, but I'm very well. I want to talk about *you* and your desire to refuse these invitations."

Marah's lips thinned both at Victoria's dismissal of her attempt to help and at the subject she had turned to in order to distract Marah.

"Well, I don't want to accept them," she protested.

Victoria folded her hands. "And why not? There is no reason you couldn't go. We could find a suitable chaperone even if Justin or I couldn't accompany you due to the marquis' condition. Alexander and Chloe will be back in Town soon, I'm certain they would gladly do it."

Marah shook her head. "But these people aren't inviting me to their parties and balls because they find me charming or interesting, Victoria. They are inviting me because I'm like a sideshow at a circus to them! They now all know who my family is, so they want to stare at me and speculate. Or they think by befriending me they can somehow obtain the influence of my grandmother and my uncle."

Victoria sighed. "You know, I was almost as sheltered from this world as you were when I first returned to London. I didn't know how to take the women of the *ton* or how to make myself comfortable at their gatherings. But I have learned a few things in my time here."

"I would say so! You are obviously very well-liked and popular now," Marah interrupted with a smile of pride for her friend.

Victoria blushed. "Thank you. But I was trying to say that any popularity I've gained also hasn't been because they like me as a person. Or at least, it wasn't at first. They invited me to their gatherings because I was the Earl of Baybary's mysterious wife, a woman who had been hidden away for years. They wanted to see me so that they could tell their friends about me. I was part of your circus sideshow as well."

Marah frowned. "I sense a lesson coming in all this."

Victoria laughed. "You know me well. And the lesson is that their disingenuous reasons for inviting me into their circle soon faded. I made some true friends and the rest fell away once they found something else of interest. It might be good for you to go to a few of these functions, let them get their staring and whispering out of the way and then try to obtain something of value from the experience. Like some more friends."

"I have friends. I have you," Marah protested.

Victoria laughed. "Yes, but if you think you might one day live in London, even part of the time, you will want to know more people than just me. I will bore you terribly if you spend every day with only me."

Marah dipped her chin, uncomfortable with the idea that perhaps she was missing something by avoiding the events she had been invited to.

Victoria smiled. "Just think about it. I'll have

Crenshaw set the invitations aside for a few days and we'll decide later."

"I can't promise I'll change my mind," Marah said softly, picking at her sleeve hem with distraction, though she was happy that this part of the conversation seemed to be coming to an end at last.

But Victoria plowed ahead into even more dangerous waters. "I-I saw you kissing Caleb."

Marah swallowed hard and slowly lifted her gaze to her friend. "Which time?"

Victoria's eyes widened. "Oh dear, two I suppose, how many times have there been?"

Marah shut her eyes and was assailed by a running set of images of Caleb's mouth meeting hers, sometimes with passion, sometimes with gentleness, but always with a sweetness she craved . . . she even dreamed of it.

"More than two," she admitted on a whisper. She took her friend's hands as heat flooded her cheeks. "Oh Victoria, what you must think of me!"

Victoria's brow furrowed. "Oh for heaven's sake, you know what I went through with Justin, I could never judge you in a hundred years for what you feel or for your attraction to a man. You two share a past, I know from personal experience how powerful a thing that can be."

"But I told him I wanted to forget that past," Marah said with a heavy sigh. She flopped back in the settee and covered her eyes. "I was so inflexible about it. I said I wanted to be acquaintances, nothing more."

Victoria chuckled. "Well, you are very *good* acquaintances, I suppose."

Marah glared at her. "Don't jest, this is a serious predicament. I told him that and I meant it when I said it. But then I allow his kiss. I want it, I've even instigated it."

"There is nothing wrong with that," Victoria insisted with a shake of her head.

"But there is!" Marah groaned. "Caleb Talbot has more than proven that he isn't a dependable man. He is wild and untamed, he goes out every single night and probably goes to bed with every courtesan in the city."

Victoria gave a thin, irritated frown that let Marah know she believed that was what he was doing, too. Her heart sank despite herself, but she ignored it, fighting to keep the jealousy from her voice as she said, "Oh it doesn't matter anyway."

"Why?" her friend asked softly.

Marah frowned. Sometimes it was hard to remember why, especially when Caleb was standing right before her. But she made herself focus on her dreams, on the goals she had set for herself *before* she had been forced to face Caleb again.

"After I returned to Baybary two years ago, I took a good look at myself," she explained, thinking about the difficulty of that time for her.

She had been hurt and feeling quite stupid that she had allowed herself to believe she might have a future with a man like Caleb. There had been many tears and angry outbursts.

"I thought about the men in my life, the ones who had let me down," she continued.

"There haven't exactly been many," her friend said softly.

"Perhaps not, but the ones who *were* in my life all did. They left, Victoria. My father left, Caleb left . . . they are not dependable. I realized that if I was to be happy, truly happy, I needed a man who wouldn't offer me surprises."

Victoria's brow wrinkled. "Sometimes surprises are the best part to a marriage."

"For you, perhaps. You were lucky to discover that the love of your life was already your husband," Marah said with a quick smile. "But that isn't true for most women."

"No—" Victoria began.

Marah arched a brow. "We live in a society of arranged marriages. And being in love with one's spouse isn't in fashion. Or at least they say that in order to justify their lack of feeling. Come, you can't be blind to that."

Victoria shook her head, her eyes sad. "You may be correct that *some* of those around us live that way."

Marah rolled her eyes at the hard-won admission and continued, "Well, I realized that since the possibility of finding a great love was rather slim, I should instead find a man who could be my friend. A man who was dependable and good. One I could stand sharing a home and children with. And I think I have done that. I can't spend any more of my energies on Caleb and his kisses. They will lead to nothing but hurt. I *must* refocus myself on Emerson."

A sigh was her friend's answer and Marah looked at her sharply. Victoria's lips were pursed and her expression gave all her thoughts away.

"I realize you have put a great deal of stock into Emerson Winstead," Victoria said in an oddly placating tone. "But don't you fear he may be no better than those who sent you all the invitations over the last few days?"

Marah stared at Victoria. "Are you asking if I believe that Emerson may want me for what he can obtain from our marriage?"

Victoria hesitated, but then she nodded.

Marah leaned back in her chair and pondered that idea. "It's no secret that Emerson is building his investments."

"And that he would like to have entry to higher society," Victoria added quietly.

Marah shot her a look. "He is bringing himself up in the world, Victoria. That is something to be admired."

"I agree, as long as he doesn't use *my* friend to do so."

"No, I don't think that is the entire story." When Victoria's eyebrows lifted, Marah shook her head. "I'm not saying that he isn't interested in my connections. I realize he wishes for Justin to invest in his shipping ventures and I'm certain he hopes our friendship will influence that goal, but it isn't as if he's kept that secret."

Victoria frowned. "No, he is quite open about his requests. That is true."

Marah nodded. "And he became aware of my family relationship to the Breckinridge title some time ago. We've spoken of it once or twice, but when I change the subject he always respects that.

Victoria, I think he truly *likes* me. He was a solid and steadfast friend after my grandmother's death and he's never been anything but kind to me."

"Have you kissed him?" Victoria asked softly.

Marah's gaze darted to her. Her cheeks heated. "N-no. I don't think we've progressed so far in our relationship yet."

"In a year?" Victoria asked, and she sounded truly surprised.

Marah pushed to her feet and paced to the window. She was trying hard not to remember the day in the park a week ago when she'd thought Emerson might kiss her and had been relieved when he hadn't.

"I wasn't trying to explain our attraction, Victoria. I was trying to set your mind at ease that I recognize he might have some interest in my connections, but I don't think it follows that we couldn't be happy together."

Victoria nodded her head. "Perhaps. But we all know Caleb doesn't give a damn about connection."

Marah stared outside.

"No," she mused softly. "He didn't know that my father was once the Earl of Breckinridge. When he found out, he didn't care except to worry about how that revelation affected me. Actually he was quite kind about it."

"Which is why you kissed him," Victoria whispered.

Facing her friend, Marah shrugged. "I suppose."

But that wasn't true. She had kissed Caleb because she wanted to. Because she needed to. She might deny that to her friend, even to Caleb, but she couldn't deny it to herself. She had given up trying.

But wanting something and pursuing it were different beasts. She *wanted* a lot of things that weren't good for her and she denied herself. She had to remain strong now.

"But all that is over now," she said quietly.

Victoria stared at her for a long while, as if she were trying to decide if she should argue the point or not. But finally she simply nodded.

"If you say so." After a moment's silence, Victoria continued, "Lady Stratfield invited us for supper tonight. She asked especially for you to join us."

Marah's cheeks heated with pleasure at this unexpected news. "She asked for me?"

"Yes," Victoria said with a smile. "She so enjoyed making your acquaintance the last time you were a member of our party. I think you made everything a little lighter that night."

Marah nodded before a terrible thought entered her head. "Do—do you suppose she knows about me? About my family?"

Victoria got to her feet and moved to the window with Marah. She took both her hands and smiled at her. "Don't read poor intentions into every lady of elevated status. You know that is your grandmother's bias coming to the surface."

Marah frowned. As much as she hated to admit it, Victoria was right. Her maternal grandmother had made clear her thoughts about those with rank.

Victoria continued, "I'm certain my mother-in-law *has* heard the gossip about your family connections. Even in her sequestered state, she is one of the most important women in Society. Her spies are everywhere and keep her in the know about such things. Honestly, I think the gossip helps to keep her from drowning in her heartbreak."

Marah hated the thought of Lady Stratfield, who she had liked so much, looking at her with different eyes. Perhaps judging her or seeing her as a new person.

"Don't look so worried," Victoria said. "I can assure you she cares nothing about that."

"How can you be certain?"

"Because she raised Caleb. And if he doesn't care . . . she doesn't care." Victoria grinned.

Marah pondered that for a moment as Caleb's reaction to the revelations about her played in her head once more. Then she nodded. "Very well, I'll come with you."

Victoria smiled as she enveloped Marah in a hard hug. "I'm glad. You won't be sorry."

But as her friend called for Crenshaw to send word of their additional guest to the Stratfield house, Marah stared at her reflection in the window. Whether she was sorry she had taken the invitation remained to be seen and depended upon one person.

Caleb.

Chapter 12

Marah sighed as the family retired to the drawing room for drinks after one of the most delicious meals she'd ever eaten. In fact, her entire evening with the Talbots had been wonderful with one glaring exception. Caleb had been seated down the table from her and he had openly stared at her the entire duration of the meal.

She was certain that he wasn't escorting *her* to the parlor, but his mother, only because his sister had taken Marah's arm before he could intercede. And he hadn't looked very pleased about that fact.

Tessa squeezed her arm gently and drew Marah's attention to her as they walked.

"I took your arm because I wanted to have a moment alone with you, Miss Farnsworth—" Tessa said as they walked. "I mean, Lady Marah."

Marah sighed. Though no one had spoken directly of the revelation of her family connections, the entire household, down to the servants, was now calling her Lady Marah. She rather hated the sound of it, it was so foreign and strange.

"Well, I'm happy to speak to you," she said with a forced smile. She could only hope Tessa wouldn't broach the subject of the Breckinridges. She wasn't up to discussing her estranged family: the topic only inspired painful thoughts.

"I wanted to tell you that you made quite an impression on my father the last time you visited with us," Tessa said as she followed Victoria and Justin into the drawing room.

Marah tensed slightly. Tessa had been so against her intrusion into her father's chambers, she hoped the young woman didn't still harbor resentment over the fact that her opinion hadn't been heeded.

"I liked him a great deal," Marah said slowly.

Tessa released her arm and faced her. "I apologize for my outburst that night. I can be quite . . . *protective* of both my parents, but especially my father."

Marah thought she saw Tessa shoot a quick glare toward Caleb, but she wasn't certain because it was so brief an expression.

"Why wouldn't you be?" Marah asked. "Under the circumstances, your protectiveness only makes you an excellent daughter."

Tessa blinked and Marah saw the beginnings of

tears in her dark eyes, but she smiled nonetheless. "Thank you for your understanding. But in this instance, I want you to know that I was wrong. I—"

Before she could finish, Caleb slipped up to the two of them and grinned at Marah. "Great God, Marah, mark the date. My sister has admitted she is wrong. This is a great moment in family history."

Marah stared at the unwarranted harshness of his tone toward his sister. Caleb had a glass of wine in his hand and she had seen him drinking at least two more at supper. Apparently the spirits had loosened his tongue in a most unpleasant fashion.

"Caleb—" she began in a hushed tone.

Tessa's lips thinned as she speared her brother with a pointed glare. "This was a private conversation, brother. You were not invited to it. Not that it has ever stopped you."

He turned to her with a laugh. "Come on, Tess, you know it's true. You *never* admit fault, you never have probably since you were old enough to speak."

"Caleb," Marah said. "That is enough. Your sister was being quite kind to me and she doesn't deserve your—"

Before she could finish, a servant hurried into the room. "I'm sorry to interrupt, my lady," he panted, addressing the marchioness.

She looked at the man and her cheeks paled. "What is it?" she whispered.

"It's the marquis, madam. He seems to have taken a turn."

"Call for the doctor," Justin called as he sprinted for the stairs. "Hurry!"

Marah stood stone-still as the rest of the room erupted into action. Tessa burst into the tears she had been trying to hold back and was ushered away by Victoria. Servants banged doors in the hall and called out to each other. But all the action seemed to be in half time, slowed until Marah turned her face and found the marchioness still standing in the middle of the room, staring at the place where the servant had first come in. She hadn't moved, she hadn't seemed to have breathed, since that moment.

"Caleb," Marah snapped, stepping forward to shake his arm, for he, too, was just standing still, numb.

"Marah?" he whispered, his tone a horrible question she couldn't answer.

Her heart broke for him, but she managed to keep from offering comfort. He needed to *give* solace rather than receive it.

"Your mother," she murmured, turning him to

make him look at her. "Take her upstairs. Take her to her husband."

He stared at his mother and then his gaze darted down to her. "I don't know, I—"

Marah grabbed his arms and shook him gently. "Stop acting like an angry, spoiled child and start acting like a son. She needs you. Whatever she has done in the past, she needs you. For once in your life think of someone else and go to her."

He stared at her for another moment, but then he walked to his mother.

"Mama, let me take you up," he said softly.

The marchioness shook her head as if she was just waking from some kind of dream. Or nightmare. She stared up at her younger son.

"Your father—" she began, and then her knees buckled.

Caleb caught her, steadying her as she somehow managed to gather herself.

"My father needs us both now," he whispered. "Let me take you up to him."

Lady Stratfield nodded. "Yes. Yes, take me to him."

Marah stood there, silent, watching as Caleb all but carried his mother from the room and up to her beloved husband. The man she might never see again. And as they disappeared from view, Marah bent her head and let a few tears fall. For the marchioness. For Caleb.

Even for herself.

Since the announcement that his father had taken a turn for the worse, when he had gone upstairs with his family hours before, Caleb had seen Marah come and go. She had escorted the doctor to the group when he arrived. Later she had ensured they were all brought tea and a few cakes, which everyone picked at but no one bothered to eat.

She had also been responsible for trading wet handkerchiefs for dry and had comforted all the women in the room. She had even passed by him during the third hour of their vigil and briefly held his hand, squeezing his fingers and making him feel, just for a moment, that perhaps everything would be all right after all.

Finally, after the hours had blurred together and time had ceased to matter, the doctor rose from the marquis' bed and stretched his back.

He turned toward the family, gathered in small groups around the room. Marah was in the doorway, away from them, but ready to assist if she was needed.

"This slip is the most grave yet," the doctor said quietly, as to not disturb the sleeping patient. "But

I think the worst has passed. His Lordship seems to be stable now and is sleeping as comfortably as we can expect."

At her husband's bedside, Caleb's mother reached out to stroke a finger over his thin, pale hand.

"Do you hear that, my love?" she whispered, her tone broken and cracking. "You have come through this yet again."

The doctor gathered his things, and Justin and Victoria offered to take him out. As they left the room, Caleb looked at his mother. She would stay at his father's side for the rest of the night, he was certain. He wasn't about to tell her she shouldn't, even though he found himself worried about the deep circles under her eyes.

Instead he approached his sister, leaning on a wall near his father's bed, almost as if it were the only thing holding her upright. Now he felt terrible about the mean-spirited teasing he had indulged in earlier. His frustration had made him cruel and he hated himself for it. With trembling fingers, he touched her arm. Tessa looked up at him with a surprised jump.

"Caleb," she said as she wrapped her arms around his waist.

He was surprised at her openness to him, but he didn't comment on it as he hugged her gently.

"I-I'm sorry," he whispered. "For what I said. For—"

"Shhh," she whispered as her embrace tightened. "I know."

After a moment, the siblings broke apart. Tessa stepped back and looked past him at their mother.

"I'll stay with her for a time, to see if I can convince her to go to her own bed. I doubt she will do it, but she needs the sleep."

Caleb was glad his sister saw the same exhaustion in their mother that he did. They were so close, Tessa probably had the best chance to make her listen of any of them.

She released him. "Now, you go home. And take dear Marah with you." She smiled across the room at her. "She has been a godsend tonight."

He followed his sister's stare. Yes, indeed she had been. He patted Tessa's hand a final time. "Tell Mother I said good night. I don't wish to disturb her."

She agreed and he left her side. At the door, he stopped beside Marah. She was holding a tray and he took it, setting it on a table beside the door.

"The servants can tend to that," he explained as he took her hand. She let him, without hesitation, yet another indication of how trying a night this had been for them all.

He took her down the stairs and into the foyer, where he sent a servant to gather her wrap. As she waited for him there, Caleb went into the front parlor. Victoria and Justin were standing with the doctor.

"I'll escort Marah home in my carriage," he said softly.

The two looked at him, Victoria's gaze particularly hard and focused, but then she nodded. "Yes, we may be here a bit longer and she deserves a comfortable bed after all her support to the family tonight."

He didn't respond as the couple returned to their conversation with the physician, but when he moved into the hall to find Marah adjusting her wrap around her shoulders, he stopped to stare. Her hair was a bit looser than it had been earlier in the evening, sending little pretty tendrils around her drawn face. She looked as tired as he felt.

But she *did* deserve something. For everything she did for everyone else, she deserved much more than he could give.

"Caleb?" she whispered.

It was the first time he'd heard her voice in close to an hour and the soft tones of it brushed across his skin and made him hyperaware of how much he wanted to touch her. Without responding, he took her hand and led her to his waiting carriage.

As they got in, she looked toward the house.

"Aren't Victoria and Justin coming with us?"

He shook his head. "They are still talking to the doctor. I wouldn't be surprised if they stay here tonight rather than coming home at all."

"O-oh," she stammered and even in the dim carriage he saw her cheeks turn pink, as if she was contemplating, just as he was, all the things that could happen when two people who had an undeniable attraction were left unchaperoned.

"Thank you for what you did tonight," Caleb said softly.

As they drove down the deserted lanes toward Justin's home, he watched the way the streetlights outside passed over her face.

She shrugged. "It was nothing."

He moved to her side of the carriage. "It was everything, Marah," he said softly. "*You* were everything."

She shivered as her hand came out to rest on his chest. He looked down at the fingers clenched gently there. She had probably meant to push him away when she did it, but now she stared up at him, her mouth slightly parted and her breath coming quickly.

"Can't I give you something in return for that kindness?" he murmured, almost more to himself than to her. "Can't I give you a gift as you have given me and all my family?"

"You only want to do this to forget," Marah said, her voice shaking.

He shook his head. "No, Marah. Not to forget."

He glided his fingers into her hair and dropped his mouth to hers. As she surrendered and her hand glided up to cup the back of his neck, Caleb realized that she was too tired to fight him. That her own desires, which she could normally control, were going to win the battle between propriety and need, at least for a short while.

So he took advantage of that surrender. He drew her even closer, until she was almost on his lap. He cradled the back of her head and kissed her so deeply that he felt like they melded into one person. She held him to her, meeting his tongue with gentle thrusts of her own.

And then she let out a sighing moan that switched off any remaining gentlemanly instincts and stirred his cock the way no other woman had been able to do since he last allowed himself to touch her like this.

They didn't have much time and Caleb wanted her so much. He wanted to feel her pleasure. He wanted to give that to her until it was all that existed in this small, cramped space.

He brought himself to his knees before her, continuing to kiss her even as he found the hem of her gown with shaking fingers. Slowly, unsteadily, he started to pull it up, bunching it at her hips.

"Caleb?" she murmured, though her body writhed as his fingers touched the bare flesh beyond her stocking.

"I won't take," he promised, looking up her body to meet her eyes. "Only give. I swear to you."

He could see how much she thought she should deny him, but he also saw something else . . . that she didn't want to. In that moment he realized that, like him, she had dreamed of the one afternoon of pleasure they had shared. She had thought of the ecstasy of that joining, and the fact made the ache in his loins all the more powerful.

He pushed her legs open and in the dim light he saw her sex glitter with moisture. He reached out to touch her there, and Marah sucked in a breath as her head dipped back against the padded headrest behind her.

He traced the open slit, feeling her heat beckon to him. When his thumb brushed the swollen nub of her clit, she clenched her fists against the carriage seat and let out a groan that sounded like music to him.

Time was ticking away. Once they were out of

the carriage, he realized she wouldn't allow this. He had to do this now or perhaps never do it again.

He dropped his mouth to her and pressed a wet kiss to her lower lips. She arched up into him, his name gurgling from her mouth as he licked her sex from top to bottom. She thrashed against the carriage cushion, her legs already shaking like she was close to release.

He glided a hand to her and pressed one finger deep into her clenching sheath. She lifted her hips as he breached her, and her breathy moan was all he needed to tell him she had been waiting for this. For him.

He pumped in and out of her gently as he continued to lick and suck her. He felt the carriage moving, bringing them ever closer to the house. He latched on to her swollen clit and began to suck as he worked his fingers in and out of her body, gentle, yet demanding at the same time.

He felt the moment just before she came. Her entire body stiffened and her nails dug against the leather of the seat as she wailed out a sound of release and then her body was rippling around his finger and her face contorted with pleasure and relief.

The carriage pulled up to the door now and Caleb quickly smoothed her gown down around her. He got to his own seat just as the footman opened the door for them. Caleb got out first and waved the servant away as he put a hand back in for Marah. She stared at him, at his waiting fingers, for a long time before she finally gripped his hand and stepped onto the drive. There was no mistaking her trembling as she pulled her hand free of his.

They were silent as they entered the house together. Crenshaw was there to greet them.

"Lord and Lady Baybary sent word," the butler said with a drawn frown. "May I inquire after the marquis?"

Caleb nodded with a smile for the man who had served his father as well as he now served his brother. "He made it through the crisis, thank you."

The butler gave a relieved sigh and seemed to droop.

"You may retire now, Crenshaw," Caleb said, returning his focus to Marah. In the brighter light inside he could see how her cheeks remained pink with pleasure and embarrassment. "I don't think Lord and Lady Baybary will return tonight and you should have your rest."

The butler bowed and left them alone. Slowly Caleb moved on her.

"Come with me to my room, Marah," he whispered.

Her gaze darted up, wide and surprised and also

filled with longing. But she shook her head. "My servant would know. *All* the servants would know."

"It doesn't matter," he coaxed as he reached for her hand.

She pulled away. "It matters to me. You may not care if you ruin yourself, Caleb, but I *can't* let you ruin me. I'm sorry about what I just allowed to happen."

He frowned as she backed up, holding up her hands as a shield. "You don't mean that. You wanted me, you wanted what happened."

She nodded. "Indeed, I did. And I didn't turn away from you. But I am not an animal, Caleb. I sometimes want things but I don't follow through because I know they are wrong for me or for the others around me."

"Unlike me," he said, stinging from her rejection and still on edge from the evening's earlier events.

She nodded without hesitation. "Yes. I have watched you wreck yourself every night since our arrival."

He pushed out a burst of unhappy laughter. "I am nothing different than I was when you met me two years ago. And you liked me then, you even called me charming."

"Is that what you think?" Marah asked with an incredulous shake of her head. "Do you really believe that by doing the same things and being with the same people that somehow you are the same? You aren't. I see you going out every night, you drink to excess, and you are cold to your mother, and often to your sister. There is *nothing* charming about any of those things. You may have fallen back into your old life, but there is no happiness in that fall. No joy."

He stared at her, stunned by how accurate an assessment she made of him. Somehow his soul was an open book and she could read it without effort.

"And yet you still want me," he pointed out, determined to expose her as deeply as she had exposed him. "Even as you are courted by another man, even as you tell me again and again that you 'can't' or 'won't' surrender yourself to me."

Her cheeks grew even darker.

"What I want is very different from what I need," she finally whispered.

He cocked an eyebrow. "I think I just gave you what you need."

She frowned. "No. What I *need* is the kind of man who won't run when there is trouble, like my father did. Like you did. I need someone who can be a friend to me and a partner. Someone steady and decent—"

"What an awful life that sounds like," he interrupted as he folded his arms.

She shrugged one shoulder. "Perhaps to you. You are right that I've claimed I can't want you and then turned around and allowed you privileges I shouldn't have. I have been confusing and misleading and for that I am sorry. But this ends now, Caleb."

"You've said that before," he replied.

She nodded. "But this time I mean it."

She turned without further comment and walked down the hallway and up the stairs. He watched her go with a new and strange desperation clawing at him. Marah might have said she was ending things between them before, but this time he'd seen something different in her face when she said it.

This time he feared it might be true. And only when he tested her resolve would he know for sure.

Chapter 13

Emerson took the cup of tea Marah had poured for him and gave her a wide and generous smile that held none of the hesitation she felt beside him.

"Thank you, my dear," he said as he took a sip, then set the cup aside. "And I apologize again for how long it's been since I called on you. I have been mobbed by the increasing demands of my business, but I will endeavor to make you more of a priority from now on."

Marah shifted in discomfort on the settee across from him, but somehow managed to put a smile on her face. "Think nothing of it. I have been quite busy myself."

He smiled and then began to talk about his investments further. Somehow Marah managed to nod and did her best to appear interested, but in truth her mind wandered.

Wandered to last night. She hated herself for thinking of the way Caleb had spread her open and pleasured her until she could hardly see, hardly think, hardly breathe. Here she was, sitting with a man she one day hoped to marry, and yet it was Caleb's breath on her inner thigh that she incessantly thought about.

But she had ended it with him. This time for good. To prove it to herself, she had invited Emerson to tea. It was best to put all her attention and energy on him. It was the only way to keep her sanity.

"And that is why I believe it is actually a good thing that your identity as the late earl's daughter has come out," Emerson said with a benign smile.

Marah blinked, pulled from her reverie. "I-I beg your pardon?"

He frowned and for a moment she thought she saw irritation in his expression but then he wiped it away.

"I was saying that my sources tell me your identity as the late Earl of Breckenridge's daughter has been recognized by the *ton* at large."

Marah stared at him. "Wh-where did you hear that?" she asked. "How?"

Emerson arched a brow. "Gossip from your realm *does* filter down to the lower class, my dear. And since I do have a particular interest in you, I tend to hear things about you, to ask about you."

Marah stared. She supposed she should be flattered by his attentiveness, but she wasn't. The idea that he would run around trying to find gossip about her made her feel violated rather than cherished.

"You must realize that this is a difficult and painful situation for me," she said through clenched teeth. "When I revealed to you a few months ago that I had a relationship to that family, I also told you they had abandoned me in every way that mattered. The fact that the entire *ton* now knows that fact and is discussing it with such zeal brings me no pleasure."

"I understand that must be true," Emerson said as he reached out to take her hand. "But with the death of your maternal grandmother, you are all but alone in this world."

"I have Justin and Victoria and my other friends," Marah insisted, shaking her hand free of his. "They would protect me and take care of me just as family would."

He nodded. "Of course, but I think it would be foolish to completely cut yourself off from any chance of a reconciliation with your father's relations. And you never know, they may be more open to your presence now. Seeking them out could be very advantageous to you."

Marah frowned. Caleb and Victoria had both

made clear their concerns about Emerson and his true intentions. Now their comments met with her own doubts and she found herself questioning his every statement.

She swallowed. "I suppose it would be good for you as well, if I one day reconciled with my family. If you continue to have intentions toward me, a reunion could one day align you with a most powerful family, with great resources for you to tap for your business."

Emerson stared at her for a moment, and in his eyes she saw hints of emotion. A bit of outrage, even a touch of hurt. Those things confused her even further.

"Do not think so low of me," he said softly. "Or mistake my intentions. When I met you, I had no idea of your family affiliations. I didn't care. I only think about your comfort and well-being when I recommend you open yourself to a rebuilding of your family. If I overstepped a boundary by making the suggestion, I apologize."

"No, it is I who should apologize," Marah said with a shake of her head. "These have been difficult days."

"For all of us," came a voice behind them. Marah turned to watch as Caleb entered the room without waiting for an invitation. "Hello, Winthrop."

Marah's lips thinned. Even after her dismissal of him last night, the man *refused* to honor her request and let her go. And why? He had no honorable intentions toward her, that was clear enough. And yet he was like a spoiled child with a toy. He didn't want it, but he didn't anyone else to play with it, either.

"Winstead," she snapped, folding her arms and glaring at him.

Seemingly oblivious to her angry stare, Caleb flopped himself into a chair and started perusing the tea cakes the servants had brought to accompany their refreshments. As he gulped one down in one bite, he said, "Whatever you say. So, how's business, Emerson?"

Emerson glared at him with as much heat as Marah was. "Very good, thank you."

"Growing?" Caleb asked, though this time he shot a meaningful glance toward Marah.

She gasped in outrage. Had he been eavesdropping on her private conversation? How dare he!

Emerson seemed to recognize that fact, as well, for his eyes narrowed. "Indeed, it is. But I don't think you really care about the state of my affairs, Mr. Talbot."

Caleb's eyes actually sparkled, as if he'd been

waiting for this showdown and now he was excited to finally begin it. "Don't I?"

"No." Emerson folded his hands in his lap. "I think you barged into this room and intruded upon our privacy solely to express your superior attitude toward me. You wish to judge me simply because I was born outside of your precious Upper Ten Thousand."

"You know me very little," Caleb said with a dry laugh, "if you think that is true."

Emerson gave a shake of his head. "Perhaps you are right about that, Mr. Talbot. Perhaps I'm far off the mark about your reasons to dislike me. But I am not blind. If you don't despise me because of my lack of rank, then perhaps it has more to do with the fact that you look at Marah with wolf eyes."

That stopped Caleb mid-bite of a second tea cake. Slowly he set the sweet down and faced Emerson fully. "Watch yourself now, friend."

Marah had been watching the exchange with stunned disbelief, but this was enough. Rising to her feet, she snapped, "Both of you, just stop it!"

The men looked at her, and it was clear that they hadn't even been thinking about her while they snapped at each other. They were just barbarians, banging their chests and marking their territory.

"Emerson," Marah said through clenched teeth. "I would very much like to take a walk if you would be obliged to escort me."

Emerson rose with a quick bow. "Of course, my lady. I would be honored."

"Good," she said. "I'll just have a quick word with Mr. Talbot and then join you in the foyer."

Emerson hesitated and she could see that her beau didn't like the idea of leaving her alone with a man he saw as a rival. But if she had her way, that would be finished. Now.

Finally he nodded. "As you wish, Lady Marah."

He left the room and as soon as he was gone, Caleb leaned back in the chair and looked up at her. Marah waited for him to mock, to tease her about Winstead, but instead he said nothing. Only burned holes in her with those piercing eyes.

"Please," she whispered. "Why can't you honor my request? Why can't you let me go?"

He straightened up, and his expression became even more serious. "I don't know, Marah."

His quiet answer troubled her more than any long explanation would have. She shook her head.

"If you cannot back away and let me be, I-I will have no choice but to quit this house and return to Baybary."

He stared at her. "You would do that?"

She hesitated. The last thing in the world she wanted to do was leave London. Even though she had resisted coming when Victoria initially asked, now that she was here she didn't want to go. She wanted to be here for her friend as the family struggled with the slow passing of Justin's father. And when she admitted the truth, she wanted to be there for Caleb, too.

But she couldn't. Last night had proven she had no self-control when it came to the man. And he refused to practice any himself because he was bound and determined to prove he hadn't changed because of the past.

"You leave me with no recourse," she answered softly. "I am not like you, Caleb. I *will* do something to better myself and my position. Even if it means parting myself forever from my friends and from you. Good day."

Unable to say more without fear of saying too much, Marah turned and fled the room, into the arms of another man who made her feel no strong feelings. Not lust, not anger . . . but certainly not love, either.

Caleb sat in the dark, a bottle of whiskey dangling from his fingertips. But despite the fact that the bottle had been open for over half an hour, he hadn't taken a drink. He had intended to do so. To drown himself and all his feelings in the numbing delights of a fine year, but when he touched the bottle he saw Marah's face.

You may ruin yourself, Caleb, but I can't let you ruin me.

That was what she had said to him the previous night. Those words rang in his head.

He stared into the fire as the door opened behind him. He didn't move and hoped whoever had intruded upon his thoughts would leave him in peace.

It wasn't to be. Justin stepped up to the chair and looked down at him in surprise. "Hello, brother. I didn't realize you were in residence tonight."

Caleb lifted his face to look at his elder brother. "Did you think I was out carousing?"

Justin smiled as he sank into another chair that faced the fire. "It has been your way of late." He motioned to the bottle in Caleb's hand. "May I have a glass of that?"

He handed it over. "You may have it all, I don't want it."

Justin stared at the bottle, still full, and a small smile touched his face. Caleb frowned at the relieved expression. Apparently his brother shared Marah's sentiment that he was wrecking himself with drink and frivolity.

"Would you like to crow about my abstinence?" Caleb asked, his tone peevish as he sank deeper into the chair, with folded arms.

Justin shrugged as he set the bottle down on the floor beside him without taking a drink of his own. "I only worry about you, Caleb. You returned to London vowing to reclaim your wicked life as if nothing had changed. But you don't seem to be having much fun at it."

Caleb scowled. Again his brother reminded him of Marah's accusations. "Well . . . it isn't very fun," he finally admitted.

Justin looked at him in surprise. "No? You could always stop."

Caleb was quiet for a long while. "You sound like Marah," he finally said softly.

His brother remained silent and Caleb sighed.

"She thinks I'm a coward, you know. And that I'm ruining myself."

"Aren't you?" Justin asked.

Caleb stared at the flames. "I have tried, but I fail even at that."

"You have failed at ruination." Justin laughed softly. "Isn't that a success?"

"Not if one is trying to forget. To numb," Caleb said with a sigh.

Justin's laughter faded and his nod grew somber.

"I'm sorry. And Marah has spoken to you about all this?"

"You sound surprised," Caleb said as he brought his gaze level with Justin's.

"I suppose I am." His brother shifted. "I know you two bonded together after she was attacked two years ago, that you told her your secret, but I didn't realize you had remained so close that she would venture such a strong opinion about your life now."

"We made love that day," Caleb admitted.

Justin blinked. "What day?"

"The day Victoria was kidnapped and I told Marah about our father." He swallowed. "We made love."

His brother was silent for a long time and Caleb held his breath as he waited for the stunned censure, the judgment.

Instead Justin sighed. "Well, I feared as much."

Now it was Caleb who couldn't mask his surprise. "You did?"

"It was obvious *something* had happened between you," Justin said with a shrug. "But when you didn't speak to me about your conquest, I thought perhaps it hadn't gone so far as that. Why *didn't* you tell me about Marah?"

Caleb stared at the flames again. In them he

could see Marah's sweet surrender that day long ago. Now it merged with her whispered moans in the carriage the night before. All of it tormented him beyond reason.

"I suppose what happened between us seemed too . . . too sacred," he admitted softly.

"You must have cared for her," Justin said, his dark eyes focused entirely too intently on Caleb.

He shrugged. "I believe I did. No, I know I did. But my world was upside down. I hurt too much already, I was so confused that the way Marah made me feel when I was near her was too much. So I ran."

The room was silent for a long time.

"She is right," Caleb finally whispered. "I *am* a coward when it comes down to it. And she is finished with me now. She has said it before, but this afternoon she meant it."

Justin tilted his head, and Caleb could see his brother was incredulous about the idea that Marah could simply let him go. But Justin hadn't seen her face when she declared she would quit the house if he didn't agree to her terms. Justin hadn't seen the steel in her eyes.

"But I think she might be right," he continued, unwilling to argue the point with his brother.

"About what?"

He sighed. "Perhaps I *should* do something. I

came here hoping I could live in the past, go back to the man I was before I discovered the marquis isn't my father. But it hasn't worked. So possibly it's time to stop pretending I can be the man I once was and start figuring out the man I should be."

Justin's eyebrows lifted and his tone was impressed when he asked, "And how can I help you in this endeavor?"

"I need a place to let until my own home's renovations are finished. I will hurry that process along now, so I should only require another residence for a few weeks, perhaps a month at most."

"You wish to leave this house?" Justin asked.

He nodded. "Yes. I think I've hidden here long enough. And it isn't fair to Marah. She wishes to be free of me. Perhaps it's time to think of what is best for her for once. Help me find a place, Justin. I think it's time for me to start over."

Chapter 14

Marah spun around the dance floor in Emerson's arms, but each time she pivoted, her gaze was drawn to Caleb. He stood nearby, at the edge of the floor talking to a small group of men. He never looked at her. He didn't even seem to know she was there.

She forced her stare back to her partner and smiled. He returned the expression just before the country dance steps forced them to part and each join a line composed of other couples. She took the opportunity to draw a breath. This was for the best.

She'd been repeating that phrase for days, though, and she didn't quite believe it yet.

"Lady Marah," said a woman beside her, clapping her hands as a couple bounced through the corridor created by the rest of the dancers.

Marah jolted. She still wasn't accustomed to hearing herself addressed in such a manner, but she forced a smile toward the older lady. "Yes, Lady Greensboro?"

"I hear you are staying with Lord and Lady Baybary."

Marah nodded. "Yes, they are dear friends."

"Then you have probably had much occasion to spend time with the earl's brother, Caleb Talbot," the woman said, and her eyes lit up with something almost . . . predatory.

Marah shifted, thinking of her times with Caleb. His kiss, his touch, his comfort.

"Y-yes, I know the gentleman a little."

"My daughter has taken an interest in the man," Lady Greensboro explained as they inched closer to the front of the line where Marah would rejoin Emerson and dance to the end. She wished the movements would advance a little faster. She really didn't want to hear this.

"Oh, yes?" Marah managed to choke out.

Lady Greensboro motioned across the room to a very pretty brunette standing with a group of girls. She was hardly out of the schoolroom and had a fresh, appealing way about her as she giggled into her hand.

Instantly Marah despised her.

"She is lovely," she said, hoping her tone didn't reveal the depth of her jealousy.

"Indeed, a Diamond of the First Water this season!" her mother gushed with pride. "Perhaps you could give us a little insight into Mr. Talbot's pursuits, his interests, his character?"

Marah swallowed. She had told Caleb she wanted to part, *truly* part. That she couldn't be his comfort or his lover or play any other confusing role in his upturned life that had no room for her in any permanent sense.

But this was going too far. To be asked to give courtship tips to another woman who wished to pursue him? She wasn't capable of such a thing.

They were almost to the front of the line and so Marah gave a little shrug.

"I'm sorry, my lady, I'm afraid I wouldn't know." She swallowed and gave the lady a side glance. "Mr. Talbot was often out until the wee hours and he— he left the earl and countess's house a few days past for his own quarters."

With that, she stepped into the middle of the space between the dancers, caught Emerson's waiting hands, and skipped with him down the middle corridor to the end of the line.

As they parted again, she sighed. She wasn't particularly proud of what she'd just done. After all, her little comment about Caleb being out all night might deter a perfectly nice match for him.

But luckily the music ended just as they took their places and she wasn't forced to continue her conversation with Lady Greensboro.

"Are you having a good time?" Emerson asked as he slipped her hand into the crook of his elbow and guided her off the dance floor.

"Indeed," Marah lied with a smile. "The party is very lovely."

"And *you* are the belle of it," Emerson said with a beaming smile. "Everyone seems to wish to talk to you."

Her smile fell as she contemplated her sudden popularity.

"Yes," she groaned with a shake of her head. "They do want to 'Lady Marah' me to death. I'm only surprised no one invited my grandmother to see what our reactions to each other might be."

Emerson's gaze lit up. "Do you think someone might attempt that?"

Marah stared at him, so interested in the idea of her reconciliation with a woman who had never been concerned for her whatsoever. He claimed his concern was purely for her happiness but Marah wasn't stupid. As Victoria kept pointing out, as Caleb mentioned constantly, Emerson would bene-fit greatly from a match with her . . . and even more so if her relationship to the house of Breckinridge was repaired.

"I hope not," she said softly. "It would bring me no pleasure for such a thing to transpire in such a public way. If I were to wish to meet with my grandmother or my father's other family, it would be done in private where no eyes could watch and judge our every reaction."

She couldn't stifle a shiver at the thought.

Emerson nodded swiftly. "Of course."

They stood in silence for a few moments. She had once thought the silences between them to be comfortable. When she first met him, she had marveled that she could sit quietly with the man for half an hour. Now things had changed, though. She was beginning to wonder if Emerson remained quiet with her because he could think of nothing interesting to say when it wasn't about his business.

She scanned the room, looking for a good reason to part company from him for a while. Obviously she was feeling peevish and there was no reason to poison the evening with such unkind thoughts. Her gaze lit upon two gentlemen standing by the punch bowl and she smiled.

"Emerson," she said, "Might you fetch me a refreshment? I'm parched."

He smiled. "Of course." He looked toward the table and his eyes lit up brightly as they had when her grandmother was mentioned. "Why look, it is the Duke of Orling and his twin brother."

Marah's smile widened. Good, so he had noticed. Her plan was working.

"Oh, you wished to talk to them about some shipping interests, didn't you?" she asked, all innocence.

He nodded. "I could do so under the onus of fetching you a cup."

"Yes, you could. Why don't you do that? I am perfectly content to wait for my drink."

He smiled at her in thanks and then disappeared into the crowd toward his potential business interests. Marah stared at him as he went. When she said to Victoria that she believed Emerson liked her, she knew that was true. But she also knew he loved his business, as did he love the idea of elevating himself into higher society.

With her, he had the chance at both. But what would *she* gain from the match? A steady partner, yes. But would there ever be anything more between them? Could she expect passion to bloom at some point? Or even something so deep as love? If they were lucky enough to have babies, would he be a good father or simply see any children they shared as a way to further advance himself?

"Here." Marah turned to see Victoria approaching her with a glass of punch in her outstretched hand. "You looked parched and Mr. Winstead seems to be involved in deep conversation with the Twin Dukes."

Marah laughed at the nickname for the two men, who did look remarkably alike, even down to their matching mannerisms. "How do people tell them apart?"

"I'm not sure they do." Victoria sighed. "There is a rumor that they each hold the title half the year and trade off. Apparently even their wives can't tell the difference."

Marah turned toward her friend with a shiver. "So they . . . um . . ."

"I have no idea if they switch wives when they switch positions in Society. I don't want to know." Victoria laughed but then the laughter faded. "You pretend to be happy, but I could see from your face while you were dancing that you weren't. How can I help you?"

Marah shook her head. "I'm just being foolish, that's all. There is nothing to be done about it."

Victoria slipped a hand through her arm. "Let's step outside and get a bit of air."

Marah hesitated. Did she really wish to go outside and spill her soul to her best friend? If she started talking about her troubles, she feared she wouldn't be able to stop this time. It wasn't that she didn't trust Victoria with them, but she didn't really want to say what was in her heart out loud.

Victoria faced her. "Marah?"

"Very well," she whispered. "To the terrace it is."

"Right in the carriage?" Victoria whispered as they stood on the veranda twenty minutes later.

Marah nodded, the heat of her blush burning her cheeks. As she had suspected, the moment she started talking, everything she had concealed came spilling out in one burst.

"Yes, I'm afraid so."

"And how was it?" her friend asked. "Both two years ago and a few nights past."

Marah's gaze lifted to her friend and she exhaled a shocked breath. "Victoria!"

"It's a legitimate question," her friend protested at her tone. "Physical compatibility *does* play a role in a happy union."

Marah's lips parted. "It was . . . wonderful. Both times. But there isn't going to be a happy union, at least not between Caleb and me. You know this."

Victoria caught her hands.

"Oh, why? You obviously care for Caleb. And he turns to you when his heart is hurting, which means he feels something more for you than mere physical attraction. Why *can't* you make a future with each other?" Victoria smiled. "You would be my sister then."

"As much as I would love to be your sister," Marah said softly, "Caleb and I aren't well suited. He may come to me when his heart hurts, as you say, but he never remains by my side once he has what he desired."

"He comforted you at my tea last week," Victoria interrupted.

Marah stopped. Yes, he had done that.

"I did appreciate it, but I can't pretend it means more than it does," she said. "Caleb wants to be free. He is just as likely to bolt when he is hurt as he is to face whatever trouble there is and fight. When we first connected two years ago, I was foolish enough to think there might be a future and when he ran, it . . . it made me question myself. I cannot do that again."

Victoria frowned. "I'm sorry. I'm sorry I didn't know and couldn't help you."

Marah shrugged. "What could you have done? I was a young woman who made a foolish mistake with a handsome man. These things happen. I learned from it. The experience forced me to see that I couldn't depend upon a person like Caleb. I needed someone who would *never* run. Whose affections and attentions would be calm and steady. So I-I thank Caleb."

Victoria shook her head. "You are a poor liar, Marah, you always have been. Caleb Talbot terrifies you because, yes, he left and it reminds you of your father and his lifetime of abandonment."

Marah turned away slightly, but her reaction didn't stop Victoria, who continued softly.

"But you *aren't* happy that he left the house. And you *aren't* happy that he seems to have taken your dismissal of him to heart this time. You don't *want* him to give up on you."

Marah blinked as she looked out into the starry night. "Perhaps you are right. But since I cannot have a man who will actually fight for me . . . then I'll have to settle for the man who won't make me always fight for him."

Victoria sighed heavily. "And that is Emerson."

"That is Emerson," Marah agreed.

Victoria was quiet for a long time and then she slipped up beside Marah and her arm came around her. "I won't interfere, as much as I would like to do so," she said softly. "But please do me one favor."

"What is that?" Marah asked, turning her face toward her friend with a shaky smile.

"Emerson hasn't offered for you yet. Until he does so, will you promise that you won't close the door entirely to the possibility of love?"

"Oh, Victoria—" Marah began.

Her friend covered her hand gently and her green eyes were bright in the light of the lanterns on the terrace. "I understand that the idea of it is frightening and that you believe it to be impossible. But will you promise me that?"

Marah swallowed. "Until Emerson has offered for me and I've accepted, I suppose I cannot truly rule *anything* out."

Her friend smiled as she released her hand. "Good. Now I must return to the party. I promised Justin I would speak to Lady Hightrail about something to do with his mother and she always leaves these things before they become a crush. Will you return with me?"

Marah shook her head. "No, you go. I want to stay outside for a while. The night air is so lovely."

With a smile, Victoria left her. But as Marah returned her attention to the sparkling night sky, it wasn't the air she was contemplating. Instead, thoughts of the past and the future melded and danced within her head.

And she was more confused than ever.

* * *

When Caleb came out onto the terrace, he wasn't looking for Marah, but the moment he saw her, standing in the distance, gazing up at the stars, every other thought fled. He had made a promise to leave her alone a few nights before, but seeing her made that vow difficult to keep.

Impossible.

"Marah?" he said.

She jumped a little before she turned toward him. "Caleb. Er, Mr. Talbot."

He frowned at her reversion to propriety. "There is no one else on the terrace," he said softly.

"Caleb," she corrected herself with a blush.

"Are you well?" he asked, wrinkling his brow at how pale she looked even behind her current blush. "May I bring you anything?"

"No," she rushed to reassure him. "I'm perfectly content, thank you. I was just enjoying the summer sky. It is rare to see so many stars when one isn't in the countryside. I have missed them while the city lights blocked their glow."

He stepped up beside her and looked up with her. She was correct that the night sky was uncommonly bright. He so rarely took the time to look at it, he was surprised by how pretty it really was.

"Beautiful," he murmured.

"Did you ever learn the constellations?" she asked.

He glanced down at her from the corner of his eye with a sheepish shrug. "I'm certain I did, but I have forgotten them over the years. I'm afraid I would make a terrible sailor and dash my ship within hours."

She laughed, the sound as light and fresh as the breeze. "Well, that there is Cygnus."

"The swan," Caleb murmured as he looked where she indicated. "Though it looks more like a kite cross bar than a bird to me."

"I suppose it does." Marah smiled and pointed to another part of the sky. "And Capricorn."

Caleb tilted his head at the shape she traced in the sky. "Headless bat?"

"It always looked like a heart to me," Marah said softly. Then she shook her head. "Did you come out here to find me?"

"No," Caleb said, lifting his hands. After their last conversation and his decisions since, he didn't want her to think he was disregarding her request, even though he wanted to. "Actually I was looking for—"

He broke off. It wasn't particularly good manners to tell one lady that he was seeking another. But it was too late. Marah's face fell slightly.

"Oh," she said.

"I promised the next dance to Lady Greensboro's daughter," he hastened to explain.

Marah's cheek twitched almost imperceptibly. "Alicia? Well, she *is* very pretty. Very young and so pretty."

Caleb tilted his head. Was that jealousy he heard?

"Lady Greensboro has an eye toward you matching with her, you know," she said with a sniff.

He leaned back a fraction, surprised at this revelation. "She does?"

"Yes. She was quite bold about it while we were dancing near each other earlier."

He shook his head. "Well, she would be less so if she knew the truth, I think."

"About your father?" Marah asked.

He nodded. He had been thinking about his father a great deal, both the one who had raised him and the idea of finding the one who hadn't. Marah's accusation that he was a coward who hid from the truth still stung.

"You could always keep the facts of your parentage from any potential bride if you felt it would damage your chances. She needn't ever know the truth," Marah said. "I would certainly never share your secret if that is your worry."

"I would never think so low of you," he said

softly. "Of course you wouldn't. It isn't in your nature to sabotage any other person, even one who perhaps deserves it."

She shifted slightly and her gaze dropped away. Caleb looked at her. He hadn't thought much about marrying or settling down in the last few years, his mind had been far too occupied with other things. But he couldn't picture sharing a life with a woman who didn't know or couldn't accept his past with as much ease and grace as the woman he stood near did.

"I-I'm going to speak to my mother about it," he finally admitted.

Marah stepped away from the terrace wall with a gasp. "About . . ." She looked around her swiftly and dropped her voice. "About what caused her to stray?"

He nodded but his heart began to beat faster with just the idea of doing such a thing.

"You were right about what you said to me a few nights ago. I can't pretend the truth away. And until I know all the facts about what happened the night I was conceived, I won't be comfortable with who I am. I won't be able to decide who I *should* be."

In the dim lamps, Marah's expression softened. "I think it's a very good idea, Caleb. You are owed some explanation."

"Yes. And perhaps then I can do as you suggested."

"What is that?" she asked, her head tilting.

"Move on," he responded.

She stared at him for a long moment. "Yes. Well, that's for the best, isn't it?"

He didn't answer.

"You should go in," she said, turning her face. "I can see the current dance is almost over. You should find your partner before the next begins."

Caleb nodded. There was so much more he wanted to say, but didn't. Couldn't. So he bowed slightly and left her alone on the terrace. Wishing he still had her as a confidante and a friend.

Chapter 15

Caleb shut the door to his father's chamber as quietly as he could and then leaned forward until his forehead touched the barrier. He let out a long sigh that expressed all the emotion he had been hiding during the previous hour when he sat beside the marquis, who was lost in what seemed to be a permanent sleep since the last attack that had nearly taken his life.

Behind him he felt a gentle touch on his arm and he straightened up to find that his mother was standing beside him, her upturned face reflecting the same emotions in his heart: love and loss.

"Hello, my dearest," she said softly.

He rubbed his tired eyes. "Mother."

When he lowered his hand he found she was staring at him, her unwavering gaze holding his. For a long moment they stood like that, really looking at each other for the first time since he had come home and tried his damnedest to distance himself from her.

"Will you join me for tea?" she asked as she motioned toward a chamber behind her.

Caleb shifted. If he went into her room, he knew the subject he would eventually broach.

"Please," she added.

He found himself nodding as he followed her into the parlor. He took a place on the settee beside the fire in the private sitting area she had set up in what once would have been the dressing room of this chamber. The door behind her was closed, but he assumed it led to the place where she slept.

"Why are you no longer staying in the chamber attached to your husband's?" he asked in as much of an attempt to delay the inevitable as out of curiosity.

She took her own place and poured him tea. As she added cream and sugar from memory according to his taste, she sighed.

"I didn't wish to give up my room, but with your father's illness and increasing decline, that adjoining chamber was sometimes better suited for a doctor or even to store items for his care where they could be easily accessed. So I moved to this room across from his. I didn't want to be more than a step away from him."

Caleb looked around. The room had been meant

for a guest or even a child, not a marchioness. "It is smaller."

"The size matters little," she said with a shrug. "I don't mind it. And now I find I'm happy I no longer stay in my old chambers."

"Really?" Caleb asked with incredulity.

She nodded. "I think it would be worse for me somehow if I was still in the chamber next to his. Those rooms hold such happy memories for me, I don't want to think of them this way. I'm trying not to forget the happier memories as the end approaches."

Tears filled her eyes, but she blinked and they cleared as she handed over his cup.

"Thank you," Caleb said, his voice gruff at her blatant display of heartbreak. It wasn't false, he knew that for certain, and her unwavering devotion to his father only raised more questions about the past.

"Ever since you returned to us, I have wanted to ask you a question," his mother said, almost as if she read his mind. "A few times I almost did, but you push me away before I dare. I feel your anger with me like a pulse beneath your skin."

Caleb frowned. He had tried to be polite when he could, but as with many things it seemed he was a rousing failure. "I am sorry, my lady."

She shook her head. "No, I'm certain you have your reasons."

He looked at her. "And is that your question?" he asked. "What those reasons are for my behavior toward you?"

She shook her head. "No, I would not press for your confidence."

He was surprised by that reply. "Then what do you wish to know?"

"I have wanted to ask you why you ran away from London so suddenly? And why you cut our family off for so long?"

Caleb sighed as he set his cup aside. He could hear Marah's voice in his head as he stared at his mother. *You deserve to know the truth*, she had said to him at the ball, and her permission to pursue the past had actually meant something to him.

Well, now was the time.

"The two questions are related, both the one you ask me now and the one I thought you would," he said softly.

"I see." His mother nodded slowly. "And what is the answer to them both?"

He stared at her. Since the time he had found out that he was a bastard, he had pictured what he would do if he broached the subject with his family. In his mind, he had confronted his mother over and again, in so many ways that his head spun from them. But now that the reality of the confrontation had come, the proper words eluded him.

"Please," she said softly.

"I left because I-I found out about my father," he finally said, ignoring the way his heart leapt to double time and his stomach turned.

She looked at him, her brow wrinkling with confusion. "What about your father?"

He stared at her. "That he is not the marquis who lies in that bed across the hall, madam. I don't know whose blood runs in my veins, but it isn't his."

She bolted to her feet and all the blood drained from her already pale face. Her lips shook, as did the hands she had fisted at her sides. The seconds dragged into minutes as she grappled to remain composed.

"I see," she finally whispered, and her voice trembled. "I-I see. Well, then your anger is understandable."

Caleb shut his eyes. "So, you do not deny it."

She moved forward and quietly closed the door, giving them privacy and sending a subtle message that they were only to be disturbed in an emergency.

She turned back to him and finally answered, "I wouldn't dare insult you by denying it." Her voice caught and she drew a harsh breath. "It is true."

Caleb couldn't speak. Of course he had known this was the truth for a long time. But now there wasn't even the tiniest hope that it wasn't.

She moved back to her seat across from him. "How did you find out?"

He lifted his gaze to her. She wasn't going to like his answer, but honesty was the only thing he could offer and hope for the same in return.

"Justin found out when Victoria's late father apparently uncovered the truth and blackmailed him with it. There were letters between her mother and you?"

His mother's face paled further. "Y-yes. We had once been good friends."

Caleb nodded. "That was why Justin married Victoria despite her father's hatred of our father, not because he wanted to end the 'war' between them as my brother told us all at the time of their sudden union."

His mother's face twisted in agony, just as his had when he realized his brother had made such a sacrifice to protect him. In that, they shared a reaction.

"Oh, dear God, no!" she whispered "Poor Justin, to have had to endure such a thing."

"Yes. He kept it all a secret for many years to shelter us all from the truth and its potential consequences," Caleb mused. "But I don't think Justin would mourn the ultimate results. After all, Victoria knew nothing of her father's deception until much later. She was as much a victim of those circumstances as my brother was. And my brother is clearly very happy in his marriage."

His mother nodded and her face relaxed a fraction at that thought. "More than happy. He loves Victoria with everything in him. She is his perfect match."

Again Caleb's thoughts briefly turned to Marah, but he pushed them away. Only one man in a thousand found what his mother described.

"But if your brother kept this a secret for so long, what drove him to tell you?" his mother pressed.

He shook his head. "His revelation of the secret was unintentional, I assure you. When he obtained the letters back from her father, he attempted to burn them. But I found them and confronted him, forcing him to tell me what he knew."

"I can imagine it was terrible for you," his mother whispered as she covered her eyes. "We never intended for you to find out."

Caleb stared at her at that statement. "We?" he

repeated, filled with confusion and suspicion.

She nodded as her hands dropped away from her tired face. "Yes. Your father and I."

Caleb's mouth dropped open, and for a moment he couldn't find his voice. When he finally did, he said, "Are you telling me that the marquis *knew* he wasn't my father?"

Her eyes narrowed ever so slightly. "First, he *was* your father in every way that mattered. He never considered himself anything but, even though he knew he couldn't have been from the first moment I confessed to him that I was with child."

Caleb shook his head. This flew in the face of everything he'd believed, everything he'd told himself for two years.

"No, no, you lie," he said, his voice low and rough.

Somehow his mother managed to maintain her calm. "I can understand why you must feel that way. You have carried betrayal and anguish with you for two long years without an explanation beyond those letters that were . . . misleading. I can only imagine what stories you told yourself about how I betrayed your father with no remorse and then hid the truth in some dastardly attempt to save myself from his wrath."

Caleb shifted. Her frank assessment of his very

thoughts made him uncomfortable. And even more so since she was on the verge of denying the beliefs he had carried with him for so long.

She shook her head. "But I assure you that when I tell you that my husband knew that you weren't his son even before you were born, it is the truth. And if the marquis were conscious right now—" She broke off on a harsh sobbing breath. "If he were able, he would confirm everything I say."

Caleb got to his feet and paced the length of her sitting room. His mother seemed to be honest, and as angry as he had been, he couldn't believe that she would be able to lie to him in this highly emotional state and not reveal some indication of it in her voice or mannerisms. So could what she said be the truth after all?

He turned on her. "Let us set aside for the moment whether your husband knew or didn't know about my parentage. I still want to know what in God's name happened to bring this thing about. You seem to love the marquis now, and I recall you two being affectionate and caring toward each other during my childhood. So what could have happened to make you stray? To betray your husband in such a devastating and ultimately *permanent* fashion?"

His mother's eyes came shut for a moment and her lip trembled ever so slightly. "It is very simple, my dear. I didn't. I never betrayed him. I never strayed."

Frustration mounted in Caleb's chest. He had asked her these things to have understanding and answers but her every response only created more riddles to solve, more questions to ask.

"I read what was left of the letters, madam. And that is not what you wrote in your own hand to Victoria's mother. So please explain yourself, I tire of talking in circles with you," he snapped, his tone far sharper than he had intended.

She flinched. "I'm not trying to talk in circles. It is a complicated situation and a very painful one. But despite what those letters said, I didn't go out looking for an affair."

Caleb stepped toward her, gentling his tone as best he could. "Then what *did* happen?" She was silent, her chin dipping as she stared at the floor beneath her feet. "Please, I have a right to know."

His mother swallowed, and when she spoke again her voice was strained and filled with undeniable pain. "My own father had his own vices. Gambling was his main one. Despite the sorrow his faults brought our family, I loved him very much. So when I was sent a mysterious message saying that someone knew something that could destroy him, I foolishly went to the meeting place of their choice thinking I might be able to assist him in some way."

Caleb cocked his head. His maternal grandfather had died a few months before he was born. He had never known the man and his mother had rarely spoken of him.

"And?" he encouraged.

She shivered. "When I arrived a . . . a man was there. He offered me some evidence that my father had involved himself in some very underhanded dealings indeed, and told me that if I did not give him what he wanted, he would reveal the truth to the world at large, thus ruining my father's reputation."

"What did he want?" Caleb asked, though he suspected he knew the answer.

She caught her breath before continuing, "Me. He wanted me. He had been pursuing me for some time, despite my marriage, and I had refused him at every turn." Her eyes hardened, a strength entering them that awed Caleb. "That night I refused him as well. I was aghast at the idea of betraying my husband. I told him to ruin my father if he had to, but that he couldn't have me. It threw him into a rage and he caught me before I could get out the door and then—"

She broke off, her cheeks darkening to red. Her posture was ramrod tall and strong, her chin lifted with pride despite the humiliation of her story.

"He—he forced you," he said softly.

She nodded slowly but didn't speak.

"But the letters," he whispered.

"Yes, the letters," she murmured as she turned away. "I *did* write to Victoria's mother and confessed that I feared you were not my husband's child. She assumed I had entered into an affair and . . . I couldn't bring myself to write down the truth. It was so ugly and so painful. So I allowed her to believe the worst of me. I thought she would destroy our correspondence, I never thought it would fall into the hands of her husband, a man who despised your father."

Caleb stared at his mother. Her pale face held no signs of deception, only pain and muted memories that were too horrible for him to imagine. And if he couldn't bring himself to picture them, he could well believe she wouldn't want to write down the truth. That she might mislead a friend rather than relive such a nightmare.

"So this person . . . this *man* raped you," he repeated, the horror of that statement sinking in.

That meant he was a product of something so vile, something so horrifying he could scarcely comprehend it.

Here he had been judging his mother for doing

something horrible to his father, something appalling to him. And in truth he himself had done the greatest wrong to her of all. Just by being born.

Caleb's stomach revolted against the misery of what had been revealed by turning and churning, threatening to cast up what little he had fed it that day. He swallowed hard past the bile that collected in his throat.

"My God, Mother," he whispered when he could find his voice.

She stood up and slowly moved toward him. "Please don't look like that. It was a long time ago, Caleb," she said softly. "I made my peace with it."

"How?" he asked on a gasping breath. "How in God's name could you when you had to look at me every day?"

"You think I could regret you?" his mother asked with a shake of her head to accompany the question. "I couldn't. You were the only good thing to come of that horrible night."

Caleb clenched his fists at his sides. "How could you say that? How could you *not* regret me after what you endured?"

She grabbed for his hand and held it tightly in her own. He looked down into her face and saw all her love reflected there in undeniable, unwavering terms. It shamed him, for he had withheld his own from her for so long out of a misguided anger over a "betrayal" that had never occurred. He hated himself for doing that and so much more.

"You are my son, my sweet boy. From the moment you were put into my arms by my husband, by your *father*, I loved you with all my heart and my soul. I looked at you and saw hope and joy and mischievous wonder. You were a gift to help me heal. To bring your father and me back together after a long period of separation and pain when he found out I was attacked."

Caleb shut his eyes as his thoughts turned to the man who had raised him. "The marquis. My God. How could he . . . why didn't he . . ."

She nodded, understanding the questions he couldn't manage to voice in his utter horror.

"When I returned home after the . . . *incident*, he could tell something had been done to me. When he heard the story, he wanted to kill Lor— the person who had done that to me." She swallowed, as if the words she was saying caught in her throat. "But he couldn't. The secrets that vile man had tried to blackmail me with to make me his were still in his possession, waiting to be revealed. Your father could see how much I had suffered and I think he didn't want to make me suffer more, especially since it might not have even mattered against such a powerful man as the one who attacked me."

"He was powerful?" Caleb asked, grasping on to this first bit of knowledge about the man who had truly fathered him, although that idea now made him sick, not satisfied.

She nodded. "Very. And blackmail was the way that . . . *thing* operated."

"So the marquis was forced to stay silent. And when you realized you were with child, forced to be father to the son of a monster," Caleb said softly.

She shook her head. "No, not forced. There were other options, Caleb. I proposed that I hide away during my pregnancy so that no one would know I was breeding. I even offered to give you away to another family to raise so that the marquis wouldn't have to see you, to face you. But he refused that idea immediately. He said that the law would see any child born of our marriage as the product of our marriage and he would also see you that way. I doubted he could, but he was . . . *is* a remarkable man."

"Yes," Caleb whispered.

She smiled. "When you were born, the doctor put you in his arms first and he looked at you with such joy, such love. No less than what I saw when he touched Justin or with Tessa. When I asked him about it later, he told me that enough ugliness had come from that terrible night and that he wouldn't allow even one more moment of it to touch our family, to touch *you*. We never spoke of it again. Even in moments of frustration with me or with you, he never said a word about it. To him, you were his son. And that was the final word on it."

Caleb kept his gaze on his mother, but he didn't see her. Instead he thought of his father, he thought of being raised by the man in the bed across the hall who had treated him with nothing less than the just and loving hand that he gave his other children.

"Remarkable," he murmured. "And there was . . . there was no chance I could have been his son in truth?"

His mother's face grew sad. "No. In the months before you were conceived, your father had been ill. We hadn't shared a bed during that time. But you *were* his son. And after you were born, we found a way to love each other again. To bond together as a family that was even stronger than before. Your sister was born after, and we even tried for another child after her, but weren't successful."

"He was utterly selfless," Caleb whispered. "He loved me even though I represented his deepest pain. *Your* deepest pain. I don't know if I could manage to be so good, to be half the man he was . . . *is*."

She smiled. "Oh, my dearest boy, you could be anything you wish to be. You have more of the marquis in you than perhaps you know."

She was smiling at him with such openness and love, even though he had just forced her to relive one of the worst moments of her life.

"Mama," he whispered as he took both her hands and held tight. "For two years I have judged you . . . I've allowed my anger to consume me when it was *I* who owed you an apology."

"For what?" she asked as she reached up to touch his cheek. "None of this is your fault and it never could be. I only hope that finally airing this matter will provide you with some peace."

He nodded. "Yes, I think I can find peace, if only I can persuade you to answer one more question."

She hesitated. "I'll try."

"Who was he?" Caleb asked. "Who was this person who was so powerful he could silence you and stop my father from taking revenge on him? Perhaps *I* can obtain some measure of justice if I know his identity."

His mother shook her head. "He is dead now. It won't matter."

Caleb swallowed. Dead. He hadn't thought of

that possibility even in all the years he'd known the truth. Just as he had imagined confronting his mother, he had pictured facing the man who had fathered him. And once he heard her tale, he had allowed himself brief fantasies of destroying the bastard who had created him. But now . . . now all his chances for both answers and revenge were gone.

"I'd still like to know," he said softly. "It is the only missing piece left for me."

She hesitated. "He was . . . he was the last Duke of Billingham."

Caleb blinked in disbelief as he remembered the old man whose name she said. "But he was—"

"Yes, he had an exalted reputation he certainly did not deserve," his mother said with bitterness to her tone. "But I think his heir does. Simon Crathorne seems like a good man in truth, not just rumor. I hope you won't think to take out your anger at his father on him."

In truth, Caleb hadn't thought that far down the road, but now he did. He thought of those who shared the Billingham blood. Simon, the new duke, had always been a good enough fellow when Caleb encountered him. He was closer in age to Justin than to him and he thought the two had been friendly in school. And there was also a daughter, Naomi, who had married and become Lady

Westford. These people were his family, as much as Tessa or Justin.

And then there was one more issue. . .

"Last year I remember hearing about some odd confrontation at a ball where some crazy person accused Billingham of fathering a bastard . . . the Duke of Waverly, wasn't it?"

His mother sniffed. "Yes, I was in attendance at the event. I wouldn't doubt that what that madman said was true, though the two dukes handled the situation with great aplomb and the rumors died off almost instantly thanks to their frank and direct denials."

Caleb winced. He had met the Duke of Waverly at a country gathering shortly before that scandalous party. He had always hated the other man for being a pompous, judgmental sod, but Waverly had tried to apologize. He had seemed . . . *different*, even though Caleb dismissed him at the time.

Now he wondered if Waverly was yet another brother to him.

"They may be my family," he whispered, almost more to himself than to her.

His mother jerked out a nod. "I suppose they would be," she admitted. "Does it help you to know that?"

He thought of it for a moment. "It does in some

way. I've often wondered where I belonged since hearing this secret."

"You belong with us," his mother said softly. She hesitated, and her voice was strained as she continued, "But, Caleb, if you desire to form some kind of relationship with them, I want you to know that you have my blessing."

He stared at her. "Truthfully? You would not be unhappy if I made some contact with them?"

She sighed. "No. I always feared the idea that you would discover the truth, but perhaps we were wrong in keeping it from you. Perhaps you had a right to pursue the past if it would help you."

He moved toward her and for the first time in two years he hugged her without hesitation, without thoughts of her betrayal troubling his mind.

"Thank you for your candor," he said softly. "I realize how difficult it must have been for you."

His mother smiled as she backed away. "No, my darling. What was difficult was losing you for so long."

He returned her smile. "Well, I'm back now."

"Yes, you are." She laughed. "Perhaps for the first time since your arrival, you're back with me."

Caleb smiled as she poured him more tea. But even as they settled into far less painful conversation, he found himself thinking of Marah. She had been a sometimes silent companion with him on this journey to discover who he was. And now that he knew, he found he wanted to tell her.

He found that she was the only one he felt he should tell. And he wondered if she would allow him that if he tried.

Chapter 16

Marah felt Caleb's eyes on her as they sat at Justin and Victoria's table having supper. It was odd. Emerson was sitting on the opposite side of her, but she didn't feel the same draw to look at him as she did with Caleb. She didn't feel his eyes on her when he looked her way.

She should, shouldn't she? Wasn't that important?

"Marah, are you quite all right?" Emerson asked.

She blinked as she returned her attention to him. "Of course, very well."

"I only ask because you haven't touched your dinner."

She glanced down at her plate and found he was correct. She had been so wrapped up in her thoughts that while everyone else at the table was half finished with their meal, she had yet to pick up her fork.

"Goodness, my mind must have wandered," she said with a blush as she picked up her fork and made every effort to concentrate on eating and stop thinking about Caleb at the other end of the table.

As the meal came to its end, and everyone rose to make their way into the drawing room for after-supper brandy and friendly conversation, it seemed her every effort was thwarted.

As soon as they stood and Emerson offered her his arm, Justin cleared his throat and said, "Mr. Winstead, I have been hearing so much about your business. I wondered if you and I might have a moment in private to discuss it further."

Marah darted her gaze to their host. He was smiling at Emerson but she saw that his eyes moved to the end of the table and his brother. But when she looked at Caleb, he seemed all innocence, casually fiddling with the sleeve of his finely tailored jacket.

Emerson lowered his arm and didn't even look at her as he said, "Of course. I would greatly love to speak with you about what I do and perhaps even tempt you with some investment opportunities."

Justin's responding smile was thin. "Indeed. Victoria, would you entertain our other guests?"

Her friend smiled as if on cue. "Of course, Justin. We shall see you both in the drawing room when you've completed your business."

As the two men left the room, Marah glared from Victoria to Caleb and back again. There was something quite rehearsed about this entire exchange. Like it had been preplanned. She opened her mouth to confront them, but before she could, a servant entered the room and gave a quick bow.

"Er, Lady Baybary, Crenshaw is having a bit of difficulty with a household matter. Do you think you might come and offer your advice?"

The maid sent a quick glance at Marah that confirmed all her suspicions. As Marah scowled, Victoria nodded. She didn't even pretend to be surprised by this odd intrusion.

"Of course." She turned to Caleb and Marah. "Perhaps you two could make your way to the drawing room. I shall be along shortly."

Then she exited the room without waiting for either of them to respond, and Marah found herself alone with Caleb. She turned on him with her arms folded.

"I congratulate you on that wonderful performance you just inspired in our friends, and even their servants. Have you ever thought of directing on the stage, Caleb?" she said with an arched brow.

He shrugged. "If we had been alone with Justin and Victoria, I wouldn't have gone to so much effort, but would have simply asked you to walk with me or grant me a brief audience alone. But with Winifred here—"

"For God's sake, Caleb, *Winstead*! His name is Winstead, it has always been Winstead and your continual mispronunciation is both childish and ridiculous," she snapped, though she had to admit that this newest "mistake" of her future fiancé's name was quite amusing.

"Of course," Caleb said with an apologetic bow. "But whatever name I call him by, it is clear to me as it must be to you that he doesn't like me. I didn't want to ask you for a moment alone in front of him and create more of a scene later that I know would make you uncomfortable."

"So instead you created a foolish diversion that only proves you still have little respect for my wishes or thoughts," Marah said with a sigh.

"I have a great deal of respect for everything you said to me last week, actually," Caleb protested softly but firmly. "But what I wanted to talk to you about tonight has nothing to do with you and me. I arranged for us to be alone for a brief time because something has happened that I cannot address with my brother or anyone else in the world."

Marah's brow wrinkled and an unwanted feeling of concern and empathy for the man before her rose up in her chest.

"Something has happened?" she repeated softly. He nodded, and in that moment she saw an unguarded pain and confusion in his normally cocky stare. "You see, I took your advice, Marah. I spoke to my mother, so I now know the full truth about my father. And I realized that there was no one else I could share that fact with but you. So have I broken our friendship so irretrievably that you will not hear me? If I have, then I apologize and I'll call Victoria back immediately."

Marah pursed her lips at him. She should have remained angry at his manipulation of the circumstances, especially since poor Emerson was likely wildly pitching an investment opportunity to Justin, who had no real intention of making any kind of partnership with him.

But instead something else filled her. A sense of curiosity about what exactly had happened that could send Caleb to these lengths. What could he want to tell her that he couldn't share even with Justin?

"Very well." She sighed. "I'll go to the parlor with you and hear what you have to say. But nothing more, Caleb. It will go no further."

"I understand," he said, his relief clear on his face as he motioned to the door. "Thank you for doing this."

She nodded as they walked without touching to the parlor. And she hoped that she wasn't being duped by Caleb. She feared she was still too weak to deny him even if manipulation was his motive.

Marah stared as Caleb finished telling her about his encounter with his mother the previous afternoon. He was leaning on the mantel in a typically nonchalant pose, but from his stricken face and empty eyes she could see how much the words he spoke hurt and sickened him. And how could she blame him?

"So that is all I know. And you see now why I wouldn't want to tell Justin this," he said. "He had to carry the consequences of this secret for too many years as it was. It would do him no good, nor any to my mother, to reveal to him that she was attacked in such a manner."

She nodded. "Yes, Justin seems to hold none of the ill will toward her that you did. Victoria told me that once their own marriage was a happy one, Justin softened his stance toward your mother. He forgave her in his heart and determined that whatever the marchioness' reasons were for straying, they were her own. If you told him what you now know, I think it would only hurt him. Anger him. And with Billingham dead, what good would that do?"

Caleb nodded. "I'm relieved you see my position. It strengthens my resolve on the matter. But the last twenty-four hours I have held this secret inside of myself and I suppose I am too weak to keep it. I had to tell *someone*, and you are the only one who knows everything about my past, Marah."

She smiled despite herself but it quickly fell as she thought of his story once more.

"Billingham, who would have ever thought?" she whispered with a shiver. "He is spoken of so highly, even so many years after his death."

He nodded. "Yes, the man was very well respected and hid his true self with the skill of the finest actor ever to stride the boards. It sickens me to think that I am the spawn of such a creature."

She moved toward him. "But it may not be so bad. You once told me you wanted to know this 'other' family, and even your mother thinks that your half brother and sister are decent people. You knew them before, you interacted with them."

"Yes, the new duke, Simon, was always a more than decent fellow, despite his unfortunate choice in best friends . . . although Waverly may be his brother, so perhaps there was little choice after all." His voice grew distant with an awful thought. "Unless all of Billingham's decency is as pretended as his father's. *Our* father's."

"You could find out," she suggested softly.

His gaze darted to her. "What?"

"If Billingham and this Waverly person were confronted about their father's penchant for fathering children out of marriage last year and they defused it so easily, it could mean that the accusation came as no surprise." She looked at him evenly. "You *could* approach them, Caleb."

He blinked and she could see both how bewitching and how terrifying a concept her suggestion was.

"Approach them," he repeated softly.

"I like to think I know you, at least a little," she said quietly, moving even closer as she reached for his hand.

"You know me as well as anyone could," he agreed, watching as her fingers tangled with his gently.

"You ran away not from one family, but two," she continued. "And now that you are facing some of your past, I think you should face all of it. If the Billinghams refuse to acknowledge you or behave as though you are wrong . . . well, then at least you'll know."

"And if they don't?" he said, lifting her hand to bring it against his chest.

She swallowed, her tongue suddenly thick and her throat dry. "Th-then you will have the opportunity to belong to two families." She frowned, reminded of her own lack of relations and support. "I can imagine that would be a great comfort."

He gave a noncommittal grunt. She could see his torn emotions in his bright blue eyes. Uncertainty. Worry.

She smiled in a way she hoped was reassuring. "But you don't have to decide today, Caleb."

"No?" he whispered, still holding her hand.

She shook her head. "No. I can only imagine your mind is spinning from all you've heard. Give yourself some time before you decide anything."

"Sound advice," he murmured, but his tone was strained, and not just by his upset.

In that moment, Marah fully realized their position. Her hand was tangled with his, their bodies close together. Once again she had somehow become tangled in his web. And unfortunately, she liked being there, despite her protests to the contrary and her attempts to distance herself from him and her own desires.

Yet every time she was put in a situation to test her resolve, she failed miserably. Why, at that very moment what she wanted to do more than anything was to lift up on her tiptoes and press her lips to his. She wanted to feel his arms come around her as he molded their bodies to one.

Her breath came short as the little rational part of her that remained told her to back away. Let go. Stop torturing herself with things she couldn't, shouldn't, *wouldn't* ever have.

"Caleb," she whispered, tugging at her fingers.

His eyes came shut and she thought he murmured a low curse before he released her hand and backed away.

"Thank you for listening," he said as he turned away from her. "I needed to talk about this and you offered me your attention although I don't deserve it."

Marah tilted her head. "Caleb—"

But before she could finish, the door to the drawing room swung open. Both of them turned to see Justin standing in the doorway. His face was pale, drawn and streaked with pain.

"Oh no," Caleb groaned as he moved forward.

At first Marah didn't understanding his reaction. But then it dawned on her. The marquis . . . their father. . .

"Caleb," Justin choked. He stopped to scrub a hand over his face. "Caleb . . ."

He strode forward toward his brother and the two men embraced. Marah lifted a trembling hand to her mouth, unable to stop the tears that fell at the unguarded moment of emotion and love that flowed between the men.

"Is he . . ." Caleb asked as they parted. "Is he gone?"

Justin drew in a breath that seemed to echo in the room as he nodded in an odd, jerky fashion. "I-I just received word."

Victoria was there then, appearing from the hallway to draw her husband into her arms. They stood together, her sobs muffled into his shoulder and the tears a man like Justin Talbot never shed flowing freely and silently.

Marah moved forward, ready to offer the same comfort to Caleb, but before she could, Emerson stepped into view in the hallway behind Victoria and Justin. Her heart sank. In truth, she had all but forgotten he was here for this very private family moment. His presence felt like an intrusion, although she recognized that hers was no better. After all, she was only a family friend. She meant nothing more to anyone than that.

"I am terribly sorry for your loss," Emerson said, looking first at the earl and his wife, then to Caleb, and finally to Marah with a gentle smile that made her ashamed of her ire at his presence. Here he was trying to console her and her thoughts toward him were unkind.

Victoria lifted her head from Justin's embrace

and nodded toward Emerson with possibly the first real smile she had ever gifted him.

"We do thank you, Mr. Winstead. I'm so sorry that this has cut our engagement with you short."

"Think nothing of it. I shall take my leave of you with my sincere sympathy."

"Allow me to show you out," Marah said, finding her voice and her manners in the same moment.

She couldn't help but look at Caleb as she slipped past the small group. He watched her, silent, his eyes hollow and pain-filled.

In the foyer, as the servants hurried around getting Emerson's jacket and called for his carriage, they stood together.

"I'm so sorry about tonight," Marah said softly.

She supposed she was apologizing for more than the tragic end to the evening. Emerson might not know it, but she was apologizing for forgetting him and resenting his disruption of a private moment that was not his fault.

He shrugged. "I suppose you shall be very busy in the next few days."

She nodded. "I would think so," she said quietly. "Victoria and Justin have been nothing but kind and generous to me. I will need to be there for them."

And for Caleb, she silently added. Caleb, who would probably need her more than ever. And despite her declarations to the contrary, she couldn't imagine simply abandoning him to his grief without *some* attempt to offer her friendship.

She would just have to be certain that friendship was as far as it went.

"May I call on you tomorrow afternoon, still?" Emerson asked, hesitant.

"Tomorrow?" Marah asked, bringing her thoughts back with some effort, to the man before her. "I-I don't know—"

"Please," he insisted. "It is events like this that sometimes make us see clearly. I would like to call on you. After all, you will be running around offering everyone comfort. Perhaps I can give you a little of the same. Will you see me?"

Marah nodded because she could think of no reason to refuse. "I will try to be here to receive you at two for tea, will that be satisfactory?"

He nodded briefly as he took his hat from a footman who scuttled away immediately, leaving them alone.

"Marah," Emerson said softly, moving a little closer. "I realize how this news grieves you."

Marah began to answer, but before she could, Emerson cupped her cheek with one hand and leaned in. His mouth touched hers with gentleness and finesse, and Marah shut her eyes as she fully recognized that after a year of friendship, after months of awkward courtship, Emerson was finally making his move.

She tried to lose herself in the kiss. To let it comfort her, as he suggested. But instead of feeling desire or relief she felt . . . nothing.

The kiss was perfectly pleasant, with just the right pressure and gentleness. But she wasn't stirred by it in any way.

After a brief moment, Emerson stepped back. "I'll see you tomorrow."

She nodded and then he was gone, hurrying to his carriage with a lighter step. He waved and then the vehicle pulled away, leaving Marah in the foyer to stare into the night and contemplate what had just happened. She might have stood there forever, but Victoria bustled into the front hall.

"We're going to the marchioness and Tessa," she explained.

Marah turned to her friend, and Emerson and the confusion he had caused by his unexpected and lacking kiss vanished. She held open her arms wordlessly and Victoria stepped into them. Her friend caught her breath, trembling as Marah hugged her.

"Of course you are," Marah said softly as she

stroked Victoria's shiny dark hair. "And I'm going with you."

Victoria drew back with a look of surprise and utter relief. "You will?"

"Of course. Perhaps I can help in some small way. At the very least, I want to be there for you."

Victoria tilted her head. "For only me?"

Caleb and Justin came into the hallway toward them. Before they got too far, the butler, Crenshaw, stopped them. He said something to Justin, and the earl smiled sadly and squeezed the butler's arm gently. Caleb reached out to shake his hand.

"Of course I'll be there for the whole family," Marah said, distracted as the two men continued their journey up the hall.

"Yes," Victoria said as they all hurried as a group to the carriage that was waiting. "I'm sure *everyone* will appreciate it."

Justin helped his wife up and then Marah. The two men climbed in afterward and the carriage raced forward. And though Marah was beside her friend and Justin was the one across from her, she couldn't keep her eyes off Caleb, who was staring out into the dark night.

He was heartbroken. And she knew that there was no comfort she could offer that would ever change that fact.

Chapter 17

Marah walked through the eerily quiet hall-ways of the London home of the Marquis of Stratfield and his wife. Only now that marquis was Justin, not the generous man she had met just a short time before. She shook her head at the thought, for she knew it wasn't a title Justin had wanted to be elevated to so soon.

Behind a few doors she heard the soft crying and whispers of servants. The sound both broke her heart and made her smile, albeit sadly. The late marquis had clearly been a very good man to in-spire such loyalty and love among those who had worked in his home for so many years.

Otherwise, though, there was little sound. The very walls of the house itself seemed to be in mourning.

The marchioness had been given something by her late husband's doctor to help her sleep and had been almost forced away from his room, where his body still lay. The most senior servants would soon come in and lovingly prepare him for his burial.

Tessa had gone with her mother to her chamber. She said it was only for a while, but Marah had a sneaking suspicion that the young woman wouldn't leave her mother tonight. And it would be good for them both.

As for Justin and Victoria, she wasn't certain where they were. Justin had been sequestered with the doctor for almost an hour after their arrival. Even when the physician had departed, Justin had busied himself with estate paperwork before Victoria took his hand and led him away. They hadn't been seen since and Marah could only hope that her tired friend had been able to convince her heartbroken husband to join her in the bed that had been prepared for them.

No one was going home tonight. Marah had a chamber ready for her as well, and had been told to ring for a servant whenever she was ready to be undressed. She wasn't sure if she would take that kind offer. It seemed on this night, of all nights, she could tend to herself.

Besides, there was still one person whom she hadn't yet accounted for. One person she shouldn't seek and yet was compelled to do so.

Caleb.

He had sat with his father's body for a long time, the door closed as he privately said his good-byes. When he came out, she'd seen his crumpled face, and the pain in it had been palpable. She'd left him alone for a little while, determined to speak to him after he'd had a bit more time to digest what was happening, but he had crept away at some point when she was out of the room.

He wasn't downstairs. She knew because she had searched every room. She moved up to the second floor with its family and guest chambers. Creeping past the shut door where the marchioness and her daughter slept, Marah listened at some of the other doors. At one chamber, there was no mistaking the low, soothing tones of Victoria's voice answered by the soft and gravelly grief of Justin's. She moved swiftly on, not wanting to intrude on their privacy.

A few doors down, she opened another chamber and found what she sought. The dressing room was dark, but beyond it she saw a fire lit in the grate. Moving into the room, Marah shut the door behind her.

Caleb stood by the window in the bedroom, his back to her as he gazed out the window into the dark night outside. Since entering the room, he had removed his jacket, which was tossed on the floor alongside his boots. His shoulders slumped, his posture telling a story of grief she doubted he would ever fully express.

She could have backed away. She knew she probably should have. But everyone else in the family had someone to turn to in this moment of heartbreak and loss except for this man. And she cared enough about him to know that he needed support and attention as much as anyone else. Perhaps more, since his relationship with the marquis had been the most complicated.

"Caleb?" she whispered.

He jumped with surprise at her voice, but didn't turn to face her.

"My earliest memory of my father is standing at this window," he said, his voice soft.

Marah moved forward and stood beside him. "Oh?"

"I must have been unwell, because I recall standing here in my nightshirt watching him down in the yard with Justin. I think they were playing around with the cricket mallet."

Marah smiled. "The marquis did that often?"

"Yes." Caleb's voice was rough. "He did. He truly seemed to enjoy his children."

Marah nodded as an encouragement for him to continue with his story.

"He must have sensed I was watching because he

turned around and looked up at my window. And he waved to me and smiled."

Tears stung Marah's eyes but she blinked them back. This was Caleb's pain, and she had no right to cry and force him to be the one to console her.

"He loved me," Caleb whispered. "Even though he knew I wasn't his. Even though I was the result of the worst experience of my mother's life, of his life. I am not even half the man he was."

Marah touched his arm and gently drew him to face her. "Don't say that."

He looked down at her, utterly beautiful in his sorrow. His bright blue eyes were filled with true emotion and the cocky shield he normally raised around him was long gone. What she saw before her was his real and true heart. And it melted her own even when she knew she shouldn't allow it.

"I must say it, Marah, it is true," Caleb said with a shake of his head. "What have I done? What have I *ever* done that is meaningful? That is good?"

She had never seen him broken, not truly broken like this. She lifted her fingers to cover his lips.

"You saved me," she whispered. "When you found me tied all those years ago, you saved me."

"No, you are scarred," he protested as he took her fingers and gently pressed them away from his lips, though he didn't release them. "And by me, as well as by the men who tied you so cruelly. I *know* I hurt you back then. I was selfish and wrong and I—"

Marah lifted up and pressed her mouth to his. She did it because she didn't want him to berate himself anymore. She didn't want him to twist the afternoon they had shared and somehow make it ugly. It wasn't. When she was honest with herself, it was one of the few times in her life she had ever felt alive and wanted and loved and cherished.

The aftermath was something else, but that day was glorious and so she kissed him so that his words and denials and self-abuse wouldn't tarnish her memories. Or his.

But the moment his arms came around her and his mouth parted over hers, she forgot that. All she knew was that his kiss was home to her. It was food when she was starving and liquid in the desert. She clung to him and opened her mouth to him, driving to meet his tongue with hers.

He pushed her toward the bed and they fell across it. Caleb's mind was clouded with grief and anger, but when he touched a woman . . . no, it wasn't *a* woman. It was *this* woman. When he touched this woman, everything bad, all the heartache that was lodged in his chest like a hard cruel fist, dissolved.

All that was left was her.

He arched against her, feeling his cock rub on her body as their fingers tangled, and he lifted her hands above her head. She offered no resistance, rather she mewled in pleasure and encouragement as he plundered her mouth and used her body to make his pain go away.

And the more he lit on fire, the more he forgot his pain. And also what he should and shouldn't do.

His fingers found the sloping neckline of her gown and he pulled until more and more of her breast was revealed. He buried his mouth there, tasting the delicate flesh as he fumbled with the buttons around the back of her gown. Finally the silk gaped and he was able to tug it down, revealing her breasts.

Marah's head hung back over her shoulders, her back arched as he held her breasts together and sucked one hard nipple and then the other. Just as he remembered from that stolen afternoon years ago, she responded to his touch with heat and fire, arching into him as her fingernails dug against his shirt and scraped the skin of his arms beneath.

His hands were moving of their own accord now. He shoved at her skirt as he continued to suckle and pleasure her breasts. Her legs parted as he got the wrinkled fabric to her hips and he stepped into the space she had created. Now when he arched into her, he felt the heat of her body through his trousers and it burned at him like silken fire.

Fire that raged out of control when Marah sat up to press her eager mouth against his, hard and hot. Her hands found his waistband and she slipped the four buttons there free. The fabric fell away and his hard, heavy cock sprang to attention against his belly.

She looked down at him for a long moment and he wasn't sure what she would do. He readied himself for her to push away, to run away as she realized just how far they had gone. Instead she licked her lips reflexively and then she reached down and gently traced the curving slope of his erection with one fingernail.

He made a garbled groan that made her smile before she cupped him with a soft fist and stroked him from base to head in a smooth motion that nearly made him lose his mind.

He hadn't had a woman's hands on him, touching him so intimately, since the last time he had made love to Marah. He couldn't find interest in anyone else. Not after her.

He'd tried a hundred ways to explain it, but now, with her stroking him dangerously close to completion, he realized it was because Marah was the only one who could make him want anymore. This uncommon woman had stolen his desire and now she held it captive.

He pushed her backward, sliding her along his bed as he covered her with his body. His cock nudged at her sheath, wet and ready for him. It took every ounce of control to keep from driving forward and filling her.

Control she did not share. With a whimper, Marah lifted her hips, and suddenly the tip of his erection was enveloped in wet heat. It was too much. Control shattered and he slid the rest of the way home until he was fully seated within her weeping, hot body.

Marah lifted her hips, crying out as they were joined once more.

Restraint had never been a friend to Caleb. He had struggled his whole life to control his desires and actions, to withdraw even when his heart told him to drive forward. But now . . . well, in the heat of emotion, his ability to back away was crushed. He forgot right, wrong, should, and any promise he had ever made to respect Marah's wishes. Now that he was buried inside her, all he wanted to do, all he *could* do, was claim her.

He withdrew, reveling in the slick slide of her arousal, the clinging heat of her sheath. She dug her fingers into his shoulders with a whimper as he came dangerously close to exiting her body. Then he glided back home again, her sex squeezing around him exquisitely.

Forward, back, rolling his hips, he drowned in pleasure, both in his own and in that he saw on Marah's face. She met his every stroke with an eager one of her own. Her hips ground against his, her sheath held his body with wild pressure and abandon. Thrust after thrust he saw her moving closer to the edge and then, with a cry that seemed to touch him to his very core, her face contracted and her inner walls pulsed with release.

The feel of her coming, the sight of her ultimate release drove him over the edge. His thrusts became erratic, his hands tightening on her hips as he slammed into her and raced toward his own edge. Just before he reached it, he withdrew from her trembling, clenching body and spent himself with a grunt.

Exhausted by the night's events, by the pleasure she had given him, Caleb fell across the bed beside her.

The room was quiet as they lay on the bed facing each other in the warm glow of the firelight. Marah didn't try to fill the space with chatter or questions and for that he was glad. Pleasure had numbed his other emotions for a moment, but now that it faded, the pain returned. And so did his long-repressed sense of responsibility.

He stared at Marah. Her dress was half around her waist both at the top where her breasts were bared and the bottom where it only half covered the smooth curve of her hips and backside. Her hair was tangled, her mouth swollen. Anyone who looked at her would know what she had done.

What *he* had done.

He reached out to smooth a lock of hair away from her face. Even after seeing the pain his moment of weakness two years ago had caused, even after promising Marah that he wouldn't go so far again . . . here he was. With no promises, with no thought to the consequences beyond preventing a child, Caleb had thrown caution to the wind and once again used this woman to drown his pain.

The marquis wouldn't be proud of his actions. That was the one thing Caleb knew.

"Caleb?" Marah finally whispered, her soft voice cutting through the silence.

He smiled to reassure her. But as she slipped off into exhausted slumber, Caleb's smile fell. Tonight he had crossed a line. Now he had to decide what to do about it.

*　*　*

Marah slipped downstairs, praying she would find Caleb waiting for her at the breakfast table. She had woken in the middle of the night to find him gone. He hadn't returned.

She opened the doors to the breakfast room but found only Victoria, Justin, and Tessa inside. She smiled softly at them, hiding her reaction. They all had enough to deal with, she wasn't about to pout about her own evening.

She didn't regret what had happened. She had come to Caleb's room telling herself it was only to check on his well-being but deep down she knew the truth. For weeks the tension between them had been rising. She could push it away all she wanted, but all her denials were lies.

She had wanted Caleb last night. And she had felt them make a connection as they made love. She had allowed herself to hope . . . only now he was gone. Again.

Sitting, she said, "How are all of you this morning?"

Tessa's smile was sad. "As well as can be expected, I suppose. Mama refused to come down, but I was about to take her some food in the hopes she will try to eat it."

"Give her my love," Marah said softly.

Tessa's face softened as she reached out to cover Marah's hand with her own. "I will. I'm sure it will mean a great deal to her. She likes you very much."

Marah blushed as Tessa pulled away. She liked the marchioness, too. Dowager marchioness, she supposed she was now. For her best friend now had a new title.

She looked at Victoria as Tessa moved from the table to gather a plate for her mother. Her best friend looked tired, but there was still a glow to her.

"Is there anything I can do?"

Justin was the one who shook his head. Although he had tossed his napkin across his plate, Marah could see he had only pushed his food around. He hadn't eaten.

"No," he said softly. "There are some things to be taken care of here and people will begin to call today."

Marah nodded. "Perhaps I'll return to your home and refresh myself while you handle those things. I could return later."

Victoria smiled. "Yes, I think that might be best. There is no reason for you to stay."

Marah tensed at the reminder. No, with Caleb gone, she supposed there wasn't. She wasn't part of his family, no matter how kindly she had been accepted by them.

Justin nodded, distracted as he picked at a loose thread on the tablecloth. "Tessa will be with Mother most of the day. God knows where Caleb is. His note wasn't clear."

Marah lifted her gaze to him slowly. "H-he left a note?"

"For me, yes." Justin sighed. "He said he needed a walk. I hope that isn't some kind of twisted euphemism for a whiskey or a woman."

Victoria's hand came to cover her husband's arm gently. "Justin."

His gaze darted to Marah. She hoped she was covering her reaction to his statement. Her stomach turned as she tried to keep smiling benignly.

"I'm sorry, Marah. I am distracted, I shouldn't have said such a thing. Not in front of you."

Marah pushed to her feet, uncertain if he meant because she was an unmarried woman or because it wasn't nice to rub Caleb's apparent penchant for indiscretion under trying circumstances in her face.

"It matters little, Justin, I assure you." She touched his hand briefly, then hugged Victoria. "I shall return home. Please send word if you need anything at all."

She nodded. "Yes. And I may return myself, later."

Marah slipped from the room and signaled to a

servant to have the carriage brought around. But as she waited, she had to work to keep her shoulders straight and her expression blank.

Caleb had left her bed for a "walk" and never said a word. When he left a note it was for his brother, not her. And that made his intentions more than clear. Once again she had fooled herself into thinking that sex meant emotion.

But she wouldn't repeat that mistake. Not again.

Chapter 18

Marah nodded to her maid as Betsy finished the last touch on her hair. With a curtsy, the girl left the room. Marah sighed as she settled back in her chair and looked at her reflection in the mirror. After a hot bath and fresh gown, she felt better.

Well, that was a lie. She didn't feel better, but she felt like she could pretend again. She would have to.

The door behind her opened and she turned. "Did you forget something, Betsy?"

Her maid bobbed out a quick curtsy. "No, miss. Crenshaw was coming up to announce a visitor and I told him I'd pass the message along to you."

Marah got up, smoothing her gown. "A visitor. Does the person not know that there has been a death in the family?"

"It isn't a visit for the house, miss, the gentleman is here for you," Betsy said with a little knowing smile. "I believe it is Mr. Winstead."

Marah swallowed hard. She had forgotten that Emerson had promised to call on her this afternoon. Her mind flew, once more, to images of last night. Caleb's mouth on hers, his hands on her, their bodies moving together.

"Miss?"

Marah blinked, clearing her mind with difficulty. "Will you inform Mr. Winstead that I shall be down directly?"

Her maid nodded as she backed from the room. Once she was gone, Marah turned toward the mirror to find her face was bright red and her hands shook. This would not do.

Wetting a rag in the basin by her bed, she cooled her face with the water. Finally, when the color had faded, she drew in a long breath. There was no reason for her to be embarrassed or ashamed. She had no understanding yet with Emerson and while her actions were certainly imprudent, she didn't regret them.

Even now when the consequences were bitter indeed.

Straightening her shoulders, she left her chamber and made her way downstairs to the front parlor where she was certain Crenshaw had left her caller. As she entered the room, a forced smile on her face, Emerson got to his feet.

"Marah," he said as she crossed to him and took his extended hands. "After last night, I must inquire as to how you are."

She froze and then calmed herself. Emerson was asking about the marquis' death, not confronting her about her actions. She had to remain calm.

"It was a trying night," she admitted as she freed her hands from his and motioned him back to the settee. She took her place in a chair near his and smoothed her skirts. "But more for the family than for me. I only wish I could be of more assistance, but there is no real way to ease their grief."

Emerson nodded. "I'm certain you were more than helpful."

She smiled. Oh, how little he knew.

"I'm only sorry that the tragedy cut our night short," she said, trying to steer the subject away from the comfort she had offered. "I hope you weren't too put out."

"Of course not," Emerson said, smiling up at the servant who brought them tea. Once she was gone, he sighed. "Actually it is sometimes these kinds of moments that solidify our thoughts."

"What do you mean?"

Marah tilted her head as she picked up the teapot and poured them each a cup. Emerson took nothing in his, so she offered it to him as it was. He took it, but set it aside. She shrugged and prepared her own with cream and sugar.

"The marquis' death," Emerson explained. "It is only a reminder of how fleeting life is. And how short a time we have to share it with those in our lives."

Marah nodded, though she was confused by Emerson's rather passionate words about a man he had never met.

"When I thought of those things after I left you last night, it gave me a perspective I perhaps hadn't had before," Emerson finished.

"Perspective?" Marah said as she took a sip of her tea.

He took a deep breath. "Marah, we have known each other for almost a year. I moved slowly in my courtship of you because I believe the best marriages are partnerships, rather than passionate unions. But I cannot wait any longer. I would ask you to be my bride."

Marah choked on her tea and nearly sent her mouthful of it shooting across the room in a most unladylike fashion. As she coughed, Emerson reached into his pocket and withdrew a handkerchief, which he offered to her.

When she could finally breathe again, Marah stared at Emerson. For so long she had been telling herself that his proposal was what she desired, and yet when he offered it, she had been taken completely off guard.

"I can see you are not convinced," he said, his mouth becoming a thin line of displeasure. "Perhaps my position in life is not as unimportant to you as it once was?"

"Oh no, it isn't that," Marah said, rushing to soothe what were clearly hurt feelings and ruffled feathers. "In no way is my hesitation a reflection on you! I must admit that I did not expect you to say this to me today."

His face softened a bit. "I realize the timing is inopportune with your dear friends entering mourning. We won't be able to celebrate our engagement with the joy I had hoped, nor with the parties I'd planned, but I still believe this is the best time to ask you this question."

She still hesitated. Less than twelve hours ago, she had been in another man's bed and she had let herself hope, foolishly, for a future with him that was built on the very opposite virtues from those Emerson represented.

"Marah, I think you know what I can offer you as a husband," he said softly. "I am not titled, but I'm moving up in the world. As my wife you would never have to worry about money or pretty baubles."

"Those things don't matter to me," she said with a shake of her head. "I was raised simply."

"But I do think that the stability that promise implies *does* matter to you," Emerson pressed. "I am not a rake, Marah. I would be a faithful husband, one you could depend upon through good times and bad. That is what I can offer you. If you will say yes to me."

Marah shut her eyes. This man had just laid out every reason she had for wanting him, he had reminded her of how he was different from Caleb. And since Caleb had just proven, once more, that he wasn't dependable. . .

Well, she would be a fool not to take the offer before her.

"Yes, Emerson," she said, opening her eyes to look at him. "I would be honored to be your bride."

He clapped his hands together and the pleasure on his face was very real. She smiled in return, though she was stricken by the oddness of this moment. She had just agreed to marry this man, yet she felt no thrill in her stomach about that fact, nor any desire to launch herself across the table and into his arms.

"Great God, this is good news," Emerson said with a laugh. "And now we make our plans. A special license might be best. Given recent events, reading the banns might be unseemly. But we could have a quiet, private ceremony in a fortnight or so and then in a few months hold a large celebration of the union and invite everyone important."

Marah blinked. "You would wish to marry so soon?" she whispered.

He nodded. "I see no reason to wait. Do you?"

She swallowed. "No, Emerson."

But the moment she had said it, the reason she had been pretending away walked into the parlor with Victoria on his arm. Caleb.

Marah couldn't help but catch her breath as she pushed to her feet and sent a furtive glance toward Emerson. Guilt overwhelmed her, but it wasn't guilt that a man she had made love to had just come face to face with her fiancé.

No, she felt guilty that Caleb had found her with Emerson.

Caleb came to a stop in the parlor, his expression blank as it moved to her. "Good afternoon," he said softly, not directing the comment to anyone in particular, though his attention didn't waver from her.

"Hello," she squeaked in answer.

Emerson didn't seem to sense the tension between them, for he came forward. "My dear Lady Baybary . . . or should I call you Lady Stratfield now?"

Victoria paled even further. "I think Lady Bay-bary for now."

"Of course. Once again may I say how sorry I am for your family's loss."

She nodded, but Marah could see how much of a struggle it was for Victoria to mask her dislike for the man. She tilted her head. She hadn't realized how little her best friend thought of him. Even with her discouragement of their match, she had never seemed to have an aversion to him.

"I hope that the news I'm about to tell you might soften that pain," Emerson said.

Both Victoria and Caleb looked at him. Marah stepped forward, parting her lips in the hopes she would find something, *anything* to say that would stop Emerson from revealing their arrangement.

But there was nothing that would have worked. With a smile, Emerson said, "I have just asked Marah to marry me, and she has agreed."

Caleb kept his gaze on Emerson Winstead for probably a full minute as he tried to comprehend the explosive words he had just heard. Slowly he let his gaze move to Marah. She stood a few feet away, her chin dipped and her hands clenched before her.

She didn't appear to be pleased by her beau . . . no, her *fiancé's* declaration. In fact, she looked nothing at all like the woman who had opened her body and her heart to him just a few hours before.

Victoria began to talk. Caleb was sure she was congratulating the couple, but she was just a mumbling voice in the periphery of his mind. All he could see, all he could focus on was Marah.

He had taken her to his bed and known it was wrong. Not because he didn't want her, but because she was owed more than a night of passion. The walk he had gone on in the middle of the night, the one that had lasted for hours, had helped him conclude that.

In those miles he had covered, he had recognized that he *had* to offer for her hand, to do the honorable thing. But first he planned to court her as she had always wished he would. The way she deserved.

Only now . . . now she was marrying another man instead. His numbness at that fact faded and was replaced with anger. Anger so powerful that it was more like rage. He looked at Emerson Winstead, still chatting amiably with Victoria, and Caleb wanted to tear his head from his shoulders.

"Caleb," Victoria said softly, her fingers clenching on his arm. "Is there anything you would like to say?"

He gently released his sister-in-law and stepped toward Emerson. Though the man's face remained utterly unmoved and amiable, his eyes reflected triumph. Once again, Caleb suppressed the urge to attack.

"With Miss Marah staying here, my brother is, I suppose, her guardian in some ways," Caleb said, his voice ringing hollow in his ears. "Since he isn't available, *I* would like to speak to you privately."

Both the women gasped at the same time, but Winstead didn't react in the slightest. "Of course, Mr. Talbot. I'm happy to discuss anything on your mind. Lead the way."

Marah moved forward and now her gaze was fully focused on Caleb in the way she had been trying to avoid before. "Cal— Mr. Talbot, there is really no need—"

He took a step toward her and it stopped Marah in her tracks. "Oh yes," he said, speaking low so as to control his tone. "There most definitely is. Excuse me, ladies."

He turned on his heel and marched from the room, steering them toward Justin's study. Once there he wasn't certain of his plan, but he wasn't about to simply offer his congratulations to this smug prick. Not before he had some say in the matter.

Chapter 19

"**H**e's going to kill him," Marah moaned as she paced the room, wringing her hands together before her. Whenever she pictured the time Caleb and Emerson were spending together, it ended in fisticuffs.

Victoria sank into the settee with a tired sigh. "Which one?"

Marah stopped and sent a glare toward her friend. "Caleb is going to kill Emerson, of course."

"And why would he do that?" Victoria said softly. "You have told me time and time again that Caleb cares nothing for you. And that you cannot allow yourself to care for him. And apparently you meant it, for you have accepted the marriage proposal of another man."

Marah winced at her friend's frank summation of her past statements. Hearing them come back to her was rather stinging. She came to the settee and sat beside her friend. "I accepted Emerson's marriage proposal because he is the only one making one."

Victoria's eyebrow lifted slowly and Marah shook her head. "Th-that didn't come out the way I meant it."

"And how *did* you mean it?"

Marah swallowed. "Of course there are other reasons for my accepting Emerson's offer. It wasn't only because no one else has wished to marry me in the past."

"Oh yes, I had forgotten Mr. Winstead's very romantic stability and dependability." Victoria rolled her eyes. "Marah, be honest with yourself. Is that the kind of union you really wish for? Empty, passionless, cold? Caleb—"

Marah shut her eyes. "Caleb and I made love last night."

Victoria stopped speaking, her eyes going wide as she simply stared at her friend. "*Last night?*"

Marah nodded, her cheeks burning with humiliation at that admission and the one she had yet to make. "Afterward, I-I thought perhaps we had a chance to make things right between us. I thought I felt a connection just as I thought we had made one two years ago. But I was wrong, yet again. As soon as I fell asleep, he left my side, he left the *house* with no explanation or even apology."

Victoria clenched her fists, and her outrage on Marah's behalf was plain. "Oh, Caleb! That ass!"

"No," Marah said, covering her friend's hand with her own. "Blaming him isn't fair."

"Oh yes, it is." Victoria snorted. "And I shall tell him so myself."

"No, please don't defend my honor to him. I came to him at the depths of his grief. I knew what could happen." Marah sighed as she recalled how nervous and anxious she had been coming to his chamber. "I suppose I *wanted* it to happen."

Victoria's anger softened. "Oh, Marah."

She nodded. "It was a foolish desire considering our past. But I believe you are right, even though he refuses closeness beyond a certain point, Caleb *does* have a deeper feeling for me than Emerson probably ever will. But obviously that isn't something we can build a future on. Caleb may confess his sins to me, he may take his comfort in me, but he doesn't see me in his future. I am and always have been a temporary consolation to him."

Victoria squeezed her fingers gently. Marah recoiled from the pity she saw in her friend's eyes.

"Don't look at me that way, I have accepted it." That was a lie, but Marah hoped if she kept saying it that it wouldn't be one day. "*And* I have accepted Emerson. That is the end of the story."

Victoria pursed her lips. "I wish it wasn't," she said softly. "But if this is your decision, I respect it. And I will do everything in my power to ensure you receive the happiness you so richly deserve."

Marah covered her friend's hand with her own. "Thank you. Now, you look tired. Will you tell me how Justin, Lady Stratfield, and Tessa are faring?"

Victoria nodded slowly and Marah forced herself to forget about Caleb, forget about Emerson, and be the support her friend needed. As she had said, her decision was made. There was no going back now and she refused to have any more regrets than she had been lamenting already.

Caleb handed over a glass of whiskey to his unwanted companion and then took a place behind his brother's big desk in his study. He rather liked staring over the expanse of oak at this man who would steal Marah away. It made him feel like he had power.

Unfortunately, in this case, that might not be true.

"You don't approve of my match with Marah," Emerson said as he took a sip of his drink and smiled.

"I suppose I don't," Caleb acknowledged.

He set his own drink aside. He needed a clear

head for this situation. And he hadn't actually gotten drunk since Marah's last chastisement of him for his lack of control over a week ago.

"And yet I sense there isn't any way on this earth that I could change your mind about your opinion of me and my impending nuptials to Marah." Winstead smiled. "So I question why you would bring me here under the pretense of verifying the correctness of my proposal to her."

Caleb fisted his fingers on the desktop before him. This man's calm only served to enrage him further, but he fought to control it. An explosion was what Winstead wanted so that he could use Caleb's behavior to underscore his own steadiness to Marah.

"You *are* direct, sir," Caleb said through clenched teeth. "I will return the favor. You see, I believe you asked Marah to marry you with ulterior motives in mind. Things you perhaps haven't expressed to her fully during your 'courtship.'"

"Such as?" Winstead took another sip of his whiskey and set the tumbler aside.

"Your unending ambition for one," Caleb said softly. "I believe you are as interested in Marah for her late father's name, her potential family connections if you manipulate those ties into being resumed, and her powerful friends like my brother and his wife. A marriage to her, especially since she is gaining attention during her return to Society, would elevate you substantially."

"Of course it would," Emerson admitted, his tone as cool as a winter wind. "How foolish I would be if I didn't consider those things when looking for a potential mate. When I met Marah, I had some concept that she would elevate me, but her newfound interest from Society is a definite windfall."

Caleb was flabbergasted that Winstead would admit such things freely and with no touch of remorse. "How dare you?"

"It isn't as if Marah isn't aware of my ambition," Winstead said with a shrug. "I *do* like her a great deal, and I haven't kept any of my intentions a secret from her in all the time we have been acquainted."

"So you believe that the openness of your aspirations makes it appropriate to marry her for these purposes, without thought to her happiness or her comfort outside of the monetary realm?" Caleb asked, still in utter disbelief.

Winstead folded his arms. "You see, my friend, this is where we differ. I don't see Marah's happiness as being compromised by a union based upon practical considerations. In fact, I believe these sensible ideals can only make her more satisfied as time goes by. You, on the other hand, are driven by excessive passions."

"And you don't believe Marah shares in those passions?" Caleb said with a snort of derision as he thought of her ardent display in his bed the previous night. She had been as swept away by desire and need as he had been.

"I do, actually," Winstead said with a concerned frown. "That may be her only imperfection. Still, I believe that once Marah is my bride and those passions are no longer fed by bad influences and silly, romantic fantasies, they will fade."

Caleb stared. "You are saying you will crush an integral part of her spirit?"

"Not crush it," Emerson said with a shake of his head. "But without encouragement it will wither on its own."

"How could you not wish for her to have passion?" Caleb asked with real shock. "How could any man not look at her and desire her?"

"I *do* desire her," Winstead said with a confused tilt of his head. "To a reasonable degree. I'm certain we will be compatible in all ways, including the physical. But a wife has too many important duties to be seen as an object of pure lust. I want her to give me heirs, of course, but I wouldn't want her to keep me in bed all day and all night."

Caleb shut his eyes at that thought. If Marah was

his, that was *exactly* what he would want her to do.

"You are a mercenary," he growled.

Winstead shook his head and for a brief moment Caleb saw anger flash in his eyes.

"No, sir, I am not. I am merely honest. But just because I have indulged you in your little interrogation doesn't mean that I appreciate it. I wonder what right you truly think you have to question my intentions when your own have been so base and unkind?"

Caleb straightened up. "What the hell are you talking about?"

Winstead arched a brow. "I hate to speak so candidly, but this is my future wife we are discussing. It is plain to me that the two of you have shared far more than a mere friendship in the past. In fact, I strongly suspect that you may have taken advantage of her 'excessive passions,' perhaps more than once. If this is true, that means you were utterly ungentlemanly in your conduct."

Caleb had no retort. Winstead was correct that in the past he had let Marah down in the worst way possible. And he had done it again last night. He had meant to make it right, but she hadn't waited.

And why should she? He had given her no reason to have faith in him.

Winstead smiled. "I will take your silence and your sick expression as a yes to my charge. So I ask you, sir, when you have made no attempt at decent courtship, what right do you have to question my own? Marah apparently enters our marriage already soiled, yet I still accept her. I would never throw her past mistakes back in her face, in fact I will never even mention them to her. I think that balances out any other unsavory thoughts you may have of me. Now, if you will excuse me, I have other appointments today and I believe our conversation is finished."

Caleb got to his feet. "You—"

"What?" Winstead snapped as he clenched his fists at his sides in perhaps the first truly emotional display of their acquaintance. "Nothing you can say will change the fact that I have *won*. This is over. Good day."

With that the other man exited the room and left Caleb steaming. He stared at the open door.

"Oh no," he murmured. "Until she is your bride, *nothing* is over."

Having said farewell to Winstead and with Victoria gone upstairs to rest for a while before she returned to her mother-in-law's home, Marah was desperately trying to find something to do to fill her thoughts. So much had happened in the last twenty-four hours that her head spun from it all.

She looked down at the book in her hand, but couldn't concentrate on the story. She had read the same page at least ten times.

"I need to speak to you!"

Marah looked up as Caleb stormed into the parlor.

"I'm sorry, I'm busy," she said, making the attempt to sound calm when just the sight of him made her heart roar to double time. "I'm rather engrossed in this story."

"I heard an engrossing tale a short while ago, as well," Caleb said, clearly in no mood to be deterred. "About a man who asked a woman to marry him with every intention of using her connections to raise himself up in Society."

Marah threw the book aside. "I assume this tale stars a man named Emerson and a woman named Marah?"

"Indeed it does," Caleb said. "Marah, he is using you! You cannot marry him."

She threw up her hands in frustration. "As if you have any say! Did Emerson actually tell you he intends to use me?"

To her surprise, Caleb folded his arms and smiled. "Why yes, he did."

That stopped Marah in her tracks. Of course she knew of Emerson's desire for social advancement, but the idea that he had confessed something so crass to Caleb, of all people . . . well, it stung a bit.

She swallowed. "Well, it isn't a great secret. Many marriages are built on similar practical desires. I'll obtain a stable future and he will have a wife who offers him the chance to elevate himself."

"And *that* is all you want?" Caleb asked, his disbelief plain on his face.

Marah hesitated. She couldn't lie. *Want* wasn't the word she would use to describe the marriage she had just described and agreed to. But unlike Caleb, she couldn't build her life on *want* at the exclusion of all else. She had personally felt the consequences of such actions her entire life.

"It is all I can wish for," she finally said.

He didn't speak. It surprised Marah, for Caleb was never at a loss for words. Finally, after what seemed like an eternity, he shook his head.

"You call me a coward," he said softly. "And perhaps I am. But so are you, Marah. So are you. Good day, my lady."

He gave her a swift bow and then left the room. She heard him in the foyer calling for his horse and then he was gone. For the first time, she actually felt like he *was* gone.

She had spent weeks telling herself, telling him that this was what she wanted. But now that she had it, now that she had everything she swore she desired, she felt empty. So she sank down into her chair, covered her eyes, and had a good cry.

Chapter 20

When Caleb entered Justin and Victoria's home with his mother on his arm, it felt like it had been a year since he had visited there, not mere days. He hadn't wished to return at all, not after his last encounter with Marah, but there was little choice. His brother and sister-in-law were hosting a small gathering after his father's burial. He was expected to attend.

His mother gently squeezed his arm and smiled up at him, though there was little joy in her pale face, made even starker by the heavy black she wore to honor her husband.

"I would like to speak to Reverend James," she said softly. "His words at the grave were so moving."

Caleb nodded as he released her. "Of course. Would you like me to go with you?"

Tessa stepped up. "I'll go with her," she said as

she took her mother's arm. "Perhaps you could see about getting her a chair?"

Caleb looked around. Even though Justin had only invited close friends of the family, there was little room in the parlor. The doors had been thrown open between the connecting chambers so that people could pass in and out at their leisure, but the uncomfortable crush remained. He supposed it was a testament to the marquis' character that virtually everyone who had been asked to attend had made the trek from wherever they were to do so. Some people had even come from the Continent to pay their last respects.

"Of course," he said as they moved off to find the reverend.

Within a few moments he and Crenshaw had managed to obtain a very comfortable place for his mother. During that time, though, Caleb had been overrun with mourners who told him stories about his father or expressed their condolences with watery eyes. It was all too much.

Across the room, he motioned to Tessa and she acknowledged his indication of the place he had found for his mother. His one duty fulfilled, Caleb turned toward the terrace. He needed some air.

He stepped outside and looked around with a sigh. The afternoon was waning, so the air was beginning to cool slightly. Compared to the hot parlor, it was heavenly, and his headache, which had begun at the gravesite, faded a bit.

Behind him the terrace doors opened and voices echoed as a few more people stepped outside. Unwilling to converse with them and hear their condolences repeated ad nauseam, Caleb slipped down and around the corner out of sight from the party. Only to find Marah sitting alone at a small round table.

He came to a halt as her eyes came up and met his. She sucked in a breath of surprise as great as his own. Slowly she got to her feet.

"H-hello."

He nodded in acknowledgment. He'd seen her at the burial, of course, but he had stood with his family while she kept toward the back of the crowd who had come to pay their respects. This was the first time they had been near each other since he had called her a coward.

A sentiment he now regretted. He had said it in anger and disappointment, but it was far from gentlemanly. Even if he believed it was true.

He was trying to decide if he should broach that subject when Marah said, "How is your mother?"

He sighed. Perhaps it was better to simply let it

rest. "She is . . . as well as can be expected. Have you spoken to her?"

"Not yet," Marah admitted, fidgeting nervously. "I will, though."

"She would like that," Caleb said, and it was the truth. His mother clearly liked Marah and enjoyed the time they spent together.

"I-I was watching you today," Marah admitted.

Caleb cocked his head. "Yes. Does Winstead approve?"

Her gaze came sharply to him. "Winstead isn't here. He wasn't a friend of your father's, and this gathering is for friends of the family alone. Even if he was, I am not owned by him."

Caleb turned away. She soon would be, if Winstead had his way. "Well, in your keen observation, what conclusions did you arrive at?"

She moved a little closer. "You're troubled."

He faced her with an arched brow. "It *was* the funeral of the man who raised me."

Her expression tensed at his peevish attitude, but then she whispered, "I've heard that the Billingham family has returned to London. I assume you've heard that as well."

Caleb tensed. He had, just the previous day.

"Yes," he admitted. "Apparently they have been

summering with the Duke of Waverly and his bride. She is breeding and I have been told they returned to London as a party for the last few months of her confinement."

"What will you do?" Marah asked.

He looked at her. He had been so shocked by the idea that his half brother . . . perhaps *two* of his brothers were now just a breath away, he hadn't actually considered what to do about it.

"Nothing, I suppose."

She made a soft sound of distress and moved on him. "No, Caleb."

He wrinkled his brow at her reaction. "You disagree?"

She nodded. "Very much so. I've seen you struggle with what you know for so long. I know, even if you refuse to admit it, that you are curious about these people, this family. Until you confront your past, you'll never find any peace or comfort in the future. I believe you should go to them."

He swallowed. "Face them."

She was silent as he paced away to look out over the grassy garden of the estate below. She had said her piece and now she didn't push him, didn't encourage one way or another.

"You've seen the way I am with my family," he

said softly. When he turned, she was looking at him evenly. "Before I left, my parents disapproved of the reprobate life I led. My father and I had several confrontations about it and he was forever scolding me about my choices. Since my return I have hurt my mother and angered my sister, not to mention frustrated poor Justin to distraction."

Marah smiled, and the expression lightened his heart considerably. "And?"

He sighed. "I suppose when it comes down to it, I worry about this other family. What if I am trouble to them, not something they welcome? What if the new Duke of Billingham doesn't even know what or who his father was and this shatters his view and his life?"

Marah hesitated. "I suppose those things could be true. You might enter their family and be a thorn in their side. You *are* one of the most infuriating men I've ever met."

Caleb chuckled and it felt so good to laugh. He realized it was the first time since his father's death that he had done so.

"*But* despite all those things you said, the family you were raised in still loves you." She smiled again. "It was clear your father harbored no ill will, Justin adores you and worries about you constantly, your mother understands, and Tessa forgives, even if it is despite herself. Why do you assume any new family would be different? Yes, you might quarrel with them, in fact I'm sure you will, but you will also have the opportunity to have a second family. I don't think you should turn that down."

Caleb frowned. She was offering him a rather pleasant future on a silver platter. Making him believe, in some small part of him, that he could formulate a relationship with his half brothers.

"How do you suppose I could approach them?" he asked.

She smiled. "The person who told me they had arrived also said that the group takes a daily walk in Hyde Park. You should go and 'stumble' upon them."

Caleb shook his head. "I cannot—"

She moved closer again. "I would go with you. If you are escorting the best friend of your brother's wife to shop for some wedding clothes, your presence there will be understandable."

Caleb kept his face very still. Wedding clothes. Great God, the very idea made his stomach turn.

"And would you really force me to help you pick out wedding clothes for your sham of a marriage with Winstead?"

Her face went very still and he saw both the anger and the sadness in her eyes. He wasn't completely certain if they were directed entirely at him. There was some self-reflection to her countenance as well.

"I am only presenting you with an excuse for being with me," she said softly. "I am offering to be your friend since I know you cannot turn to Justin with this matter."

Caleb bent his head. She hadn't deserved his earlier barb. When he looked at her again, he offered a sheepish smile. "If I have ever earned your friendship, I appreciate it now. If you are certain you don't mind coming with me, I would welcome your presence."

She nodded briefly. "Shall we say at two o'clock tomorrow?"

"Yes. But I have a question," he said, moving toward her another half step.

"What is that?"

"Why do you not take your own advice?" he asked. "You, too, have a second family. One you have been estranged from through no fault of your own. Don't *you* wish to make some kind of connection with them?"

Marah shut her eyes. He saw the struggle on her face and the pain. She might pretend that her lack of bond with her father's family mattered little to her, but he could see what a lie that was. And her pain cut him as deeply as his own.

"With me it is different," she murmured as she shook her head. "Complicated."

"Is my situation not complicated?" Caleb asked softly.

She hesitated and he could see she had no retort for that.

"Marah . . ." he began.

"They don't want me," she murmured as she stared down at her feet.

He stepped toward her, longing to comfort her in this moment of exposed emotion. Her gaze came up to meet his and she shifted, looking around as if she had just recognized the inappropriateness of being alone with him in a darkened corner of a terrace. He felt it, too, and was well aware of how easy it would be to kiss her.

Marah blushed and stepped away. "I-I should return and make certain Victoria and your family don't need anything. Good night, Caleb."

He nodded as she slipped away, but he was perfectly aware that tonight wouldn't be good. He was certain he would dream of his meeting with the Billinghams. And of Marah. Always of Marah.

*   *   *

She shouldn't have agreed to do this. It was utterly wrong. Marah knew it was wrong because when Emerson had sent her a message that morning asking her to join him for a ride, she hadn't told him the truth about what she was doing. The lie and the fact she felt she had to tell it were evidence enough of her guilt.

If she needed further proof, there was her fluttering heart as she and Caleb took a leisurely stroll around the park. Her hand was tucked in his arm and she could smell the warm, masculine scent of his skin. She wanted to lean into that, lean into him. It took all her self-control not to do so.

They crested a small hill and Marah looked around. Caleb had been quiet during their walk and on the ride over in his carriage. Now she felt the tension coursing through him.

"There," he said softly.

She followed his gaze. There on a blanket about a hundred yards away was Simon Crathorne, Duke of Billingham, and Rhys Carlisle, Duke of Waverly. Their wives were also with them and the small party seemed to be sharing a late luncheon.

"Perhaps this is a mistake," Caleb murmured as he came to a sudden stop.

Marah squeezed his arm gently. "It may be, indeed. But why don't we make it just to be sure?"

He smiled down at her and for a moment she forgot everything else in the world but him. Yes, all this might be a mistake, but she refused to regret making it.

Slowly they approached the group. Billingham saw them first and from the way he slowly straightened up and stared at Caleb, it was clear he recognized him. But why? Because he already knew the truth? Or was his sudden awareness only because he had heard of the marquis' sudden passing?

"Good afternoon," Caleb said as they reached the blanket.

The gentlemen on the blanket rose, as did Lady Billingham. Lady Waverly stayed where she was, laying a hand on the slope of her pregnant belly as she looked up at Caleb and Marah with a warm, if curious, smile.

"Talbot," Billingham said.

Was his voice gruff with hidden emotion, or did he just need to clear his throat? Marah racked her brain with every little motion, every turn of his head. She could only imagine Caleb was doing the same.

"Billingham," Caleb said in return. "Waverly."

There was a long, awkward silence as the three

men stared at one another. Finally it was Lady Billingham who broke the tension. "Hello, you must be Caleb Talbot."

Her outstretched hand seemed to break the odd spell over the three men.

"I'm sorry, my love," Billingham said with a smile for his wife. "I have taken leave of my manners. Mr. Caleb Talbot, may I present the Duchess of Billingham, and there on the blanket is the Duchess of Waverly."

"Forgive *my* lack of manners in not standing," the pretty lady on the blanket said with a laugh as she covered her swollen belly with one delicate hand. "I'm afraid I carry quite a load with me."

Marah smiled. It was difficult not to when Lady Waverly was so open and fresh, her laughter filled with sweetness and welcome.

"And this is Miss Marah Farnsworth," Caleb stammered.

Marah smiled. He hadn't introduced her as Lady Marah. The ladies and gentlemen said their hellos to her and if any of them had heard the stories of her relationship to the house of Breckinridge, no one was impolite or direct enough to address the subject.

"Why don't you two join our party?" Lady Waverly said. "We have more than enough food. And you were friendly with our husbands as children, were you not, Mr. Talbot?"

Caleb shot her a side glance and Marah could see he was asking her permission to stay. She nodded. "We would love to join you if it's no trouble."

They sat down on the blanket. The gentlemen were ill at ease with each other, talking of crops and weather and politics. Marah smiled to encourage Caleb. This was a mere first meeting. If it went well, she had no doubt there would be others. There was no hurry for him to ask about their family connection.

"I have heard you were recently engaged, Miss Farnsworth," Lady Waverly said as she handed over a plate of delicious-looking finger sandwiches.

Marah nodded as her attention was brought back to the women. "I am, Your Grace."

Lady Billingham smiled. "You and Mr. Talbot look well together. It is a fine match."

Marah paled. "I, er, you misunderstand, Your Grace. It is not Mr. Talbot to whom I'm engaged."

Lady Billingham drew back and she and Lady Waverly exchanged a look that was both incredulous and knowing. Marah shifted. It was like they were having a little conversation with their eyes and she was the subject.

"I apologize," Lady Billingham finally said with

a smile. "I assumed without asking. I should know better."

Lady Waverly also smiled as she took a sip of her tea. "Now, why don't you tell us all about yourself? The instant I met you, I was certain that we are destined to be close friends."

Marah cast a quick side glance at Caleb, but he seemed to be lost in conversation with his brothers. She didn't dare interrupt and perhaps break a bond being built slowly but surely.

So she smiled at the ladies and was welcomed into their conversation. She found she liked them both immensely. Lady Billingham, with her blond hair and bright eyes, was sharp and witty. Lady Waverly, the darker of the two women, was immediately friendly, putting Marah at ease with just a glance. She could feel the strength of their friendship, but was never excluded by it.

She was shocked when over an hour had passed and the men began to pack up the picnic basket carefully.

Billingham exchanged a quick look at Waverly and then he smiled at Marah and Caleb as they got up from the blanket. "We would very much enjoy it if the two of you would join us for supper tonight."

Marah's lips parted. She had accompanied Caleb

in order to put him at ease, but spending an entire day with him, a night with him . . . that idea did not seem wise. Especially when she considered what had transpired the last time they were alone in a carriage together.

But he looked at her from the corner of his eye, and his bright blue gaze pleaded with her. "I cannot speak for Miss Marah, but I would greatly enjoy that. Marah?"

"Please do say yes," Lady Waverly said as she clasped Marah's hand gently. "With my confinement advancing, I see so few people. Rhys is overly protective."

She winked, and her husband, the Duke of Waverly, laughed. In that moment Marah was struck by how his smile was like Caleb's. There was no doubt, this *was* Caleb's family.

"Y-yes," she found herself stammering, still in shock. "I would greatly enjoy that."

Caleb stepped up beside her and she felt the gentle warmth of his hand at the small of her back. The return of the support she had just offered, despite her hesitation.

"We will see you at my London home at seven," Billingham said with a smile.

Then the other group headed off toward their

carriage, leaving Marah and Caleb alone.

"We didn't speak of our relationship," he said as he took her arm and led her back down the hill toward his vehicle.

She smiled. "I saw it in Waverly's face."

"What?" Caleb asked with a half glance at her.

"You," she whispered as she stopped and reached up to briefly touch his cheek. "Your smile. Your laugh. It was there. I have no doubt you will soon resolve this matter and I think in a way that will be very happy for all of you. They will welcome you into their fold."

He looked at her as she dropped her hand away. "You seemed as comfortable as can be with their wives."

She smiled. "How could one not be? They are the best that the word *lady* implies."

"As are you," Caleb said, leaning closer.

Marah caught her breath. She so wanted the kiss she could see in the promise of his gaze, but she drew away.

"Come, I shall have much explaining to do if I am to join you tonight."

She moved toward the carriage. It took a moment for Caleb to do the same, but he helped her up without a word and joined her. She sighed as they pulled away from the park. She had vowed to separate herself from this man, but yet continued to involve herself in his life and his happiness.

The question was, could she stop that now that she was to wed another? And did she truly wish to?

Chapter 21

Caleb couldn't keep his eyes off of Marah as they stood in the parlor of the Duke of Billingham's London home, sharing a spectacular bottle of port with his two brothers and their wives after a delightful supper.

His attention to her was foolish, considering where he was and with whom. He forced his focus back to the men. He was really beginning to like them both. Even Waverly, whom he had despised as a boy because of his arrogance, had been softened by his marriage to a lady no one could disapprove of. Lady Anne Waverly was as kind as she was beautiful, as was Lady Lillian Billingham.

He belonged here. He felt it in his bones. And yet instead of pondering that, he found himself looking again at Marah. Her blond hair had been done up in a complicated and pretty fashion and she wore a fine deep blue gown that brought out the brightness of her eyes and the porcelain paleness of her skin.

Even in a room with two duchesses, she was the most regal and stunning woman.

"I was sorry to hear of the passing of the marquis," Billingham said softly.

Caleb couldn't help but look at the black band he wore on his arm to express his grief. In the midst of all this attempting to find out who he was and where he belonged, he couldn't help but continually wonder if his father would have been hurt by his actions.

He swallowed. "He was the best of men."

Waverly nodded somberly. "He was indeed. I had a great deal of respect for him."

Caleb shifted, and the tension in the room seemed to mount. Even the ladies had stopped speaking and were now staring at the men in waiting.

"I actually heard something recently about my father that made me love and respect him all the more," Caleb began.

Billingham eased closer, as if anticipating what was about to come. "Did you?"

"Yes." Caleb's voice caught, but he forced himself to continue. "Although he knew that I was not his son, he accepted me and loved me regardless."

Waverly's expression softened with relief, but also something more intense. "You know."

Caleb nodded again. "Yes. I know."

Billingham moved toward him slowly, his face unreadable. Caleb tensed as he reached him. Would this man reject or accept him? Deny or welcome him? His head throbbed as he awaited the answer.

"Then let me introduce you to your brother, Rhys," he said softly as his hand came out to cover Caleb's shoulder. "Welcome to our family, Caleb. As odd and secret and patchwork as it is, you are a long-awaited addition to it."

"How long have you known about me?" Caleb choked when he was able to find his voice again.

"Last summer," Rhys admitted. When Caleb's eyes grew wide, Rhys rushed to continue, "But not the night I saw you in the countryside and made my terrible attempt at apology for my abhorrent behavior. I didn't know you were my brother until later."

Caleb was speechless and numb at the reaction of the two men who stood before him, smiling and welcoming him as if this strange thing was normal. But evidently it was to them. After all, at some point they had discovered the unlikely truth that they were brothers to each other, too.

"How many others are there?" Caleb asked.

Billingham shrugged, his expression tightening with pain that had been dulled by time. "We don't know. Our father was a philanderer, a seducer, even a rapist. He loved knowing he had by-blows aplenty, all while being celebrated by everyone around him for his *piety*."

Billingham emphasized the last word with disgust as Caleb nodded slowly. He was happy he wouldn't have to crush this man with the truth about his father's . . . their father's predilection for force when a woman wouldn't yield what he desired of her own free will.

"I'm certain you have many questions," Rhys said. "If we can answer them, we would be happy to do so."

Caleb stared at the two men, overwhelmed by the acceptance he found here. He looked across the room. Lady Billingham and Lady Waverly stood with Marah between them. All three women had tears in their eyes. In that moment, she belonged in his family, both the one he had grown up in and the one he had found in this room. His heart swelled and he couldn't imagine letting her go. Not to Emerson Winstead and not to anyone else.

She smiled at him and he returned the expression softly. Then he turned to his brothers and they began to speak about their father, the lives he had destroyed, and the ones he had created.

It was late, too late, as Caleb's carriage wove its way back toward Justin and Victoria's home through the darkened London streets. Marah knew she was going to face a great many questions from Victoria, but what could she do? Once Caleb and his brothers had begun talking, she had seen the bond they instantly forged. She couldn't have taken that away from him simply because she feared Victoria's reaction to her late return.

She looked across the dim carriage at him and smiled. He didn't return the expression.

"You are very quiet," she said softly. "You have much to think about, I suppose."

He nodded. His silence confused her, for Caleb was generally gregarious. Now he just *stared*, and she shifted beneath his focused regard.

"It was a pleasure watching you with your brothers tonight," she whispered.

"As it was to watch you," he answered quietly. "You fit into both my families without a seam to be seen. My brothers actually asked if we were engaged. I think they were surprised I would bring someone to such an important meeting who wasn't my . . . love."

She tensed. His love.

"Caleb," she whispered.

He reached across the carriage and took her hands. She had forgotten to put on her gloves and his palms were rough against hers.

"Don't marry him, Marah," Caleb whispered.

Marah sucked in a breath. With a start, she tried to free her hands from his but he wouldn't allow it. He clung insistently, never removing his intense gaze from her face.

"Don't marry Emerson Winstead," he continued. "You think you know what you want, but you don't."

"You don't know that," she whispered, her voice catching. "You don't know what I want."

"Perhaps you are right," he said without missing a beat. "Perhaps I only know what I want. Would you like me to tell you?"

"No," she whispered, turning her face and once again trying to free her hand. In truth, she did want to hear his words. So desperately. But she was terrified of them, too. Of this confession when it was too late.

He kept her hand captive and used the free one to cup her chin and force her to look at him.

"I want you." He stared into her eyes as he spoke. "I *need* you. If you marry some other man, especially a man who you do not love, it could kill me where I stand."

She shook her head. "You don't mean that."

"Don't marry him, Marah," he said. "Marry me."

Marah's heart was pounding so loudly in her

head that she could hear nothing but the rush of blood in her ears. Her mouth was agape, and she hardly noticed when the carriage pulled onto Justin and Victoria's drive. As the footman came to the door, Caleb held it shut, keeping him from entering. Immediately the servant stepped away.

"Please marry me."

Her heart felt like it was stretching, expanding to fill her entire chest as emotions overwhelmed her. Joy, wonder, surprise, they hit her from every side and sent her off-kilter and dizzy. But one stood out above the fray. Stark, cold terror.

She breathed slowly and tried to regain some control over rational thought and reason. "You say this out of emotion."

He nodded.

"We cannot make these kinds of decisions on emotion," she insisted.

"This is the one decision that should be made entirely on emotion," he argued.

She sucked in a sobbing breath. "Well, I have seen the consequences of such a thing," she whispered, her voice broken and choked. "My parents married in a passion, and in the end it only hurt everyone involved. My mother died and my father regretted his choice."

"I am not your father, nor are you," Caleb said.

"You may not be my father, but you terrify me regardless," she admitted. "I've watched you walk away from me too many times to trust that you won't do it again."

"I promise—"

She shook her head. "You *can't* promise. You don't know what the future will bring. I fear you'll end up running from me again. But I also fear you'll stay. I want stability, I want calm . . . I've spent a lifetime without them. With you, I would have neither."

"Marah." Caleb stared at her, so intense that she felt like she was drowning in the stormy blue sea of his eyes. "Don't do this."

She pushed the carriage door open. His offer seemed like heaven, but she feared the potential for hell too much to take it.

"I can't," she said as she hurried from the carriage, leaving him alone behind her.

Caleb pulled into the drive of his mother's house with a heavy heart. He had a suspicion that his brother was there and he wanted more than anything to speak to Justin.

He was announced to his father's old office. As he stepped inside he came to a sudden halt. Justin sat behind the old desk, head bent over paperwork. In a flash of a moment, Caleb saw his father in his brother's face. A younger version, yes, from their childhood when he had snuck in and hidden under the desk as his father worked.

Justin looked up. "Oh, hello."

Caleb frowned. "You look tired."

Justin shrugged as he returned his attention to his papers. "It is early still."

Caleb tilted his head. "No, it isn't. It is almost midnight. You should go home to your wife."

Justin looked up again in dazed surprise. "Midnight?" He glanced at the clock. "I suppose it is."

His brother closed the folder in front of him and rubbed his eyes gently. "I've been told you went to visit the Duke of Billingham tonight."

Caleb tensed. "Have you?"

Justin smiled sadly. "I know a little, Caleb. You don't have to hide this from me."

Caleb shifted as he took a seat across from his brother. "I hope you know that just because I take a place in my other family doesn't mean I have forgotten this one. Or that I don't appreciate what a good brother and friend you are."

His brother's expression softened. "Thank you, Caleb. That means a great deal to me."

"I-I took Marah with me," he said softly.

Justin's lips thinned. "Did you? She said she was visiting an old friend in town."

Caleb nodded. "I need your advice. As my brother. As my friend."

Justin straightened up. "You shall always have it."

"I-I asked her not to marry Winstead. I told her she should marry me."

His brother's eyes lit up with unmistakable relief and pleasure. "And what did she say?"

"She refused me." Caleb winced as he recalled that moment in perfect and painful clarity. "She told me she couldn't trust me, and that I frightened her."

Justin shook his head. "I hate to say it, but why shouldn't she feel this way? After all, you ran away from her more than once. And how did you ask her to marry you?"

Caleb wrinkled his brow. "I said I needed her. I wanted her. What more could I give than that?"

Justin smiled. "For a man who has had so many lovers, you really don't know a damned thing about women."

Caleb opened his mouth to protest, but Justin waved him off with a chuckle.

"Don't argue! Think about what you said. You told her *you* needed her. *You* wanted her. There was no thought to her feelings or fears in those words."

Caleb shifted. He had never thought of it that way. "But—"

"The entire time you have known her, have you ever given her something just for her? Something that would prove you would protect her, love her, offer her strength when she was lacking it?"

With a start, Caleb thought of the question. He racked his mind for even one example of what his brother meant.

Finally he stammered, "I-I comforted her after her relationship to the Breckinridge family was revealed at Victoria's party."

The moment he said the words, he knew how ridiculous they sounded. His brother's arched brow was further indication.

"If that is the best you've done, no wonder she runs away from you." Justin shrugged.

"Oh, thank you," Caleb said with a dry smile. "That is very helpful. I'm so happy I came here to spill my soul to you."

His brother shook his head. "Think of it. Marah has suffered loss in her life, uncertainty. She craves stability, you know that, she's made it plain. If you want her, you must prove to her that you can provide that. And more importantly, if you want to give her more than Emerson would, you must be sure if you *love* her."

His brother leaned closer. "*Do* you love her?"

Caleb pondered the question. It was one he had avoided with women in the past. In his younger days, he had been interested in pleasure, not permanence. And the discovery of the truth of his birth had attacked every other notion he had of his future.

But with Marah . . . she had always challenged and interested him. Even when he ran from his past, he had kept her in the back of his mind. And since coming face-to-face with her in London, a constant refrain of *mine* had run in his head when he saw her.

She offered herself to him without hesitation. Her support, her comfort, her friendship . . . he couldn't imagine living without them. Without her.

"Yes," he whispered in wonder. "I love her."

Justin nodded. "Then you had best get to proving it, my friend, whatever way you can. Otherwise you'll lose her to a man not even fit to shine your boots."

His brother pushed to his feet and stretched his back. "Now I am going home to my wife. A woman I also almost lost due to an abominable stubbornness. Thank God I saw the light before it was too late." Justin passed him on the way to the door and squeezed his arm. "Say good night to Mother before you go. She is still awake."

Caleb nodded as his brother departed. He sat in the chamber alone for a long time, thinking of what Justin had said. When he thought of a gift he could give Marah, there was only one thing that came to mind. It might not be something she wanted, but it was something he knew she needed.

He could only pray it wouldn't be too little, too late.

Chapter 22

Marah shook her head as she adjusted her gloves and smoothed her gown.

"Victoria!" she called in exasperation toward the parlor where her friend had disappeared nearly five minutes before. "We will be late!"

Her friend's voice was muffled in the distance as she said, "I'm coming."

Marah frowned. Victoria was always on time, she never left anyone waiting. Marah would think that would be especially true of Lady Stratfield, who had invited Marah and Victoria to her home that day. There would be other ladies in attendance and Marah didn't want to be late and force the newly widowed marchioness to tend to them herself.

"Victoria," she called again, this time sharper.

"Go to the carriage," her friend said, her tone a bit peevish. "I shall be there in two shakes."

Marah glowered as she marched out the open door toward the waiting vehicle. This was utterly ridiculous. Whatever Victoria was handling, Marah hoped it was important.

The footman opened the carriage door and Marah slipped inside. Just as the door closed, she realized she wasn't alone in the vehicle. Caleb sat across from her.

"Caleb!" she gasped, but before she could say more, the carriage began to roll. "What are you doing? We must wait for Victoria! Why are you here?"

She had never seen such a serious, anxious expression on his face before, even in the carriage a few nights ago when he had shockingly asked her to overthrow Emerson and marry him. That night had hung with her ever since, keeping sleep at bay and making her pick at her food.

"I'm sorry," he said finally.

She shook her head. "You had best be. Victoria and I were going to your mother's house! She is expecting us and will be very disappointed if we don't arrive promptly."

Caleb's chin dropped. "I'm afraid I must confess a ruse, Marah. There was no invitation from my mother today."

Marah blinked. "You are not correct, I saw it myself."

He nodded. "I arranged for that."

"Victoria will be furious," Marah said as she reached for the door handle.

He caught her hand. "You will hurt yourself if you jump out of the moving carriage now," he said. "And Victoria knows perfectly well that there was no invitation."

Marah's jaw dropped. "*Victoria* was your partner in this foolishness?" She shut her eyes in exasperation. "*That* is why she was late. That's why she urged me to go to the carriage and wait for her. She wanted me to be swept away by you."

Caleb nodded slowly. Marah glared at him as she settled back against the carriage seats and folded her arms. "Well, you had best confess what your motives are for this ridiculous kidnapping. I thought we had said all there was to say a few nights ago."

He swallowed, and Marah immediately regretted speaking so harshly. Her intention hadn't been to hurt Caleb, but to protect herself.

"We did," he said slowly. "You are right that there is nothing more to *say*, at least not at this point. But I do have something I must do."

"To me?" Marah asked, feeling her eyes go wide. She wished she had controlled her tone and the physical reaction, for Caleb smiled and some of the wickedness that had once attracted her sparked in his stare. Despite herself, her stomach clenched and her body grew wet at the sight. She turned away from him, praying he wouldn't see her desire for what she couldn't have and had claimed not to want.

"Oh, there are many things I would like to do *to* you," he purred.

She blushed and clenched her hands as she refused to turn away from the window.

"But this is *for* you."

She glanced back. "For me? What do you mean?"

As she asked the question, the carriage slowed and she looked out to see they were pulling up to a great house. It was as beautifully appointed as Justin and Victoria's and even rivaled the fine house where they had visited the Billinghams.

"Where are we?" Marah asked.

Caleb hesitated as the footman opened the door. "You'll soon see."

He helped her out and they entered a sparkling foyer. There a servant bowed, though it was clear he didn't need an introduction to know who Caleb was.

"We are here for our appointment," Caleb said. "Will you let her know we have arrived?"

The servant motioned to a parlor just off the foyer, but Marah felt his eyes on her, watching her. She shifted with discomfort.

"Of course," the man said. "If you will wait here,

I shall fetch her. I know she is anxious to meet with you both."

As he shut them into the pretty room, Marah looked around her, but still had no idea where she had been taken. Her confusion was giving way to worry and anger.

"I demand to know where we are," she snapped, her tone harsher than she would have liked. There was no doubt of the riotous feelings inside her when she couldn't control her tone.

Caleb motioned her toward a settee, but she refused to move, arching a brow at him instead. He sighed almost imperceptibly.

"Look around you," he said softly. "I think you'll understand."

She stared at him for a moment, but then expelled her breath in an angry sigh and began to pace the room. She didn't understand his riddles. All she saw around her was a typical parlor as she'd seen in a hundred other houses in London. With heirlooms and fine furnishings and family portraits that—

With a start, she cut off her own thought. Hanging above the mantel was a portrait of a stern family. Their positioning was very formal, very regal, with the sense of an old and powerful tradition.

But in the middle of the portrait was a man she had seen before. In fact she had a miniature of him at home hidden beneath her bed in a box that had been left to her with *all* her dead mother's things.

She covered her mouth, stepping back away from the picture even though she couldn't take her eyes off it.

The man in the portrait was her father.

Marah turned on Caleb, her hands shaking and the blood draining from her face so swiftly that the room began to swim. As if he sensed her crisis, Caleb rushed for her.

She backed away. If he touched her now she would come undone in his arms, and she didn't want to give him the satisfaction of seeing her collapse.

"How could you bring me here?" she asked, her voice sounding odd and far away to her. "How could you?"

He reached for her, and this time she couldn't get away fast enough. His hands were cool and calming on her suddenly hot skin.

"Breathe, that's it, love. Breathe," he whispered.

She did as she was told and the room stopped tilting after a few moments.

"Why did you do this to me?" she asked again, her voice cracking.

"For you," he corrected. "For once I wanted to do something for you."

She was about to retort when the door opened and Marah spun. An older woman stood in the entryway. She was thin and petite with a bright, open face. When she saw Marah, she staggered slightly, as if she was as shocked to see her as Marah was to be there.

"My God," the other woman breathed. "You— you have his eyes."

Marah caught a sob in her throat as Caleb whispered, "Miss Marah Farnsworth, may I present your grandmother, Lady Breckinridge."

For a moment the two women simply stared at each other and then Marah managed to gather her senses and recall all the years of her life that had been filled with abandonment.

"I apologize, my lady," she said, smoothing her gown gently. "My friend made a mistake in bringing me here. I hope you do not think of this as a manipulation on my part, or an attempt to invade the privacy you so obviously covet."

She moved toward the door as she spoke, hoping she could slip past this woman and escape before she suffered the ultimate humiliation of breaking down and weeping.

Her grandmother's expression grew sad. "Oh, my dear, but you were invited here," she said, moving slightly so that she blocked the door.

Marah stopped advancing. She couldn't break free of this torture now. Helpless, she turned back and looked at Caleb. His arms were folded as he stood across the room from her. He was watching her with a gaze filled with sadness . . . but also understanding. And although she was furious with him for what felt like a betrayal, she also knew that of all the people to witness this awkward reunion, he understood her emotions better than anyone else in the world.

"Marah," he said softly, tossing a quick glance toward Lady Breckinridge. "Allow me to explain, allow your grandmother to speak. I know the desire to run away better than anyone, but from my own experience I can tell you it is a mistake. Please, will you hear us?"

Marah stared at him, then turned toward the older woman still blocking the door. It seemed she had no choice, so she nodded slowly. "Very well."

Suddenly exhausted, she sank into a chair. Caleb and Lady Breckinridge seemed equally relieved and both took places, Caleb in a chair beside her, Lady Breckinridge on a settee across from her, where she gazed at Marah with an unreadable expression.

"Let *me* begin," Caleb said, turning in his seat toward her. He looked her straight in the eye, never turning away, never wavering though Marah was sure her expression wasn't exactly a kind one.

"Please," she whispered as she fiddled with her reticule.

"Since you came to London," he said, his voice gentler than she had ever heard it. "I have watched you struggle with the subject of your father's family. It was obvious how much pain that subject brought you, but also how frozen you were by fear. Too frozen to face them."

Marah shook her head. "And so you thrust this upon me?"

"Please don't blame Mr. Talbot," her grandmother interrupted softly. "When he came to me two days ago, I was as shocked as you are that an emissary to you was reaching out to me. Only when he explained that you didn't know did it make sense. I told him that I did wish to meet you, but that I thought it would be better if you were not told the truth. After all, my prior attempts at contact had been so shunned over the years." She blinked. "Not that I blame you, my dear. I think our family did yours a great wrong. We may have deserved your censure."

"What are you talking about?" Marah finally whispered. "I have never had *any* attempts at contact from you or anyone else in your family in all my life. Even when my father died, I was forced to read about it in an announcement in a paper a few months later."

Her grandmother's lips parted. "You are saying you never received my letters?"

"Only your money, madam," Marah said, trying to keep her voice cold. "Are you saying there was more than the guilty payments I received twice annually?"

"Yes." Lady Breckinridge leaned forward. "From the moment your father died, I began writing you letters. At least a few times a year. For your birthday, I sent little gifts. I never received a reply."

By now Marah's hands had begun to shake. She clenched them in her lap, but it didn't help. They still trembled. She found herself looking toward Caleb, with her gaze beseeching him to somehow explain this to her. She didn't understand it. Not any of it.

He reached across the brief expanse between them and covered her fingers with his. "Marah, sweet, just breathe."

It was what he had said to her earlier, but now she realized she had been holding her breath. She exhaled with a huge sigh and sucked in air in a painful gulp.

"Is it possible Lady Breckinridge's letters went astray?" he asked, his tone soothing and yet somehow strong. Like he was passing her the strength she needed.

She found her voice as she continued to look at him, unexpectedly drawing calm from his presence. "For so many years? I doubt it. Someone must have intervened."

She shut her mouth. Her maternal grandmother, the woman who had raised and loved her like her own . . . how many times had she railed about men "like her father"? She had made it no secret that she felt his insistence on staying in London, on keeping her daughter from her, had led to Marah's mother's death.

"She wouldn't have," Marah whispered.

Lady Breckinridge smiled softly. "If she did, I believe it was to protect you."

Marah tilted her head. Could this woman really be *excusing* her other grandmother?

"You must understand," the lady continued, her cheeks brightening with shame. "When my son married your mother, our family did not . . . well, we could have been kinder."

"Yes, my grandmother . . . my other grand-mother told me that you shunned her. I understand you even cut your son off financially for a time," Marah breathed.

Lady Breckinridge's chin dipped lower and there

was no mistaking her upset. "My husband had some very specific thoughts on the kind of woman his eldest son, his heir apparent should marry. He was unkind and I was equally so by my silent acceptance of his behavior. Your grandmother, the one who raised you, she must have hated us for the pain we caused her daughter. I wouldn't blame her. I have a daughter and granddaughters, even a great-granddaughter. If anyone treated them in such a fashion I would tear them to shreds. Over time that has been my greatest regret."

Marah kept her gaze even. "Your greatest regret?"

"Perhaps not my greatest," Lady Breckinridge corrected, her face going sad. "When your mother, when *Emily* died, your father was so grief-stricken and guilty. He blamed himself for not taking her home to her mother for your birth as she had requested. He could hardly look at you without breaking down. And then he disappeared with you."

The other woman broke off and Marah saw a shiver work through her.

"I was terrified," Lady Breckinridge whispered. "My son was so inconsolable over his terrible loss, I thought he might do you both a harm in order to be reunited with his wife. But then he came back and told us he had left you with his wife's mother. Giving you up was penance in some way."

"My other grandmother told me he couldn't stand to look at me," Marah whispered.

Lady Breckinridge blinked at tears. "Perhaps that was true. But not because he hated you. He saw his wife in you, and his failure of her on every level."

"But he threw himself back into Society quickly enough," Marah said, clinging to the facts she had been told for so many years.

The other woman nodded sadly. "He did, but I could see he had no joy in any of it. A year passed, then two. He made no effort to find a new bride, even though he had inherited his father's title by that time. Finally I approached him about seeing you again."

Marah sucked in a breath and she felt Caleb's hand tighten on hers. She clung to his fingers like they were a lifeline as she whispered, "What did he say?"

A tear slipped down the other woman's cheek. "He wanted to go to you. To reunite with you and mend what had been broken by his grief. But before he could, he was stricken ill. He died shortly thereafter."

Marah's heart leapt. Was she really hearing these

words? These things she had prayed for as a little girl? She could scarce believe it and she whispered, "He wanted me? He was coming for me?"

Lady Breckinridge nodded. "I *did* write to you through your grandmother after his death, but she rebuked me quite harshly for the attempt."

Marah shut her eyes. Yes, she could see her grandmother, a loving but direct woman, doing such a thing.

"I think she feared we would steal you away from her. I couldn't blame her. She had been through the worst thing a parent could experience: losing a child."

Lady Breckinridge's eyes filled with tears and Marah felt her own swell with the same. She found herself looking toward Caleb. The one commonality for all of them was their grief. In that moment she felt bonded to them both. And being bonded to Caleb frightened her.

The other woman gathered herself and continued, "I never gave up hope that in time she would soften in her stance against our contacting you. Finally, when you turned thirteen, I started writing you directly. I felt you were old enough then to decide yourself if you wanted to know your father's blood. When I received no reply, I assumed you must have the same feelings toward us as your grandmother did. And when I heard you came here, but made no effort to meet, I didn't want to push you any further. But now . . . knowing you never saw my missives, I wish I had kept trying. I'm so very sorry, Marah."

Marah shook her head. Her mind was spinning with everything she now knew. "For so long I thought you were ashamed of me," she whispered.

"I'm ashamed of myself. I realize our family might not deserve it, but I hope we can establish some kind of ties." Lady Breckinridge tilted her head with a smile. "You have so much of my son in your face."

Marah smiled. "I-I would like to know you more. Perhaps hear more about my father. I only had snippets, bare facts from a woman whose view of him was colored by grief."

Lady Breckinridge nodded. "And there are others in our family who would love to meet you. You have aunts, an uncle, and many cousins who I'm sure will be very happy to see you if you allow it."

Marah shifted. "Perhaps . . . perhaps slowly. This is a great deal to grasp at once."

Her grandmother nodded. "Of course. May I invite you back to tea just with me later in the week, then? You are staying with Lord and Lady Baybary, are you not?"

Marah nodded. "I'd like that."

"Good." Her grandmother rose, and Marah and Caleb stood with her. "I would like to hug you. May I do that?"

Blinking back tears, Marah moved toward this woman she had so feared, and entered her embrace with a shiver. They stood in each other's arms for a long moment and then Marah stepped back. Both of them swiped at tears.

"Good day," her grandmother murmured.

Marah smiled. "Good day."

Caleb took her arm and led her from the room. But as they exited into the hallway, Marah looked back to see her grandmother beaming with pure pleasure. For the first time in a long time, Marah felt . . . *whole*, and that gift had been granted to her by the man whom she had accused of being incapable of giving her such concern and care.

It had been given to her by a man whom she realized she loved with all her heart and soul.

Chapter 23

Caleb sat across the carriage from Marah. She was looking out the window, watching as her grandmother's home disappeared from view. When it was gone, she looked at him and her smile was the greatest reward he had ever been given.

"Caleb," she said softly. "Why did you do this for me?"

He drew back a fraction. "You think me incapable of an act that is selfless?"

She shrugged. "I know you have the potential for great kindness. I've seen you display it. But we have quarreled. And I . . . I have promised to marry another man. So I wonder why you would do this for me after all that has transpired between us since we both arrived in London."

He was quiet for a moment. What he wanted to say was that he had done it because he loved her. Because he wanted her to be with him. Because he wanted to prove that he was the kind of man she believed she wanted . . . needed.

But Justin was right. Every time he spoke to Marah, Caleb spoke in terms of his own desires. And if he really wanted to prove that he was worthy, he had to allow her to decide that fact all on her own.

"Marah, you have given me such a gift by supporting me when I told you about my past. When I asked you to stand at my side as I found my brothers," he said. "From personal experience I know how important knowing your family . . . *all* your family is. So that is why I did this for you. Because I know you deserve some of the peace, the resolution that you have offered me without asking anything in return."

He moved toward her. She stiffened, but didn't draw back as he reached out. With the back of his hand he stroked her cheek. "Marah Farnsworth, you are the most remarkable woman I have ever known. The most remarkable woman I will ever know. You deserve everything good in this world and more."

Her lips parted and her brow wrinkled with confusion and emotion. "Caleb—"

"Even if it's not enough, even if it's never enough," he interrupted, "I wanted to try to show you what you deserve."

He leaned back as the carriage came to a stop at Victoria and Justin's home. "Now we are back," he said as he smiled at her. It took every bit of his strength not to reach across the carriage and drag her to him. Kiss her until he forced her to admit that she felt something for him.

"I hope I will see you later," he said as the footman opened the carriage door and extended a hand for Marah. She stared at Caleb for a long time and then she took the help out with a dazed expression.

"Good-bye Caleb," she whispered.

He smiled as the carriage door began to close. "Good-bye, my love."

And the vehicle drove away with Marah standing in the driveway, watching it go.

Marah stumbled down the upstairs hall toward her chamber with her mind spinning. Not only did she have thoughts of her reunion with her grandmother to cloud her mind, but then Caleb's behavior in the carriage. He hadn't pushed her. He hadn't demanded. He had simply given her this gift without asking anything in return.

And she could have sworn he called her his love. But that couldn't be correct.

She came to a stop. Down the hall was Victoria's chamber. Crenshaw had informed her that her friend had gone to read. Marah moved forward. She needed her friend more than anything right now. Her advice and her soothing nature had to help Marah sort out the confusion.

When she knocked lightly, she heard movement and low voices inside. Without waiting, she opened the door.

Victoria was in her dressing room, but she was in a state of undress. As she and her maid turned toward the interruption, Marah covered her mouth in shock. There was no denying the swollen swell of Victoria's belly and the heaviness of her bare breasts.

"Marah!" Victoria gasped.

Marah ignored her and came into the room, shutting the door behind her. "Victoria," she breathed. "A baby?"

Her friend gave a quick nod to her maid and the young woman handed Victoria a robe and then hurried from the room. When the servant was gone, Victoria approached her. As she grew near, a wide, joyful smile broke across her friend's face.

"Yes," she said with a laugh that seemed to lighten all the troubles in the world. "I'm having a baby."

Marah hugged her friend and then rested her hand on the belly she hadn't noticed thanks to her friend's well tailored, high-waisted gowns. And, if she was honest, her own distraction had probably kept from her being observant.

"Oh, why didn't you tell me?" Marah asked as the two women moved to the settee before Victoria's fire.

Her friend frowned. "I was . . . afraid."

Marah's own smile fell and she nodded. "Because you lost a child before."

Victoria sucked in a breath. That was how Marah had met her friend. Her grandmother had tended to her during her ill-fated pregnancy.

"I didn't want to raise anyone's hopes and then have them crushed if the child was lost," Victoria said softly, her hand coming down to protect the unborn baby. "And then with the marquis' illness, it was unseemly to celebrate a birth. Though we did tell his father and mother." She smiled. "The marquis was delighted beyond measure at the news. It seemed to bring him such peace before he slipped away from us."

Marah shook her head. "You brought me here for support during this trial and I fear I've been the worst friend. I've been wrapped up in my own dramas for so long that I didn't ease your pain or your fear at all."

Victoria shook her head. "You have had a great deal thrown at you since your arrival."

Marah thought of Caleb. She still desperately wanted to talk to her friend about her day, but she forced herself to focus. "How far along in the pregnancy are you?"

"Almost five months."

Marah smiled. "Then your fears should be eased. Most women lose a child in the first three months. You are well past that threshold and you look happy and healthy."

Victoria smiled and her relief was palpable. "That is what my doctor says. But I hope you might come and tend to me when the birthing begins. You have so much of your grandmother's knowledge."

Marah nodded without any hesitation. In fact, Victoria's request relieved her. "Of course!"

"That is, if your husband will allow it," Victoria corrected.

Marah blinked. Her husband? And then she realized that Victoria meant Emerson. A man she had all but forgotten.

"What is it?" her friend asked, taking her hand. "I have been thinking of you all day. Are you thinking of your visit with your grandmother?"

Marah pursed her lips. "You tricked me."

"Yes, I took part in the ruse because I believed Caleb was right that you needed to face her and you wouldn't do it unless dragged." Victoria squeezed her fingers lightly. "How was it?"

Marah sighed as she briefly recounted the visit. "I feel odd about it all. For so long to believe one thing and then . . . poof! Your life has changed."

Victoria smiled. "You sound like Caleb."

Marah nodded. Yes, she and Caleb shared that odd experience. Along with a great many things.

"Victoria, he . . . he gave me my family back," she whispered.

Victoria nodded slowly. "I suppose he did."

"And on the way home, when I asked him why, he asked for nothing in return. This wasn't a bargaining chip or a way to make me bend to his will. He seems to have done this merely to make me . . . *happy.*"

"That is a rare thing, my dear." Victoria's soft smile and distant eyes made it clear she was thinking of her own husband.

"You know he asked me to marry him a few days ago."

Victoria drew back. "What?"

She nodded. "With all that was going on, I didn't tell you. But he asked me not to marry Emerson and to take his hand instead. But I can't do that, can I?"

Victoria got to her feet. "Why?"

"Our past . . . his casual nature."

Victoria threw up her hands. "You would give away the great gift that is love for *that*? For fear?"

Marah blinked. "Am I so obvious?"

Victoria nodded. "And so is he. You two love each other. It is unavoidable and undeniable. And if you toss it aside, I shall never forgive you."

Marah started. Her friend's tone had a seriousness to it that went deeper than her words.

"Do you not remember my past with Justin?" Victoria continued. "How tumultuous our re-union was? My God, I could have lost everything if I hadn't risked my future on the love I knew we shared."

Marah nodded. "But it's different."

Victoria shrugged. "The particulars may be, but at the core the situations are the same. Love versus fear. The past versus the future. And I beg of you, don't make the mistake of throwing away all the potential for joy and happiness, all the magic and utter uncertainty that love will provide just because you are *afraid*. You'll regret it and I'll have to watch you wither under the weight of your poor choices."

Marah had had no idea that Victoria felt so strongly about this. "You have never said these things to me before."

Victoria shrugged. "I suppose I wanted you to work this out on your own. But this baby, the marquis' death, Caleb's attempt to find out who he is . . . they have all underscored to me how delicate and fleeting life is. You may only have this one chance at happiness. Please be the brave, remarkable woman I know you are and take it."

Marah blinked. Tears stung her eyes and she swiped them away. "What if I can't."

"You can," Victoria said as she wrapped her arms around Marah. "You only have to try."

Caleb strummed his fingers along the arm of his chair as he looked toward the parlor door again and again. He had been called to his brother's house for the first time in two days. The first time since he rode away from Marah with the hope that his gesture of love would make her see him for the man he wanted to be.

The door opened and he stood as Crenshaw stepped in. "Miss Marah for you, Mr. Talbot."

His heart froze as Marah entered the room. Her face was pale and her eyes unreadable as she looked at him. Crenshaw excused himself and after he had gone, Marah reached back and quietly shut the door.

Caleb held his breath. It was an inappropriate

reaction for a woman engaged to another. For an unmarried woman at all. And yet she didn't hesitate as she came forward.

She cleared her throat. "Thank you for coming, Caleb."

He tilted his head. "*You* invited me here? I thought it was Justin."

"I copied some of your earlier trickery," she said with a blush. "I thought you might not come if it was me who called you."

He moved forward, unable to resist her draw.

"Marah," he whispered. "I would come any time you called. From any distance. I would cross the world if you sent for me. I haven't always shown you that, but my intention is to try to prove it up until Winstead puts his vile ring on your finger."

Marah sucked in her breath at that declaration. "I broke the engagement."

For a moment Caleb lost all ability to move, to speak, even to breathe. A riotous joy built steadily in his chest, but he somehow managed to remain calm. After all, her broken engagement gave him hope, but it didn't mean he had earned her trust or love.

"Why?" he asked softly.

She turned her face. "I'm ashamed to say that your assessment that my union with Emerson was mercenary was correct, but it was on both our parts. He wanted to use me to further himself. And I wanted to use him to hide. But in the end, I realized I need something different in a husband."

Caleb frowned. Marah had never made it a secret what she thought she needed in a mate. Stability, which in his current state of continued upheaval, he wasn't certain he could provide to her satisfaction.

He sighed. "You need a man you can depend upon."

"Yes." She nodded and his heart sank. "But I was wrong about what that meant."

He tilted his head. "How so?"

"I thought dependability meant a man who would never surprise me or shock me. A man who would be so evenhanded that he never felt any strong emotion. But I was wrong, so very wrong." She inched closer. "A man who is dependable is one who shows up when he's needed. Who takes me in his arms and kisses me until I can't think or breathe or hurt. A man who would drag me kicking and screaming to a place I feared . . . but needed to go. And most of all, a man who is dependable is a man I know I can love for the rest of my life. But—"

She cut herself off, and Caleb somehow found his voice. "But?"

"I need to know if that man, the man of my

heart and my dreams, loves me, too." She slipped her arms around his waist and looked up at him. "Do you love me, Caleb Talbot?"

He could see the worry on her face, the last remnants of the doubt that had kept them apart for so long. And he wanted nothing more than to wipe it away, never to return.

"I love you, Marah," he admitted, brushing a lock of hair away from her forehead. "With so much power and so much depth that I feel it in my blood. I felt that love for you two years ago, but in the midst of my grief, I made the terrible mistake of running from it and from you. But I'm finished running. At least away from you. If you let me, I will only run into your arms for the rest of our lives."

Her breath caught and the joy on her face was enough to steal his speech.

"I love you," she whispered. "Will you ask me again what you asked me in the carriage last week?"

He dropped down on both knees and looked up into her face. Tears streamed from her eyes, but she was smiling so brightly that he could have stayed like that forever.

"Marry me," he whispered. "Marry me and no one else."

She nodded. "Yes. Yes. Yes."

She dropped down and her mouth met his. He

crushed his arms around her as they drowned in each other. For the first time, perhaps in all the time they had known each other, he didn't feel the undercurrent of mistrust and doubt in her touch. He felt only her love. And the warmth of the future they would share.

And as he dragged her against his body, Caleb knew that this was all he needed, all he wanted, all he could hope for the rest of his life.

Epilogue

Two Years Later

The Billingham Bastards were a most exclusive and secret club. They consisted of three brothers who never acknowledged their blood ties in public, but whose friendship was widely known. Some people shook their heads at their unlikely closeness, for the three men couldn't be more different. The Duke of Billingham was known as a fair and generous man who fought with passion for the rights of others.

The Duke of Waverly was still remembered as arrogant, but upon closer inspection many said he was a devoted husband, loving father to his two young boys, and a much improved man.

And Caleb Talbot was wild. Even now he and his wife would often shock an entire ballroom by exchanging a kiss after a dance. Or they had before Mrs. Talbot's confinement.

But none of this meant anything to the Billingham Bastards as they gathered in Caleb and Marah's comfortable parlor. Also in attendance were Justin and Victoria and their eighteen-month-old daughter, Portia, who toddled off and studied Rhys and Anne's son Ian with much interest.

"Careful," Marah laughed as the two children examined each other. "It might be a love match."

The room laughed as the nurse entered carrying a newborn baby. The women all sighed as the child was placed into her mother's arms, and Marah shivered with pure delight at the feel of her daughter's soft skin and the smell of her hair.

"This is Alice," she said to the room as she kissed her baby's forehead.

"She is beautiful." Lillian smiled and her hand came to cover her own swollen belly. In a few months she would add to this family, and Marah couldn't be happier.

After all, the family had endured a great deal lately. After the death of Simon's mother, he had let the others in on the secret of their hidden brother, the only true Billingham heir. They had met with the childlike man in his hideaway on Simon and Lillian's estate. All of them were serious about protecting him and dedicated to ensuring his happiness for the rest of his life.

But now was the time for happy thoughts. Marah smiled as Anne reached for Alice, snuggling her close as she cooed over her niece in low and soothing tones. Caleb's arm came around her and she felt the warmth of his fingers at the small of her back, reassuring and comforting as ever.

"Are you happy?" she whispered as she watched the baby be passed from one loving family member to the next.

Caleb nodded. "Indeed I am. You know, the more time we are together, the more we grow to know this extended family, the more I have come to realize just how foolish I was to run from it all."

She turned to him. "Yes?"

He smiled. "It isn't blood that makes family."

"No," she agreed as she kissed him gently. "It's love."

Next month, don't miss these exciting new love stories only from Avon Books

A Night to Surrender   by Tessa Dare
Spindle Cove is a haven for the women of England looking for something more than the brute air of pig-headed men. So when Victor Bramwell, the Earl of Rycliff, breaches its borders, Susanna Finch is hell-bent on protecting her utopia. But as the two collide, their friction becomes fiery. Who will back down when both of have so much to lose?

In the Arms of a Marquess   by Katharine Ashe
Knowing the fire that Lord Ben Dorée once set off in her heart years ago, Octavia Pierce has had little interest in anyone else. Though she claims to have put her lust for the rogue behind her, she now needs his help with a most dangerous, clandestine matter. But as they fall in league with one another, their reunion proves to spark a hotter flame than they ever imagined.

One Night in London   by Caroline Linden
After Edward de Lacey hires away Lady Francesca Gordon's solicitor to help save his inheritance, she demands he rescue her niece in return. He agrees to her proposal, but is determined to keep the beauty at arm's length. And still…their arrangement quickly ignites a passion too hot to tame.

Star Crossed Seduction   by Jenny Brown
Miles Trevelyan is looking for temporary, unattached bliss when he meets Temperance, a skilled pickpocket. Not sure what to make of the wily vixen, he falls for her. As love blooms, their desire unlocks secrets of the past better left unopened. With betrayal and treason in question, will love rise above?

At Avon Books, we know your passion for romance—once you finish one of our novels, you find yourself wanting more.

May we tempt you with . . .

- **Excerpts** from our upcoming releases.

- Entertaining **extras**, including authors' personal photo albums and book lists.

- Behind-the-scenes **scoop** on your favorite characters and series.

- **Sweepstakes** for the chance to win free books, romantic getaways, and other fun prizes.

- Writing **tips** from our authors and editors.

- **Blog** with our authors and find out why they love to write romance.

- **Exclusive content** that's not contained within the pages of our novels.

Join us at
www.avonbooks.com

AVON

An Imprint of HarperCollins*Publishers*
www.avonromance.com

Available wherever books are sold or please call 1-800-331-3761 to order.

FTH 0708